I0838318

World of Danger

UNDERCOVER MAGIC BOOK THREE

ISBN: 978-1-951738-97-6 (Paperback Edition)

Cover Design by CReya-tive Book Design

Edited by Mo Sytsma of Comma Sutra Editorial

Proofread by Dominique Laura

For Shane & Stella,

Your talent is an endless source of inspiration and a constant motivation to create characters deserving of it. I can never thank you enough.

"Whatever our souls are made of,
his and mine are the same."

— Emily Bronte

WORLD OF DANGER

CHAPTER 1
LINA

Lina stared in open-mouthed horror at what was left of her uncle. She managed one staggering step forward before her knees gave out. Nord was right there, his hands shooting out to grasp her under her arms and support her full weight. If not for his unflagging strength, she wouldn't have remained upright.

A scream tore up her throat, but an unknown force held it captive, rendering her mute. It was as if a war raged inside her, one where her conflicted emotions fought for dominance. Each one of them collided against the others, fighting to be released.

The sweltering heat of rage.

The yawning chasm of grief.

The smothering sense of panic.

Desperation. Denial. Outrage. On and on it went, each fractured feeling chasing the next.

It should have been impossible to feel that many things at once, but somehow, Lina registered every terrible sensation. What should have turned her into a howling mess left her in a shocked sort of stasis while her brain waited for one of the surging emotions to emerge as a victor.

She was distantly aware of Nord calling her name and Quinn's muffled sobs, but she couldn't seem to acknowledge anything but the dead man in the chair. As horrific the sight was, she simply could not look away.

She stared, waiting for some sign that this was all a terrible misunderstanding. For the twitch of a finger or the slight rise and fall of his chest. Something—anything—to prove that Alistair was still here. That her uncle, the man she considered her true father, was alive despite all the evidence to the contrary.

Even as her heart shattered, her mind refused to accept what her eyes could so clearly see.

The world tilted, and it wasn't until the walls became a blur that she realized Nord had scooped her up in his arms. When he hadn't been able to get through to her, he must have decided to take matters into his own hands and get her away from the massacre in her uncle's office.

He set her down gently in one of the living room's chairs, crouching so that their faces were level.

"Lina," he called as he ran his hands up and down her arms. "Look at me, Kærasta."

She tried to focus on his face, but it was little more than a hazy blur. Her mind was still occupied with the grisly contents in the other room.

"She might not be able to," came Finley's low murmur. "She's in shock."

"Can you blame her?" Quinn asked, her voice hoarse from her tears. "You saw what those butchers did to him."

Lina flinched.

"Quiet," Nord ordered, his voice low but unyielding.

"Sorry," Quinn mumbled.

"Lina," Nord tried again.

This time, she did manage to focus on Nord's face. His lips were drawn down in a severe frown, a deep line etched between his brows, his attention trained solely on her. For a man crafted for bloodshed, he sure knew how to be tender. Every ounce of his love for her was telegraphed in his gaze and the soft sweep of his thumb over her cheek.

With all that had happened in the last hour, she hadn't had a chance to get used to him without the metallic flecks of a Guardian's power around his pupils. It was odd to see the icy orbs free from the tiny pricks of color, but not uncomfortably so. In a way, he seemed almost more expressive now. Like there was one less barrier between them—if any still existed.

The warmth of his palm sank into her skin as he cupped her cheek. "You don't have to say anything, but can you blink so I know you're here with me?"

It took a second for her muscles to obey his gentle command, her eyelids feeling like sandpaper as they brushed over the sensitive tissue. She couldn't recall whether she'd blinked since finding the Drakes' present. Given the gritty, dried-out state of her eyes, she was guessing not.

Then it struck her as odd that her eyes were dry.

Her hand shook as she lifted it to her face, her fingers confirming what she'd already come to realize.

No tears.

Lina forced herself to blink a second time, willing the tidal wave of pain and heartache she was drowning in to manifest themselves in a proper display of her grief. Maybe if she could cry, it would release some of the pressure trapped in her chest. But when she opened her eyes, they were still dry.

"Shouldn't I be crying?" she asked, her voice coming out as a strangled whisper. As if the screams that had been sounding in her head had found a way to rob her of her actual voice.

Nord and Lina stared at each other for a moment, both of their gazes searching. He must have found the answer he was looking for because his expression shifted from concern to a compassion so filled with knowing that it bordered on painful.

"Don't worry about that right now. They'll come when you're ready."

As she continued to peer into his eyes, she drew in some of his endless strength and the rest of the world faded—not completely, there was no forgetting what she'd seen—but just enough that she could draw a full breath into her oxygen-starved lungs. Since even breathing required effort in this moment, Lina focused on only that until the function became automatic once more.

Then, and only then, did she allow her mind to wander. Instantly it flew back to the nightmare they'd discovered. She was overwhelmed by the images that assaulted her. Bloodied sockets that had once been her uncle's twinkling eyes. The gaping slit across his throat. The charred smell of burnt flesh.

Her breathing turned erratic once more, and the hand still curled over her bicep tightened to the point of pain. That sharp sting was enough to pierce through the fog of her grief and keep her from losing herself within it.

"Focus on me. Just me," Nord murmured.

Lina gave a jerky nod.

It could have been minutes or hours. She had no concept of time as she sat there, coming to terms with the fact that the Drakes murdered her uncle.

And that it was all her fault.

Eventually, the sound of Quinn's muffled sobs and Finley's hushed voice reached her. She blinked slowly, feeling like she was coming out of a trance.

Lina still hadn't managed to form a single tear, but that didn't mean she wasn't consumed by her grief. If she'd let it, it would likely cripple her. But now was not the time to fall apart. There was work to be done. Plans to be made.

Vengeance to be found.

The only way she could accomplish any of that was to shove the pain aside. Doing so wrapped her in a cocoon of numbness that she clung to with everything she was worth.

Numb was safe. It would help her face what came next. Dealing with the rest of her feelings would come later.

"There you are," Nord said in his husky whisper.

She swallowed, trying to ease the constricted feel of her throat. It helped a little, but did nothing for the heavy ache in the center of her chest.

"How did they even know where to find him?"

Nord shook his head, something dark and dangerous flashing in his eyes. "I don't know. But we'll find out."

"Could they have been waiting for him?" Finley asked.

"This place was protected by the Brotherhood," Nord answered. "They couldn't have found it."

"Not unless he led them straight here," Finley replied.

Lina's attention bounced between the men. "What do you mean?"

Finley looked equal parts apologetic and guilty. It was obvious to her that he was trying to spare her any further pain, but there was no getting around it. No matter how gently the words were offered, the end result would be the same.

"Perhaps all this time they'd had eyes on wherever he stashed the Codex? And when he got there, they were tipped off and ready to make their move once he freed it for them?"

"No," Quinn said with a shake of her head. "He called us once he was already on his way back. Remember? He wouldn't have risked coming home or making that call if he was being watched."

"You assume he knew," Finley said.

"Alistair was the smartest man I've ever known. He evaded the Mobius Council for years. He would have taken every precaution against the exact scenario you've just described," Quinn insisted.

"Then how do you explain this?" Lina asked, her voice hollow. As much as she wanted to agree with Quinn, the evidence clearly supported Finley's theory.

Quinn swallowed, more tears trailing down her cheeks as she gave Lina a helpless shrug. She looked as devastated as Lina felt.

Finley reached over to the end table beside them and plucked a tissue from the box, offering it to Quinn. She accepted it gratefully, wiping at her face and gesturing for him to continue. He gave both women a considering look, then turned to Nord as if seeking guidance.

The berserker must have thought so too because he gave him a slight nod.

Finley leaned forward, resting his elbows on his knees as he clasped his hands loosely together. He couldn't seem to look at them as he continued to outline a plausible version of the night's events. "They could have followed him home, waited until his guard was down and . . ." he trailed off.

"Jesus," Quinn whispered, shuddering.

Lina squeezed her eyes shut, the image Finley's words brought to mind so vivid it felt as though she'd watched it unfold in real time. It was jarring enough that Lina had to reinforce her emotional cocoon before she could open her eyes and give voice to the questions racing through her mind.

"Assuming that's the case, how would they have known where the Codex was hidden? Or that Alistair had found it in the first place? They didn't even know what he looked like because of the Brotherhood's glamour, so how could they have known Alistair was the one who went back to retrieve it?" Lina bit her bottom lip as her mind scrambled for answers. Finley was on to something with his theory, but the story wasn't adding up. They were missing important pieces of the puzzle still. "It couldn't have been about the Codex. Not entirely. This was an act of revenge, not thievery. Mikel wanted to hurt me because of what we did to his son."

"Don't," Nord ordered, his expression severe. "Do not blame yourself for this. *I* was the one who killed the Drake bastard. Not you. If anyone is guilty here, it's me."

"You only killed him to protect me," Lina said, pressing her forehead to his.

"You asked me not to, and I did it anyway."

Lina knew what Nord was doing. He was trying to force her to blame him for her uncle's death instead of herself. But it wouldn't work. He may have been the instrument of Mataius' destruction, but she was the reason behind it. None of this would have happened if not for her.

It was no coincidence that after remaining safely hidden for decades, her uncle had been brutally slain within a month of her return. Especially since he spent the days leading up to his death off on a solo mission to recover an artifact that was dangerous enough to hide in the first place. He'd risked everything—his protection, his anonymity, his life—so that she could have access to the secrets of her people. All in the hope that it would provide them with an upper hand in the days to come.

Instead, she ended up with nothing. No Codex. No Alistair. Just the Drakes and a bunch of pissed-off Guardians hunting them.

A thought suddenly occurred to her, and she straightened, her eyes finding Quinn's across the room. "Don't you think if Mikel got his hands on the Codex, he would have taunted us with that as well? He's not one to miss out on the opportunity to take a cheap shot like that."

"You think Alistair managed to keep it from them? That it could still be here somewhere?" she asked, her red-rimmed eyes flaring wide.

"You said it yourself. My uncle would have planned for every probable scenario."

Maybe even his death.

A small bubble of hope started to form within her as a new, staggering thought took hold. As it did, a laugh that was just this side of manic escaped her lips. "Perhaps he let them kill him."

Quinn's eyes narrowed. "What?"

Lina didn't like the expression on either Finley or Nord's faces, so she kept her gaze trained on her best friend. "Alistair was powerful. Far too powerful to go down without a fight *unless* it worked out in his favor. He must have known we'd find him. That you would remember the spell you two used to bring me back, that we could revive him—"

Quinn cut her off. "Oh, Lina. No," she shook her head, her expression crumpling.

"You've done it before," Lina insisted.

"It was different with you; you were still alive when we found you. And you had the Prism keeping your soul bound." Lina had to look away from Quinn's mournful expression as she whispered, "You know I would do it in a heartbeat if I could, but it's too late. He's gone, Lina."

Grief clawed at Lina as her fragile cocoon shattered. The small glimmer of hope she hadn't even realized she'd been holding on to guttered. And yet, she clung to it as part of her stubbornly refused to accept Quinn's words. Alistair would have had a plan. He wouldn't have left her like this. Empty-handed. Lost.

Alone.

As if he could sense the direction of her thoughts, Nord cradled her face in his large hands, forcing her to meet his gaze. "We will get to the bottom of this. I swear to you. Alistair's death will not go unpunished."

No, not alone. Never alone, so long as Nord drew breath.

Little shivers of apprehension worked down her spine at the unwanted reminder that without his Guardian power, her berserker was no longer immortal.

She brushed her lips against his as she shoved the thought away. One tragedy at a time was all she could manage, if you counted willingly succumbing to denial as managing.

"I don't know what I'd do without you," she whispered.

"You'll never have to find out," he promised.

Her heart throbbed like an open wound as a bitter voice in her mind hissed that it was a promise he couldn't keep. Alistair was proof enough of that.

She tried to manage a grateful smile, but it wouldn't come.

Instead, she settled for another quick press of her lips against his. A silent token of everything she couldn't express.

Lina settled her hands on his shoulders as she pushed back, startled when Nord went rigid beneath her palms.

"What's wrong?" she asked, as his eyes narrowed and his head jerked to the side.

"We've got company."

CHAPTER 2
NORD

The sound of hurried footsteps reached his ears, catapulting Nord from concerned lover to bloodthirsty warrior in less time than it took to blink. He'd been on high alert since they'd fled the Brotherhood's headquarters. That focus might have crystalized into caring for Lina's well-being after they'd found Alistair's desecrated body, but that didn't mean he'd dropped his guard.

Quite the opposite.

The Drakes' grisly threat only stoked the flames of his berserker rage. His need to draw blood was a living thing, awake and writhing inside him. It begged to be unleashed. And for the first time in as long as he could remember, Nord was having trouble keeping it contained.

No, that wasn't quite true.

He didn't *want* to keep it contained.

He welcomed the violence. Someone had dared harm what was his. He wanted to paint the walls red with their blood and pull their still-beating heart from their chest.

Nord knew that he'd never forget the haunted, wrecked look on Lina's face. Or his relief when she'd broken free of her fugue state. He intended to repay the sadistic bastards back for each second of pain they'd caused her.

Tenfold.

Violence was his birthright. The language and lifeblood of his ancestors. He'd lived, breathed, and craved it since he'd first stepped onto the field of battle. For too long, it had been locked away. A vital part of himself left to wither and decay. Even once it returned, he'd mostly kept it bound in chains forged from his own fear. In doing so, he'd denied what he was. And what he needed.

It was time to be who he'd been born to be.

It was time to let the berserker free.

When their unwelcome visitor's knock finally sounded on the door, he was already halfway to the door.

"Wait," Lina whispered from her chair, "we don't know who it is."

"I doubt anyone who means us harm would risk knocking," Quinn countered in a hushed voice.

"Who's to say the person at the door is here for us?" Finley asked. "They could be looking for Alistair. This is his apartment, after all."

Nord ignored all of them. He didn't need to know who it was, and he wasn't about to allow Lina's safety to hinge on some half-baked assumption. As far as he was concerned, the only people he trusted in this world were already in this room. Everyone else could fuck right off.

Moreover, the visitor's timing was too suspect. Anyone who dared to show their face here right now would be considered an enemy out of hand.

They could try to change his mind after his fist greeted their face.

Nord stalked the last few steps to the door, gripping the doorknob and causing the wood to groan as he ripped it open. He spared a second to let his eyes sweep down the woman who was posed with her hand still raised mid-knock.

A black leather case dangled from the forearm of her other arm. Her ebony hair was pulled back in an elegant twist, and light makeup dusted her cheeks and emphasized the lavender color of her eyes. Her clothes were expensive and expertly tailored, and diamonds sparkled at her ears and wrists.

At a glance, she didn't immediately appear to be a threat, but Nord knew better than to dismiss her simply due to her appearance. Grasping her by the collar, he tugged the woman inside and kicked the door closed behind her.

"Would you mind unhanding me?" she asked, looking up at him, entirely unfazed by his rough treatment. "This blouse is couture. I'd hate for you to ruin it over a misunderstanding."

There was a startled intake of breath, and then Quinn let out a shocked, "M-mom?"

"Hi, sweetie," the woman replied, craning her neck around Nord's bulk.

"Cora?" Lina gasped, lurching to her feet.

The woman—Cora's—face went soft, and her lips lifted in a bittersweet smile. "Oh, my Evalina, you look just like your mother. It's been far too long, sweet girl."

"What are you doing here?" Lina asked, rushing over to where they stood. A slight frown marred her face when she noticed how Nord held Cora. She slapped at his arm. "Let her go. She's not going to hurt us."

Rage continued to pump through his veins, and Nord gave Cora a long, considering once-over. "How can we be sure? She's a head of Mobius, is she not?"

"Hey," Quinn protested.

"He's got a point, love," Finley said.

"Alistair trusted her, remember? Let her go. Now," Lina added more forcefully when Nord failed to immediately comply.

He held onto Cora one second longer before letting go with an annoyed grunt. The urge to destroy things still thrummed through him. Assurances would never satisfy a bloodlust this potent. No matter who offered them.

Since he was currently without an outlet for his anger, Nord crossed his arms over his chest and tucked his hands beneath his biceps, hoping it might alleviate the temptation to start pummeling furniture. He didn't think Lina would be very understanding if he took his fury out on her uncle's things. Not even if the only alternatives were Quinn's mother and Finley. Actually, with Fin around, she definitely wouldn't forgive the decimation of Alistair's belongings.

The thought was just darkly humorous enough to blunt the sharp edge of violence surging through him. Though contained for the moment, his rage continued to simmer below the surface, waiting for an excuse to erupt.

"Mom, what are you doing here?" Quinn asked, repeating Lina's earlier question as she came to stand beside the other women in the center of the living room.

"I had a feeling I'd be needed."

Quinn and Lina both visibly reacted to the somewhat vague reply. Nord's eyes narrowed, and his gaze shot to his partner's.

Almost instantly, Finley's words sounded in his mind. *"I think we're missing something. Did you catch that?"*

A reply formed before Nord remembered he could no longer send it. His fury flared in response to the reminder of what the Director had stolen from him. Still holding Finley's gaze, he dipped his chin in a slow nod.

Finley's brows furrowed for a second at the lack of telepathic reply before his expression turned apologetic. *"Sorry, mate. Habit. Want me to stop?"*

Nord shook his head. Even if he couldn't reply, Finley's ability to silently communicate with him was still an asset. There were ways that Fin could use his Guardian abilities to open a mental link between them again, but not one that would be permanent—or that would protect Nord's privacy.

"You're too late," Lina said in a hollow voice, hugging herself as she added, "he's already dead."

Quinn's lower lip quivered, but she did not give back in to her tears as she wrapped an arm around Lina's shoulders.

Positioned as he was, Nord only had a view of Cora's profile, but there was no mistaking the flicker of pain that crossed her face. "I know, dear. But I didn't come for him. I'm here for you."

"Me?" Lina asked.

Cora nodded.

"Why?"

The older woman let out a gusty sigh. "Perhaps we should sit, hmm? Lord knows I haven't been looking forward to keeping this particular promise."

"Promise?" Nord asked, jumping on the word.

Cora's eyes flitted over to him. "That's what I said, yes."

Nord's teeth bared in a snarl. "If it wasn't obvious, I don't trust you. Perhaps you should take more care with your answers."

The woman surprised him with her husky chuckle. "My, you're exactly what I pictured." She reached out and gave Lina's arm an affectionate squeeze. "You're a lucky woman, Eva. I have a feeling that one will take excellent care of you and your heart."

There it was again. Both Lina's and Quinn's eyes widened at the declaration.

"Think she's some kind of seer?" came Finley's question in his mind.

Nord tilted his head to the side, hoping the not quite nod, not quite shake of his head would translate as a maybe.

"The Satori are known for their mental abilities. It would track."

Nord studied Cora with more interest. She didn't look the part of a seer at all. In his experience with the lot, they were either free spirits that embraced the duality of their gift, or incredibly high-strung and traumatized by what they'd Seen. Cora seemed more like a pampered housewife than someone kissed by the fates.

"You had a feeling, a-about Nord?" Lina asked, clearly stunned.

"Is that so hard to believe? People have feelings about lots of things."

"Well, yes, but . . . you're *you*."

Cora's lips quirked up. "Is that your way of saying I'm always right?"

Lina huffed out a little laugh, but grief still sat heavy in her eyes. She was doing her best to stave it off, but Nord could see that she was barely hanging onto her composure.

"Perhaps you should fill us in on these *feelings* of yours," Nord said, pushing off the wall.

"That's what I'm trying to do," Cora replied with a sweet smile that was no match for the wicked amusement in her eyes. The woman enjoyed playing with him, the same way a feline enjoyed toying with a mouse right before they ate it.

"Best get on with it then," Nord said through gritted teeth.

She flashed him a quicksilver grin. "We're going to be friends, berserker. Just you wait."

Nord fought hard to keep his surprise off his face. Seer or not, Cora definitely knew more than an outsider should.

"I doubt it," he replied.

She laughed. "You wouldn't if you knew me better. I'm never wrong about these things."

"There's a first time for everything."

She shook her head, her smile slowly fading as she moved to take a seat between Lina and Quinn on the couch. Setting the black case she'd been holding on the table, she flicked open the clasps and pulled out a thick white envelope and a manila folder.

"There's no easy way to start this conversation, so I'm just going to jump straight in, all right?" she asked, glancing at Lina.

"That'd be a nice change."

Quinn shot Nord an annoyed look, but Lina's lips lifted ever so slightly. For her part, Cora ignored him completely.

"Careful there, mate," Finley whispered as he moved to stand beside him. "She doesn't seem like one you want to piss off."

Nord spared him a quick glance. "Perhaps you're forgetting who you're talking to. I think you've got that backwards."

"That's different. You're perpetually pissed off."

He gave his friend a long look. "Heed your own advice, Fin."

Finley broke eye contact first as they both turned their attention back to the women on the couch. Cora had set the packets of paper in her lap, her hands lightly resting on them.

"Many years ago, Alistair came to me and asked if I would keep these safe for him. Then, about a week ago, he asked to meet—something he hadn't done in over a decade. I knew he was in hiding, and we'd both agreed unless it was an emergency, we wouldn't contact each other directly. So when he reached out, I knew it was important. That's when he gave me this." She reached back into her bag and pulled out an impossibly long object.

Nord instinctively reached for his magic and stopped with a disgruntled curse. The only way the object could have fit in the bag was if it was enchanted. He'd sought to check for the source of the enchantment—whether it was the bag itself or the walking stick—but once again, the lack of his Guardian abilities prevented him from following through on the instinct.

"He gave you his cane?" Lina asked, instinctively reaching for the black lacquered wood. "Why would he do that?"

"He wanted me to hold on to it for him and said I would know when it was time to return it."

Lina frowned at the silver snake that made up the handle. "I don't understand."

Cora lifted one shoulder. "I can't say that I do either. Perhaps the contents of these will prove more enlightening." She lifted the envelopes, offering them to Lina. "This one contains his will. And this," she said, tapping the thick white envelope, "is addressed to you. Neither have been opened."

"If they've never been opened, how do you know what they contain?" Nord asked.

"Because Alistair told me," she said, managing to make him feel like a petulant child with a single glance. Then she returned her attention to Lina, placing a hand on her knee as she continued in a soft voice, "He left you everything, Evalina. You're his sole beneficiary."

On the surface, Lina appeared calm, but Nord knew it was little more than a façade. She sat with a sort of rigid stillness that made her seem as though she'd been carved from glass and one careless blow would shatter her entirely. Her eyes were tight but dry, her lips bracketed by deep lines as she inhaled sharply.

The sight of her pain sent him spiraling. He wanted to let out a savage roar, forcibly remove everyone else from the premises, and take her in his arms. It would change nothing, but at least then he could hold her. Offer her comfort with his body and his words—for whatever those were worth.

It would be a damned sight better than this.

Anything would be better than being forced to memorize the way she looked, ravaged by grief and helpless to do anything to put an end to it.

He may no longer be a Guardian in name, but the vow he'd sworn to her was as true now as the day he made it. It was his duty—his right—to protect her. To ensure her every need was met and that she wanted for nothing.

Her tears. Her pain. Her pleasure. All of it was his.

If she wept, he would be the one to wipe away the tears and chase the shadows from her eyes. If her body burned with need for him, then he would slake her desire until she was little more than a boneless heap curled up in his arms. And if it was retribution she craved, then he would be her weapon.

Always.

That was what it meant to be a Guardian. That is what he swore to her when he gave her his vow.

Yet once again, her monsters eluded him.

Once again, he'd failed her.

His track record of failure ended now. He would make good on his promise, whatever the cost.

Nord's gaze swept over Lina once more. The muscles in his neck and shoulders were knotted with tension as he watched her fight through her pain and force her eyes back up to Cora's face.

"Do I . . ." Lina paused, looking pained. "Do I have to read this now?"

Cora shook her head, her expression soft with understanding. "No, of course not. But I had a feeling you wouldn't be here much longer, and that you'd need this wherever you were going. You should pack warm," she added as an afterthought.

"How can you possibly know that when *we* don't even know where we're going?" Nord demanded.

"You'll figure it out soon enough," she replied evasively. "But for what it's worth, you're going somewhere cold. I think." She tapped a finger to her painted lips, her eyes taking on a hazy quality as they shifted to where Nord stood. "A place untouched by time yet steeped in tradition." Then she blinked and shrugged as if she hadn't just spoken utter nonsense. "Wherever it is, I don't want to know the specifics."

"You're not coming with us?" Quinn asked.

Cora squeezed her daughter's hand. "As much as I would love an impromptu family reunion, you know I can't just disappear. Mikel watches me closely enough as it is."

Nord let out a soft snarl at the mention of the Drake patriarch. He couldn't know for sure whether Mikel personally held the blade that slit Alistair's throat, but the sorry excuse for a man was undeniably at the root of what had happened here tonight. As such, he'd just scheduled his own execution and landed himself at the top of Nord's list. Right next to the Director.

It might not happen tonight, or even next week, but Mikel Drake was as good as dead.

The beast within howled with a savage sort of pleasure, eager for the chance to hunt its prey. Instead of taking over, it fell silent. Content enough with the promise of imminent bloodshed that its lust was satisfied.

For now.

Nord took his first easy breath in hours, some of his tension falling away along with his berserker's rage as Lina gestured to the documents on her lap.

"What should we do if we need your help to make sense of these?"

"All the answers you need are right here," Cora said, resting her hand just above Lina's heart. Then her lips lifted in the barest hint of a smile, and she added, "But if you truly need me, you won't have to say a word. I'll already be there."

"Thank you," Lina said softly.

Cora waved the words away. "Nonsense. You're family, dear. This is what we do."

"You risked so much to come here and keep your promise. It means a lot to me . . . and him."

Some of Cora's unflappable calm cracked, and her pain shone through. "There's very little I wouldn't do for Alistair. Or for you." Her voice broke, and she paused to collect herself. "Now," she said, mask firmly back in place as she stood up and glanced around. "I believe you four have plans to make, and I have the last of Alistair's wishes to see to."

Lina made a soft sound of protest, but Cora was already heading back toward the office . . . and the body it contained. She called over her shoulder as she moved, "Let me do this for you, Evalina. It's what he wanted."

"Is she always like that?" Finley asked once it was just the four of them.

"Like what?" Quinn asked, sounding more like her usual self.

"A one-woman hurricane?"

One side of Quinn's mouth lifted. "You've been Cora'd. Don't worry, it'll pass. Most people have that reaction when they meet her for the first time. She can be a little intense."

Finley's eyes glided back in the direction her mother had taken. "That's one word for it."

Quinn shrugged. "It's the sphinx in her. Most of my family members are like that."

"Hmmm," came Finley's noncommittal reply, but Nord's attention had already shifted back to Lina.

She turned the white envelope over in her hands, her fingers running along the edges.

He crossed the room and sat beside her. "Want me to do it?" he offered.

She stared at the letter in her hand, brushing the tips of her fingers over the elegant scrawl on the front. "No. It should be me."

Nord covered her hand with his. "There's no rush. Open it when you're ready."

"But what if it's important?" she asked, lifting her grief-stricken eyes to his. "What if he left me a clue about where he hid the Codex?"

"He gave that letter to Cora years ago. I doubt any secrets it contains will be tied to the events of the last couple of weeks."

Lina seemed uncertain, but after a few seconds she nodded and released a shaky breath. "You're probably right."

She looked more than a little relieved as she set both envelopes back on the coffee table beside Alistair's cane. She stared at them hard and then reached out and pushed the pile further away with the tip of her index finger. When she caught Nord's eye, she flushed and dropped her gaze to her lap, where she'd clasped her hands together so tightly her knuckles were already white.

Nord frowned, not liking that she was attempting to comfort herself when he was right there and more than willing to offer the same. He slowly reached out and pried her hands apart, weaving his fingers through her own.

At first, her hand trembled in his, but then, after a series of deep breaths, the tremors eased and Lina gripped him more tightly. When she finally spoke again, her voice was pitched so low, he could only just make out the heartbroken confession.

"It probably seems stupid, but if I open them, it's really goodbye, you know? And I'm not ready to say goodbye to him yet." She sucked in a ragged breath. "I just got him back."

"It's not stupid at all. No one is ever ready to say goodbye to someone they love."

"How did you do it?" she blurted, looking like she wished she could pull the question back as soon as it left her lips.

Nord gave her a wry smile. "I don't think you want to try my method."

Her brows lifted. "Why not?"

"It involved a lot of bloodshed."

"I'm not opposed to getting my hands dirty."

He recognized the darkness that flashed in her eyes as she uttered words that spoke to the most primal part of his soul.

Nord turned Lina's palm over and began tracing the lines there as he weighed his response. He was the last person to dissuade her from that path if that was what she wanted. But he'd learned a hard truth when he'd walked it himself, and he'd spare her its sting if he could.

"Revenge is not an easy road to traverse. It will consume you if you let it. I won't lie, for a while, it will make you feel better because it gives you something to do with the pain. Something to focus on."

"I'm not seeing a downside here."

Nord kept his attention fixed on the play of his fingers moving over her skin, not wanting her to notice the twitch of his lips and mistake his appreciation of her sentiment. What he needed to say was too important.

"In the end, it will not bring him back."

Her fingers spasmed in his hold, but he forced himself to keep talking.

"Once that focus is gone, the pain returns. Only this time, there's nothing to bury it with. The problem with revenge is that the relief it provides is short-lived. The grief will always be there once you're done, waiting for you."

"Oh." She blew out a heavy breath. "I was really hoping you had some kind of magic cure because this"—she pressed her free hand to her chest—"is un-fucking-bearable."

Her words gutted him. He wished he had a way to take away her pain; he'd bear the weight of it for her if he could. Since that was impossible, he settled for offering a different kind of comfort and lifted her hand to press a kiss into her palm. "I know. There's a reason I left everything behind to escape it."

She looked so lost sitting there beside him, her eyes searching his. "And did that work? Running away?"

Nord shook his head. "No. Time is the only thing that ever softened the ache."

Lina's eyes fluttered closed, and she swallowed convulsively. He watched as she took several deep breaths, knowing she'd managed to win whatever internal battle she'd just waged with herself when she shot him a side-eyed glance and asked, "And you're sure ending the Drakes won't make me feel better? Even just a little?"

Warmth unfurled in his chest. She had a core of fucking steel, his woman. He was equal parts proud and in awe of her ability to pick herself up and face whatever the world threw at her head-on.

"Just say the word, Kærasta. You know I'll gladly lay the bodies of your enemies at your feet if you'd like to test it out and make sure."

Lina wove her fingers through his beard, cupping his cheek. "How is it that even at a time like this you can manage to make murder sound romantic?"

He flashed her a grin. "It's a gift."

She chuckled, and just for a second, the shadows fled. Though she sobered again almost instantly, that one moment of sunlight breaking through the storm clouds told him everything he needed to know.

His woman was hurting, but this would not be the blow that broke her.

Nord pulled her body into his, feeling his chest loosen even further when she cuddled into him and tucked her head beneath his chin. He was still holding her like that, his fingers lazily drawing patterns on her back, when Quinn cleared her throat.

"Uh, guys, I hate to break up this Hallmark moment you two are having—"

"Quinn," Lina interjected with a huff of exasperation.

The Satori heir's eyes were still red-rimmed, but her lips were curled up in a rueful smile. "You know I'm no good at living in my feelings for too long, Li. Makes me antsy. I like to get in, get out, and get over it."

"Is that some kind of catchphrase?" Finley asked.

Quinn shrugged. "Sure. Feel free to trademark it. Anyway, while you two were over here, Mr. Stick Up His Ass—"

Finley shot her a dark look, but Nord couldn't help but appreciate Quinn's bluster. He hadn't known her long, but it didn't take a genius to see that compartmentalizing and downplaying the situation were part of her coping method. Or that she was doing it for Lina's benefit.

He'd have loved her for the attempt alone, but the swell of amusement in Lina's eyes as her gaze darted between a scowling Fin and a smirking Quinn was the true gift. The animagi may not realize it, but she'd just earned herself his loyalty. It was a rare thing, and not easily given. But it was now hers. Anyone who could bring the light back to Lina's eyes at a time like this was someone he wanted to keep around.

"—and I were trying to figure out a place we could go that might fit Mom's clues. When we didn't come up with anything, I asked her if she could shed any more light on the matter."

"And, did she?" Nord asked.

"Well, that's the weird part," Quinn said, placing her hands on her hips and giving him a searching once-over.

"What do you mean?"

"She told me to ask you."

"Me?" Nord repeated.

Quinn pursed her lips and nodded. "Mmhmm. She had a feeling you'd know exactly what she was talking about."

Nord opened his mouth to deny it, but a sense of premonition crept down his spine at her deliberate use of the now-familiar expression. So, instead, he forced himself to take a second and go back over Cora's cryptic references.

When the answer came to him, he almost couldn't believe it. It was quite possibly the only place in existence where they'd be completely out of both the Brotherhood's and the Drakes' reach. The chance of that secret—buried millennia ago—being the very thing that could save them now, it was impossible, and yet . . . perfect.

He might not have even put the pieces together, except that his conversation with Lina had brought his past to the forefront of his mind. That, in addition to Cora's mention of a place untouched by time yet rich with tradition, sparked a long-forgotten memory.

"So, do you have any idea what she was talking about?" Quinn pressed.

"Actually . . . I think I do."

Three sets of eyes bored into him.

Lina was the first to recover from her shock. "Where?"

He looked at her, his voice laced with wonder as he answered, "Home."

CHAPTER 3
LINA

Lina wasn't sure she heard him correctly. "Home? You mean the penthouse?"

"Not Finley's home. *My* home," Nord corrected.

She blinked. His answer was no more illuminating now than the first time he'd said it. She knew she was operating a little slower than usual—the fact that she wasn't curled up in the fetal position right now was a feat in and of itself—but wasn't what he was suggesting impossible?

"Does it even exist anymore?" Finley asked.

There. At least she wasn't the only one struggling to make sense of this.

"Obviously," Quinn said, her arms folded across her chest and hip jutted out to the side. "My mom wouldn't have made a point to mention it otherwise."

"Did she, though?" Finley asked. "Mention it? Because all I heard were a few vague comments about cold weather and tradition."

Quinn lifted her eyes upward. "Clearly, you don't appreciate the subtle nuances of conversation with a Satori."

The look he gave her was dripping with meaning. "Clearly."

"I have to assume the gateway still exists," Nord said. "It was sealed off and hidden, but I'm inclined to agree with Quinn. Cora's hints would have been meaningless to me if not for those exact reasons."

"Gateway?" Lina asked.

"During the worst of the invasions by the English, a bunch of the tribes banded together. Our losses were great, our numbers dwindling, and joining forces was the only way to protect ourselves. While the bulk of our fighters remained behind to deal with the English army, the rest fled. It was the only way to ensure that our way of life would not be lost."

"Fled where?" Finley asked.

"Novasgard."

"Where's that?" Lina asked, her knowledge of Scandinavian geography faulty on her best day. Today was *far* from her best day.

"Another world connected to this one by a gateway," Nord said matter-of-factly, as if it was a normal everyday thing. Perhaps for an ex-Guardian used to walking between literal worlds, it was.

"Of course it is," Lina said, sitting back. With the series of strange turns her life had taken recently, that was about par for the course. At least if Novasgard was located in some other world, she didn't have to feel bad for not recognizing it.

Quinn's brows puckered. "What's a gateway?"

"It's like the Brotherhood's portals," Finley explained, "though permanent."

"How did a bunch of Vikings manage that on their own?" Quinn asked.

"They didn't. The Brotherhood helped," Nord answered.

"Why would they do that?" Lina asked, her hatred of the Director coloring her voice. "They're not exactly the altruistic type, are they?"

"Simple," Nord said. "They wanted me."

"That's how they convinced you to walk away," Finley said, sounding as if he'd finally found the answer to a question he'd long wondered.

"It didn't take much convincing. But yes." Nord's eyes flicked to Lina's, reminding her of his earlier admission about leaving everything behind to get away from his grief. "I asked them to save my people in exchange for me taking their vow."

A new life in a new world, far away from the constant reminders of everything he'd lost? Yes, Lina could see the appeal.

"This is probably a stupid question," Quinn started, glancing between Nord and Finley, "but if they were involved in its creation, won't the Brotherhood know to look for us there? The whole point of us finding a place to hide is to avoid detection, isn't it?"

"Even if they figure it out, not even their power will allow them to access the gateway," Nord said.

"Why not?" Lina asked.

"It was sealed after the last person stepped through, and only one with the blood of my ancestors can reopen it. It was a safety measure we requested so that our enemies would not be able to follow behind us."

"If that's the case, why create a gateway at all? Why not use a portal?" Finley asked.

"In the event that we managed to defeat the English army, we wanted a way to return home and reclaim our land," Nord explained. "But . . . as far as I know, it was never opened again."

The comment struck Lina as profoundly sad. How long had all those people waited for some sign that their loved ones were safe before they were forced to give up hope?

"You don't know for sure?" she asked, needing something in her life to have a happy ending.

"I've never been back," Nord admitted. "I took my vow the day the gateway was sealed, and the Brotherhood sent me off on my first mission not long after. By the time I came back to this world, there was no one left to ask."

"And you never thought to go back yourself before now?" Finley asked.

"The Director prohibited it. He didn't want my loyalties to be confused." Nord chuckled darkly. "If they only knew, huh? But, honestly, I had no desire to return. Anyone that would have remembered me was long dead. That part of my life was over."

Even amid her own tragedy, Nord's washed over her. She knew what it was like to be cut off from everything and the resulting loneliness that came from that kind of exile. It led to a singular despair that settled deep in your soul and slowly tore you apart.

No wonder they'd been drawn to each other. They might be two of the only people in existence that understood what it was like to suffer that way.

Whatever Nord might claim, it couldn't have been easy on him. That was the sort of trauma that never faded. One could only learn how to cope.

A conversation with her uncle returned to her then, completely unbidden. *"There's a lot about my past I wish I could forget, but then I would also lose the very best pieces of me. So, no. I do not wish to forget them. Instead, I choose to endure."*

Lina flinched as his voice sounded in her mind, drawing Nord's attention to her. He frowned, not liking whatever he saw in her expression, and pulled her body back into the protective cradle of his. As she settled against him and breathed in his warmth, he secured his arms around her and brushed his lips against her ear.

"Tell me what you need, Kærasta."

"How about a fucking break?" she muttered, only half joking.

His voice rumbled through her as he replied, "I wish it was in my power to give that to you."

Lina sighed. So did she. "I know," she whispered. "But even if you could, we don't have time for me to fall apart."

"Says who?"

She twisted her neck to meet his eyes. "Do you need me to make you a list of all the reasons we don't have time? The Brotherhood is on our ass, the Drakes just declared fucking war, my uncle's corpse is in the other room, and I can't even spare the time for a proper burial, let alone ten minutes to process any of it. We've already stayed here longer than we should. We have to keep moving before one of our eight hundred enemies finds us." She made to stand up, but Nord tugged her back, keeping her firmly tucked against him.

His eyes flared as he looked at her. "Understand this, Lina. When it comes to you, there is nothing I wouldn't do. No sin I wouldn't commit. The world could be on fucking fire, and I would let it burn down around us if that is what you wished." He angled his face down, his mouth capturing hers briefly. "Fall apart if that is what you need. I will be here to put the pieces back together when you're done."

A ball of emotion clogged her throat, and there was no way to form words around it. It was several shaky breaths before she could manage his name. "Nord."

"I mean it."

"I know."

He held her, rubbing her back and murmuring things she didn't really hear against the top of her head.

"We should probably get going," Finley said awhile later.

"Fuck off, Fin," Nord softly snarled.

Finley lifted his hands. "I'm sorry, mate, but it's the truth. We're not safe here."

She felt Nord tense beneath her, but she placed a hand to his chest, preventing him from saying whatever he was about to say on her behalf.

"He's right. It's time for us to go."

Nord's eyes narrowed as he looked at her. "Are you sure?"

"Yeah. I just need to take care of one last thing before we leave."

This time when she shifted away to stand, he didn't stop her.

"Do you want me to come with you?"

"No. It will only take a minute. Be right back."

Not wanting to find pity in the others' eyes, Lina avoided their gazes and kept her focus on the ground as she left the living room and walked back to her uncle's study. Her heart grew heavier with each step, and no matter her initial intention, she couldn't bring herself to push open the door.

As she stood there, she could make out the soft sounds of Cora finishing whatever it was she was doing on the other side of the door. Lina decided it was probably for the best if she remained outside. Cora might have questions she couldn't answer, but more than that, she didn't need to see Alistair's body to do what she had in mind. And she certainly didn't want to remember him that way. It'd be hard enough as it was to forget the horrific image they'd stumbled across; she didn't need another glimpse.

Placing her hand flat against the door, Lina bowed her head and drew forth the strongest memory she could find. One of her uncle before the Brotherhood had gotten ahold of him and changed his appearance. It was nothing special, just a random day where she'd come across him slouched in one of his chairs, a book opened on his lap. As he'd looked up and found her there, his eyes creased in a smile, and a laugh formed on his lips.

She held that image of him in mind as she whispered, "From the day I was born, you've looked out for me. I wasn't here to look out for you. But I can do this much now, even if it's too late."

Calling upon her power, Lina pushed the image outward, willing it into being. Cora's startled gasp told Lina when her magic had been successful. The Drakes may have left a message, but that didn't mean Lina couldn't leave one of her own. Even if she and Quinn's mother would be the only two who ever knew about it.

Alistair deserved better than for his last moments on Earth to have been spent as the Drakes' toy. After everything he'd sacrificed, he deserved to find the peace he'd sought for so many years. It might be silly, but Lina worried he couldn't do that if he was still wearing a face that didn't belong to him. Or someone else's brand.

So she restored what had been lost.

It wasn't a fair trade considering what he'd done for her when their roles had been reversed and he'd found her dead body. But it was as close as she could get. At least in death, if not in the last years of his life, Alistair would get to be himself.

Lina took a step back, letting her hand fall away from the door as she did. She spoke without conscious thought, the words both a promise and an affirmation.

"I choose to endure."

It wasn't goodbye exactly, but it was as close as she could get. At least for now.

By the time Lina made it back to the living room, Finley had already summoned a portal.

"You okay?" Quinn asked when she rejoined them.

"No," Lina answered honestly. "But I will be."

Quinn's arms snaked out and wrapped around her in a crushing hug, which Lina was quick to return.

"You guys were busy," she said as they pulled away, gesturing to the luggage stacked at Quinn's feet.

"It's not much, but Mom said to pack warm. We grabbed what we could find since it's not like there's time for us to make a supply run," Quinn said. "We'll have to make do with what we have and hope you and the Guardian can magic up whatever else we might need."

No one missed Quinn's singular use of the title. Lina's eyes shot to Nord, but his expression was closed off, his attention on the shimmer of displaced air where the portal waited for them.

Quinn winced, realizing her misstep. "Sorry, didn't mean to pick at a fresh wound."

"It's fine."

But it obviously wasn't. A vein throbbed along the side of his neck, and a slight tremor worked its way down his hand before he curled it in a fist. For a second, Lina thought he might be a hairsbreadth away from slipping into his rage, but then he shrugged and seemed to come back to himself.

"Anyway, it's the truth. No avoiding it. I may no longer be a Guardian, but I'm far from useless."

"Atta boy," Quinn said with a wink. "I'm sure we'll find all sorts of fun uses for you in the days to come."

Lina shook her head. *Leave it to Quinn to find time to sneak in an innuendo.*

"Everyone all set?" Finley asked, bringing them back to the matter at hand. "This is probably the last time we'll be here for a while."

"Here," Quinn said, kneeling down to unzip the suitcase and pass out a couple of the items they'd stashed inside. "We're about to show up in a remote part of Sweden, in the middle of the night, during winter. Probably best we suit up."

Lina accepted a pair of leather gloves and a thick charcoal gray scarf, putting them on while the others did the same around her. After shrugging into a coat Finley had transformed to fit his large frame, Nord helped her into one of her own, though it was several sizes too big.

"I thought you might prefer to wear one of his unaltered," he said.

Lina smiled gratefully. "You were right, thank you."

"Ready?" he asked, his hand running over her back as she buttoned up.

She started to nod, but a flash of something at the corner of her eye had her crying out, "Wait!" Turning back to the coffee table, she snagged her uncle's will and letter addressed to her, along with his cane. "We probably shouldn't forget these."

Quinn took them from her, carefully placing the documents inside the suitcase, and then eyed the cane clutched in her hand. "I'm not sure that's going to fit."

"It's okay. I'll hold on to it for now."

Her best friend gave her an understanding smile and re-zipped the suitcase.

Once she was standing again, Finley asked, "Now are we ready?"

The air between them grew charged as one by one, they looked at each other and nodded, the reality of what they were up against setting in once more.

"All right," Finley said, "then I guess it's time for us to go see a man about a gateway."

For the record, there was no man. Or gateway, for that matter. Not yet anyway. As they stepped through the portal in Alistair's living room and out into the chilly Swedish night, all Lina could see for miles were stars.

Well, that, and a sea of white, glittering snow.

She breathed in the cold, the icy air burning her nose and lungs and making her cough a little at the extreme temperature shift. Lina was hardly an expert, but given their location and the time of year, it had to be in the low teens. Thankfully, between the warm clothes and her and Finley's combined magic, that shouldn't be an issue.

"Brrr," Quinn groaned dramatically, eyeing their surroundings with far less appreciation than Lina.

Maybe it was because it was so foreign, and she'd long craved adventure after her years shackled to a single building. Or maybe it was because Nord had come from here, but Lina was immediately entranced.

The untouched beauty of their surroundings spoke to her. She especially loved the way it smelled. This kind of cold had a distinct aroma. Crisp and clean, it was further enhanced with the salty tang of the sea—which was currently out of view—and sweet with the sharp scent of pine. It was beautiful, unique, and a bit wild. Just like the man who once called this land home.

"We're going to have to wait until morning to make the trek to the place where the gateway is hidden," Nord said, his breath coming out in little white puffs.

"Why not just head straight there?" Quinn asked.

"Well, for one, it's the middle of the night. And two, we only had a rough frame of reference for the portal," Finley answered. "I've never been there and could only go off what the big guy could remember of the area. As you're probably aware, things have a way of changing over a thousand-plus years."

Quinn frowned as she rubbed her hands together. "Are you telling me we're lost?"

"Not lost," Finley said, pushing his hands deeper into his pockets. "Just not quite at our destination."

"Which you don't know for sure is nearby," Quinn said.

Finley shrugged. "We're pretty confident."

Quinn scowled at him. "Forgive me if I don't find your confidence overly comforting."

"You should."

She scoffed. "You just told me I blindly followed you through a portal like a fucking idiot without making sure you actually knew where you were going, and now I'm going to have to pass the rest of the night in the middle of the Swedish wilderness." She pressed the heels of her hands into her eyes and groaned. "I didn't sign up for this."

"What's wrong, sweetheart? Afraid of roughing it?"

Quinn spun to face him; her eyes narrowed into slits. "For your information, I'm perfectly fine with rough. Prefer it, in fact. It's the freezing to death I'm not a fan of."

Finley stared at her for a second, seemingly at a loss for words before he cleared his throat and offered, "We can spoon if you want. I'll even let you be the big spoon."

Quinn made a sound like she was choking. "You'd like that, wouldn't you?"

"Hey, I'm just offering you solutions to your problem. Everyone knows that getting naked and cuddling up is the best way to stay warm."

She stared at him, color high in her cheeks as she spat, "Never gonna happen."

Finley shrugged, but his lips were tilted up in a mocking smile. "Now now, you know better than to say never."

"I'd snuggle a polar bear before going anywhere near you."

His expression turned pensive. "I'm no expert, but I'm pretty sure bears hibernate during the winter, love."

Quinn let out a little growl of frustration, which only made Finley smirk like he'd just been declared victorious.

"Suit yourself. When you change your mind, I'll be right over there." He pointed to the unmarred snow a few feet away. "I won't even say 'I told you so' when you do."

"Should we stop them before it gets physical?" Lina asked.

"I think they might enjoy themselves more if it did," Nord replied.

She snorted. "No kidding. But I don't think that's the sort of activity she's got in mind," Lina said, spying the way Quinn's hands were curled into fists at her sides.

"I wouldn't be so sure. Fighting makes for excellent foreplay."

"Speaking from experience?"

"Berserker," he said by way of answer.

"Right." She let out a soft snicker of amusement and then grew serious once more. "Are you sure we're not lost?"

Nord took her hand in his and squeezed. "I'm sure. The maps might call things by different names, but the land doesn't lie. We're as close as we can be for now. I should be able to guide us easily enough once the sun is up."

"Then I guess we should set up camp until it does." Lina looked around, not noticing anything nearby but shadows she could only guess were trees. "Here's as good a place as any, I suppose. Hey," she called, catching Quinn and Finley's attention before they could start drawing blood. "Knock it off, you two. No one's going to freeze on my watch." Then, speaking directly to Finley, she added, "Help me clear a spot so we can set up some tents and maybe a fire? Oh, and use your glamour thing to keep us out of sight, yeah?"

His eyes were glowing before she finished making her request.

"On it." Within seconds a large section of snow was fading and being replaced by rich brown earth.

"I'll take care of the firewood," Nord said, moving toward the nearest line of trees.

"Talk about a bad time to leave your ax at home," Quinn called after him.

"Want me to make you one?" Lina offered.

Nord paused, not quite looking back as he cracked his knuckles and drawled, "I'll manage."

"What's he going to do? Rip branches off the trees with his bare hands?" Quinn asked, coming to stand next to Lina.

"I think that's exactly what he's going to do."

Quinn let out a soft whistle. "Damn."

"Yeah." She watched Nord's retreating figure until he blended in with the rest of the shadows. "Guess that means I'm in charge of tents."

Turning back to where Finley had been transforming snow into dry land, Lina drew on her power and called forth the image of a standard campsite she'd sketched in her mind.

"Nope," Quinn said before Lina could open her eyes. "Try again."

"Did I get it wrong?" Lina asked with a worried frown, thinking maybe her power was starting to wane after the excessive amount she'd drawn on over the last few hours and not all the tents had formed.

Instead of answering the question, Quinn asked one of her own. "Do I look like a Girl Scout to you?"

"What?"

"Camping has come a long way since you've been gone. We don't have to sleep on the floor like a bunch of prepubescent kids trying to earn their merit badges with only a flimsy scrap of plastic to protect us from the elements. We're grown-ups. Conjure us up a couple cabins with an air mattress or, better yet, actual beds."

Lina stared at Quinn, certain that in her exhausted state and after the sheer overwhelm of the day's events that she couldn't be hearing her correctly.

"Why are you looking at me like that?" Quinn asked when Lina didn't respond.

"Are you kidding me right now?"

"No. Need me to show you what I'm talking about?" Quinn offered, her eyes swirling with power as she lifted her hands toward Lina's face.

"Quinn." Lina blew out an exasperated breath and swatted her friend's hands away. "I'm not going to make you a cabin."

"Why not?" she asked, her brows slanting down.

"Uh, because it's a massive waste of energy for something you're not going to use for more than a handful of hours at most. You'll be just fine in your own tent. Hell, it's big enough for you to stand up and walk around in."

"I'm not seeing your point."

What little hold Lina had on her composure snapped. "Then let me spell it out for you, Satori. You're acting like a spoiled brat."

"Evalina Cuska, did you really just call me a brat?"

"Yes! Because after everything we've gone through today, you're over here throwing a temper tantrum for no good reason."

Their battle of wills stretched until Quinn finally gave in with a heavy sigh. "I'm not trying to be a pain in the ass. I'm not," she insisted, taking in Lina's disbelieving look. "It's just been a long fucking day. I'm tired. My heart hurts."

Lina's frustration vanished at the admission. So did hers.

"I want to curl up in something warm and soft, not spend the night digging rocks out of my ass."

Lina rolled her eyes, but she couldn't quite hold back her slight smile.

Quinn poked her. "Admit it, my way sounds a lot better than yours. Call me a brat or a snob or whatever else you want. There's nothing wrong with appreciating luxury or taking comfort when and how you can."

"Maybe not, but I'm still not going to drain what's left of my power to make you a cabin when we don't know what we're going to have to face next."

"Pfft. Your power is just fine. But . . . that's probably the smarter choice," Quinn said, wrapping her coat around her more tightly. "I guess I'll just make myself a mattress out of the suitcases. But there better be some proper blankets in there."

Lina's chest thawed. It was such a familiar argument for them to have. Not the topic specifically, but the reason behind it. Quinn preferred making demands and riling Lina up rather than talking about what was really bothering her. It had always been that way between them. That little slice of normal, in the middle of a day filled with absolute chaos, brought her the tiniest sliver of peace.

Quinn wrapped an arm around Lina's waist and rested her head against her shoulder. "We're going to get through this."

"I know."

Somehow, someway, they would. She'd prayed too hard, for too long, for a chance to live a full life. She hadn't come this far just to let some jackasses with god complexes steal her dream from her.

The road ahead might be a rocky one, but Lina would have her happily ever after.

Anything else simply wasn't an option.

CHAPTER 4
NORD

Neither he nor Lina got much, if any, actual sleep that night. Their minds were too filled with the horrors of the day they'd shared for respite. Even laying here now, Nord could recall with agonizing clarity the way it'd felt when the Director had raped his mind and carved out his power. It left him shaky, coated in sweat, and fighting hard to keep the rage at bay.

It had been easier to ignore what happened while there were other crises demanding his attention. But in the quiet hours just before dawn, there was no hiding from the truth.

Thankfully, he'd been able to distract himself from the worst of it by focusing on the woman in his arms. When the memories got to be too much, he'd tucked himself around her body and began to catalog each and every detail he could until he was firmly grounded in the present.

It worked so long as he remained intent on the sound of her soft breaths, the silky feel of her hair, the lingering scent of her shampoo. To be fair, once he'd started, staying focused was no hardship. He much preferred memorizing the things that were uniquely her than the alternative.

Nord trailed his fingers up Lina's arm, starting with the back of her hand and moving up to her shoulder. When the path became blocked by her hair, he curled his fingers around the golden strands and slid them back, letting his knuckles drag lightly across the side of her neck.

"When are you going to stop pretending you're asleep?" he whispered, before dipping his face and brushing a kiss to the hollow just behind her ear.

She shivered at the contact of his mouth, her breath hitching slightly. "I was taking my cue from you." She rolled over to face him, pillowing her head beside his on his arm. "Guess we're both terrible actors."

"You know you never need to act with me."

"Ditto," she said, extending her index finger and bopping him on the nose.

His lips hitched up as he drew his fingers down the velvety skin of her cheek, his gaze taking in the smudges of exhaustion beneath her eyes. "Well, the sun's up now. No need to fake it any longer."

Her eyes darted to the side of the tent that was only just starting to turn a lighter shade of green due to the rising sun. "That's up?"

Nord continued the gentle play of his fingers over her face, helpless against his need to touch her. "Enough to prove that we made it through the night."

"Yeah, I guess we did." She swallowed, and her eyes fluttered closed for a second. "Though it doesn't seem like much of a victory after all that was lost."

"I know. It's never easy." He ran the pad of his thumb over the crease between her brows, smoothing the skin before tracing the curve of her eyebrow. "But you should still celebrate every victory, Kærasta. No matter how small. Living to fight another day is never a bad thing."

"I suppose that's true. I just feel so guilty. And angry. And—" she broke off, looking uncertain.

"Tell me. Let me help you carry the burden."

"It's stupid."

"Your feelings could never be stupid. Tell me."

Still looking conflicted, she finally gave in to his gentle demand. "For the first time since all this began, I'm not sure I should be alive."

Nord went still.

"Don't get me wrong. I'm not saying I want to trade places with him. But, it's just . . . if I hadn't come back, he'd still be alive. The Director wouldn't have done those awful things to you . . . it just feels like I've ruined the lives of everyone that matters most to me."

"Speaking as one of those people, that could not be further from the truth."

"Look at what he did to you," she whispered, her voice breaking. "You may not have told me exactly what happened, but I'm the one that found you in that cell. I saw the aftermath. He *tortured* you, Nord. Because of me."

"No—"

"And the Drakes went after Alistair because of me. Don't you see? I'm the common denominator here. I'm fucking things up for every-body. There's no way I'm worth it—"

"Shh, stop. Lina, listen to me," he said, taking her chin in his hand and forcing her to look at him. "Have you already forgotten what I told you? My life didn't even begin until you came into it. I spent centuries alone, wandering, searching for meaning. Searching for you. You, Kærasta. I would have spent the rest of eternity searching had I not found you.

"Can you honestly say you would have wanted that for me? For him? Even knowing how it would end, do you think Alistair would have traded a single day he got to spend with you in exchange for a lifetime without you? He may not be here to answer the question for you, but I am. The answer is no, Lina. No matter the cost, I would pay it a thousand times over to keep you."

Emotion turned her eyes a deep aqua. "Nord."

He talked over her, needing her to hear him, needing her to believe. "The guilt for his death is not yours to carry. He would not have wanted that for you. I know your heart is breaking, and it's only natural to look for someone to blame. But you are not that someone. Alistair loved you. *I* love you. Do not doubt for a second what a gift it is to have known you—to have loved you. You haven't ruined my life, Kærasta. You've made it."

Her face crumpled, and he pulled her into his body, his fingers weaving into her hair as she buried her face against his neck. He held her close and pressed his mouth to her temple while her shoulders shook beneath his arm.

He held her while the sun continued to climb in the sky, giving her the space and time to fall apart, but ready to help her put herself back together.

Just like he promised her he would.

"You still haven't told me what *that's* for," Nord said while he was buttoning up his coat a couple hours later.

Lina followed the direction of his gaze, her lips lifting in a small smile when they alighted on the metal helmet with its two curving horns she'd created along with their blankets and the rest of their camping supplies. "The helmet? I thought you might want to look the part when you lead us to your secret Viking village." Then her eyes swept up his body and color flushed her cheeks. "But I'm pretty sure you have that covered with or without it."

He chuckled. "That's thoughtful of you, but I've never met a Viking that wore a horned helmet on or off the battlefield. It's not exactly practical, is it? Although . . . I guess it does have a certain sort of ferocity." He reached over and plunked it on his head, turning and posing for her with his fists planted on his hips. "How do I look?"

She let out a snort of surprised laughter, and Nord shamelessly stared. She looked so fucking beautiful in that moment that his heart ached. He'd give anything to keep it there.

Her smile stretched as she caught his gaze, and there was no missing the feminine appreciation in her tone as she replied, "On anyone else, it'd be ridiculous, but you make it work, berserker."

"Shall I save it for later then?" he asked, waggling his brows.

The pink in her cheeks deepened. "Maybe."

He winked at her. "Anytime you want to role-play a Viking raid, you just say the word. I'd be more than happy to show you how I pillage and plunder."

It was possibly the stupidest thing he'd ever said, but her reaction told him she thought it was anything but. She was laughing, yes, but there was unmistakable interest shining in her eyes.

Still chuckling, she threw one of the fur blankets at him, which he caught easily. "You're ridiculous."

"You love it."

"Yes," she agreed. "And you."

Then she took the few steps necessary to reach him in the relatively cramped space of their tent and gave him a sweet kiss. It was over before he was ready for it to be, his lips chasing hers as she pulled back.

"Where do you think you're going?"

"As much as I'd love to hide in here with you, I think we've put off the inevitable long enough. We have a gateway to activate and sanctuary to find, remember?"

The sound of Quinn and Finley moving around the campsite reached his ears, and he sighed, dropping his forehead to hers. "You're right. But one more won't hurt," he said, pulling her back and giving her a much more thorough kiss.

By the time they pulled away, her hair was disheveled from his hands running through it, her face flushed, and her lips swollen.

"Now we can go," he said, turning toward the tent's front flap. When Lina made no move to follow him, he paused. "You coming?"

"What?" She blinked. "Oh! Yeah. Right."

Quinn watched them exit the tent with a knowing smile. "Good morning, love birds."

"We weren't—" Lina started.

"Then you're a fool. I raised you better than that," Quinn mock-scolded, holding out a granola bar. "Now, eat your breakfast."

Lina accepted the offering with a slight grimace. "I don't have much of an appetite."

"Don't care. Your body needs the fuel. Eat."

"You're bossy this morning."

"This morning?" Finley drawled.

It was too early to deal with another of their verbal pissing contests, so Nord cut it off at the pass. "Fin, catch."

The Guardian grunted as the helmet Lina conjured connected with his chest. "What's this?"

"Lina and I wanted to make sure you fit in."

"You want me to wear this?" His eyes narrowed suspiciously as his gaze darted between them. "Is this some kind of joke?"

"You think the traditions of my people are a joke?"

Finley blinked and started backpedaling. "No, of course not—"

Nord maintained his stoic expression, but Lina's snort of laughter gave them away.

"Assholes," Finley muttered, his expression clearing.

Quinn was beaming. "I don't know, Fin. It might be an improvement. You could always hang on to it and use one of the horns if you need to replace that stick of yours."

He glowered at her.

She ignored him and turned to Nord. "In all seriousness, what *do* you expect we'll find once we get through the gateway? Should we be prepared for drinking horns and war paint? Or do you think things will be more, uh, modern?"

"Things will certainly have evolved. That's just human nature. But as far as what that evolution looks like, we won't know until we get there."

Quinn nodded, looking as though she expected as much. "That's good. I'm not sure I'm okay with ice floating in my bathwater. Let's hope for some sort of indoor plumbing system at the very least."

He was smiling as she turned to repack their belongings, but his smile faded as another thought came to him. He'd traversed enough worlds on behalf of the Brotherhood to know that civilization always moved forward. Progress was inevitable. He'd be surprised if the place they found was anything like the home he'd left. But there was another thing all of those worlds had in common: their natural aversion to outsiders.

"Something wrong?" Lina asked.

"No," Nord said, hoping she couldn't sense the words he'd left unsaid.

At least not yet.

DESPITE HIS ASSURANCES, THEY HADN'T MANAGED TO LOCATE THE GATEWAY within the first couple of hours.

"It might help if you told us what you were looking for exactly," Finley said, peeling off his coat and revealing the sweat-soaked shirt beneath.

Though they were near the coast, there wasn't much else in the way of landmarks to guide them besides the distant mountains and a forest of trees, which seemed never-ending. So all they had to go off of was Nord's memory of a stone archway set atop a slight hill that overlooked the northernmost part of what was now the Baltic Sea. It'd been selected due to its remote location, and apparently, not even a thousand-plus years had changed that much.

"Just keep heading east."

"We go much farther east, we're going to end up in the water," Quinn muttered as she stomped along behind Finley.

Nord pressed his lips together, a headache building at the base of his skull. He understood their frustrations. No one had planned on spending the day hiking through a snow-covered wildland, but he knew they must be close. The gateway couldn't just disappear . . .

Unless it had been intentionally destroyed.

The thought was unbidden, unwelcome, and immediately set Nord's teeth on edge.

If they'd come all this way for nothing . . . but no, Cora was the one that led them here. This *had* to be the answer. They just needed to keep searching.

When the next couple of hours passed without any sense of recognition, a part of him started to wonder if the gateway might have been disguised or hidden somehow. The former was not only possible, it was likely. The latter less so since the magic that infused it would prevent it from going unrecognized by one who'd helped create it. In either case, so long as the gateway still existed, he should be able to locate it.

So why the fuck can't I find it?

Lina slid her gloved hand into his, squeezing hard. "Don't worry. It's here, somewhere."

For all intents and purposes, he should be the one reassuring her, and yet, even with everything she was dealing with, she'd sensed he could do with a little reassurance himself and hadn't hesitated to offer it.

The feel of her hand, steady and solid in his, was enough to send the rest of the doubt scattering, and he returned her squeeze with a grateful one of his own. Nord appreciated her optimism, especially because he knew it was likely only for his benefit. She had no reason —save her faith in him—that that would be the case.

Lifting her hand to his lips, he pressed a kiss against the back of it, silently swearing then and there never to give her a reason to doubt in him.

Nord wasn't used to having someone so attuned to his needs. He'd had blade brothers who watched his back on the battlefield, but this was different. It wasn't about mere survival; it was personal. Intimate.

It was love.

He was thinking that the novelty of being loved so completely would never wear off when Finley stopped and called out.

"Hey, what's that?"

Nord angled his head, following the path of Finley's finger until he was looking at what appeared to be some sort of ruin mostly hidden amongst the towering conifers.

"I'm not sure."

He started to dismiss the piles of snowy rubble and crumbling walls. After all, it wasn't an old building they were looking for. But there was something about the randomness of the location that set the hair at the back of his neck on end.

Perhaps it wasn't random at all.

"Let's check it out," he said, heading further into the forest.

It took longer to reach the ruin than he'd expected at first glance, not having noticed the steady incline, which required them to move with care. Even so, as more of the ancient stone construct was revealed, the tingle beneath his skin intensified.

This was the place.

He didn't know how he knew. Only that he was right.

The group was uncharacteristically silent as they crested the hill and came to stand beside the first of many stone piles.

Lina was the first to break the silence. "What do you think it used to be?"

Nord shrugged, but Quinn was quick to answer. Her eyes were squinted, but she sounded certain when she said, "Monastery."

"How do you know?" Finley asked.

Quinn shrugged and borrowed her mother's phrase. "I have a feeling."

Nord couldn't say whether the phrase held as much meaning for her as the Satori matriarch, but he wasn't about to question her. What the place had once been was irrelevant. All that mattered was the secret it contained.

Now that the trees no longer obscured what remained of the ancient structure, Nord could make out the overall layout. It looked like there had once been two buildings, though only one of them had more than a singular crumbling wall left to its name.

The larger of the two sat roughly in the shape of a T on its side, while the smaller ran parallel to its eastern wall. The two buildings seemed to have once been connected by a covered path. All but two of its archways had been destroyed; what was left of the evenly spaced pillars little more than broken stumps of varying heights.

Still, it was enough to lure him forward.

Finley's hand shot out, grasping him around the wrist. "Wait. We don't know anything about this place. There could be wards or traps."

Nord let out a soft huff of frustration, but his partner was right. Better to be safe. He gestured for Finley to proceed with a search since he was without the power to do so himself. Finley walked the perimeter, his eyes blazing with silver light as he used his Guardian abilities to search for any trace of residual magic.

Once Finley completed his circuit and paused between the two standing arches, Nord glanced down at Lina. "Wait here."

She looked like she wanted to debate the issue but surprised him by haltingly agreeing. "Okay."

He knew she hated staying back, and he didn't sense immediate danger, but there were other things at play here. He'd feel more comfortable if she remained a safe distance away until he could figure out what they were.

"Find anything?" he asked as he neared Finley.

"It's clean as far as I can tell," he replied, though his eyes remained trained on the closest arch.

With each step he took, the tingling sensation grew, until it was a harsh buzz. "Do you feel that?"

Finley's expression twisted with surprise. "No, actually. It's the lack of anything that's bothering me. If the Brotherhood's magic is at play, I should be able to detect it."

Nord chewed on that, wondering if the thing that sent his pulse racing through his veins was actively hidden from the others. Magic would leave a trace, which made the possibility unlikely since Finley hadn't picked up on it.

That only left one other explanation for the very physical reaction Nord was having to the proximity of what could only be the gateway, and it was infinitely simpler and equally more complex.

The land recognized him and was beckoning him home.

Without stopping to think, Nord reached out and pressed his hand flat against one of the stones.

CHAPTER 5
LINA

"Is it just me, or is your boyfriend acting weirder than usual?" Quinn asked with an arched brow.

Lina's gaze cut over to the two men huddled together beneath the closer of the intact archways before returning to her friend. "What do you mean 'weird'?"

She waved a hand in Nord's direction. "You don't find it odd that he's over there right now lovingly caressing a pillar of stone?"

"He's not caressing it."

Though he was currently running his fingers along the inner edge of the arch and leaning forward to inspect it more closely.

Quinn snorted. "Um, yeah. He is. He's about half an inch away from making out with it, and no one wears an expression filled with that much rapturous longing unless they're fondling the goods."

"Jesus, Quinn. He's not fondling anything; he's just checking the stones for identifying marks or whatever." Lina crossed her arms and stomped her feet in an attempt to stay warm. The chill in the air was much more apparent now that they were standing still. "And even if he was, could you blame him? This is the first time in centuries he's come into contact with anything from his past. Of course it's going to dredge up some feelings."

"If you say so."

But now that Quinn had planted the thought that Nord was acting off, Lina couldn't help but pick up on little things herself. Like the sudden paleness of his skin and the feverish shine in his eyes. And there was definitely something about his expression that seemed out of place.

She wouldn't go as far as to label it 'rapturous,' but there was an unnatural intensity there. Reverence, perhaps. Like a person of faith coming into contact with a holy relic.

While Lina studied him, he pulled away from the arch and turned to speak to Finley. As he did, she could easily make out a tremor in his usually steady hands. Gateway or not, whatever he'd found was clearly affecting him.

Finley nodded along to whatever Nord was saying and then moved further away to stand beneath the other arch.

Prickles of foreboding shot up Lina's spine. Nord loved to be in control. He wouldn't rely on someone else's investigation to provide him with crucial information. He'd insist on performing the investigation himself to guarantee nothing pertinent was missed.

So why's he having Fin—

Before the question could finish forming in her mind, Lina saw the flash of metal catching light. She recognized the multi-tool immediately. It was one of those little keychain items that could act as an emergency screwdriver, spare set of scissors, a knife . . .

Just as the word came to her, Nord's right hand slashed across his left, and bright red blood welled. She'd known he'd need to activate the gateway somehow, but she hadn't expected him to maim himself in the process. And given everything else going on, she couldn't shake the feeling that the action wasn't completely intentional.

. . .

"Nord!" she cried, slipping on the icy rocks in her rush to get to him.

She went down hard, pain blossoming in her knees and palms as they connected with jagged stone. It was a comedy of errors as she tried to stand, her limbs sliding out from beneath her again and again, unable to find purchase in the snow.

Finally, Quinn grasped her around the waist and helped support her weight as she got her feet back into position beneath her.

As far as she could tell, Nord was utterly unaware of the commotion. Usually, he'd be the first at her side, his preternatural reflexes helping him catch her before she could even hit the floor. But he hadn't so much as looked in her direction as he lifted his dripping hand to the curved and pitted slabs.

"Nord, stop!" she shouted, desperation making the words shrill.

He gave no indication he'd heard her at all.

Her shouts got Finley's attention, at least. Although he was so focused on her, he didn't immediately register what had triggered her cries.

That meant it was up to her. Instinct had her reaching for her power, but she was too panicked to focus. With only seconds to act, and since Nord couldn't seem to hear her, Lina knew that the only way she could stop him was to physically restrain him. She couldn't do that from here.

Unfortunately, the slick ice and snow forced her to take aggravatingly slow steps, and she was still out of reach when Nord started to paint the archway with his blood.

Lina froze, her mouth dropping open in horrified fascination as he dipped a finger in the crimson pooling in the palm of his other hand and began to draw primitive-looking shapes onto the stones.

No, she amended, *not draw. Trace.*

The designs were chiseled into the surface, and he was filling in the hollowed-out lines with his blood.

Shock held her captive one moment longer before she broke free of its hold and scurried with as much haste as she could manage across the last few feet that separated them.

"Nord," she tried again. But even as his name left her lips, she knew it was too late.

The runes—for it was clear now that she was close enough to make out the individual shapes that's what they were—began to pulse with an eerie red light.

He dropped his hand and finally turned to face her. Lina gasped, her heart stuttering in her chest.

The light wasn't just pouring out of the runes. It was also shining from Nord's eyes.

Close enough now to touch him, Lina reached out a shaking hand.

"Lina, don't," Finley roared.

The second her fingers made contact with Nord's body, she was flung up and back. Then she was airborne, her body seemingly weightless for several heartbeats before she hit the ground with a bone-rattling thud. The air left her in a heavy whoosh, and she moaned, her body throbbing with pain.

"Don't move," Quinn ordered, panicked as she knelt beside Lina.

Quinn's face swam in and out of focus, and something warm dripped down the nape of Lina's neck, but still she tried to push herself up. Quinn stopped her with a hand on her chest.

"He needs me," Lina slurred, weakly pushing at the hand and trying to sit up. Through sheer force of will, she succeeded.

"Dammit, Lina," Quinn hissed, moving so that she was supporting most of Lina's weight.

It took a couple of blinks for the fog to clear from her eyes, but even then, Lina wasn't sure what she saw was real.

Nord was floating in the air like some sort of wingless angel. Wind tore at his hair and clothes, holding him suspended high in the sky. His head was flung back, his arms outstretched on either side of his body, blood still dripping from the gash in his hand and splashing onto the once pristine snow. Then his head lifted and slowly swiveled until his burning eyes locked with hers.

Lina felt a blast of power pulse through her body as those ethereal, glowing eyes pinned her in place.

Then Nord opened his mouth and spoke in a voice both ancient and not remotely his own. "The Warrior has returned."

Before she could do more than suck in a ragged breath, Nord's face went slack, and he plummeted to the floor amidst a chorus of horrified screams.

CHAPTER 6
NORD

The transition from wintery forest to foggy wasteland was instant. One second, he was standing beside Finley, and the next, he was here.

Wherever here was.

He'd lived among magical beings for entirely too long to treat the forced relocation as anything but what it was. A threat.

Whatever—or whoever—brought him here wanted to weaken him and prove they had the upper hand. While they may have succeeded in isolating him, no matter how they tipped the scales in their favor, one thing Nord would never be was weak.

He sought the ever-present pool of rage that burned within, calling on the berserker to come to his aid, but . . . it wasn't there.

Or, if it was, it was out of reach.

Fuck.

Alone, weaponless, and with absolutely no clue how to get back to the others, Nord weighed his options. Not that he had many. Until he figured out where he was and why, he was at the mercy of the magic that bound him.

Knowing he wouldn't find any answers to his questions by just standing around, he took a tentative step forward. He was pleased to find that he moved easily. Though, he couldn't help but note the oddly weightless feel of his limbs. Like his physical form wasn't fully materialized in this plane.

An interesting fact, but one that raised as many questions as it answered. If his consciousness had been separated from his actual body, he could be, quite literally, anywhere.

Nord continued his careful prowl forward, his mind working overtime to sort through the events of the past several minutes in an attempt to make sense of them. As best he could guess, when he touched the stone it triggered the ancient spell that sealed Novasgard and pulled him here, to this in-between place.

But why?

The magic should have recognized him and allowed him safe passage. All of this was something else entirely. But was it test or trap?

He couldn't be sure.

Thick fog swirled up his ankles, reminding him of a playful cat seeking attention and taunting him in equal measure. Something about the electric zing of raw energy crackling along his nerves felt familiar. But as soon as he had the thought, it disappeared, as if skimmed from the top of his mind.

His eyes narrowed, his distrust swelling. He did not appreciate feeling like he was here for some other being's amusement.

"Do not toy with me," he growled.

There was no answer, but then, he hadn't expected one.

He swept his eyes from side to side, trying to draw clues as to his whereabouts out of the pale gray mist that stretched endlessly in every direction. Besides a few random explosions of color that went off without warning or reason, there were none.

His steps slowed at another shower of purple sparks.

The tiny color-bursts tickled the fringes of his memory; he'd seen them somewhere once before. The harder he tried to draw forth the memory, the more elusive it became. In the end, the only thing he could tie them back to were fireworks trapped within a cloud. And while a beautiful sight, that was hardly noteworthy enough to prick at him this way.

The sparks signified something; he'd bet his life on it.

When a flare of turquoise light went off to his left, Nord turned and stalked in that direction, determined to ferret out its secrets. Just before he reached it, the last of the color faded and another memory clawed at his consciousness. One so blurred about the edges, he'd always dismissed it as a child's fanciful imagination.

Dismissed it, but never managed to forget it, even after all this time.

As the memory came into focus, Nord's breath left him in a shocked whoosh. He suddenly recalled all of it in perfect detail.

The mist. The lights. The *voice*.

Nord went still as the hairs along his arms and neck stood on end and ice shot through his veins.

He'd been here before.

The night he learned what he was.

"So you do remember who you are, Warrior of Odin."

That ancient, bodiless voice called to him through the mist, seemingly nowhere and everywhere at once.

Nord resisted the impulse to drop to his knees. There was only one woman he'd ever kneel for, and she wasn't here.

"Interesting," the voice crooned as dozens of tiny blue and green explosions lit up the fog.

"Get out of my head," he said through gritted teeth.

"But your thoughts are so loud."

Nord wasn't sure what to do with that information. True or not, after the Director, anyone reading his mind without permission felt like a violation. When he spoke next, the words were dripping with barely suppressed rage.

"Why have you brought me here?"

"You are the one who returned, seeking sanctuary from the very people you abandoned."

"I didn't abandon them," he snarled.

"What else would you call walking away from everyone you once vowed to protect?"

Nord felt the inappropriate urge to laugh. "All I've ever done is protect people."

"Not *your* people. Not the people you swore to serve. To lead."

"I never swore to lead them."

"You didn't have to. The promise is written in your blood."

Nord sucked in a breath, feeling as though he'd just been punched in the kidneys. "I ensured they were safe. I do not owe them anything else."

"But you do, Warrior of Odin. Those are his people. They belong to him just as you do. It is your duty, your destiny, to protect them. By turning your back on them, you turned your back on *him*."

Nord growled. "He turned his back on them, not me. He is the one who allowed them to die by the hundreds."

When the explosions went off this time, they were a vibrant red, reminding him far too much of blood hitting water.

"He gave them *you*. He made you, gifted you with his own strength and divine fury, and yet you ran. You let fear into your heart and ignored what you were given."

"I fear nothing!"

Even as the angry shout left his lips, Nord knew it was a lie. Fear was a silent but constant companion, especially now that he had someone in his life he could lose.

The sparks pulsed again, still red, but softer now.

"A gift can always be taken away if the recipient is deemed unworthy."

The threat, coming on the heels of the Director's actions, was too much. Instinct overshot reason as fury ignited within him. It may not have the added benefit of his berserker's power, but it was potent, and it was his.

"I have spent countless lifetimes on and off the battlefield, defending those who could not defend themselves. I used my power to save as many lives as I have claimed, all in the hope that one day I might find the one I was born to protect. Even you cannot deny the worthiness of that cause."

"You sold your soul in exchange for immortality and power."

"No!" he roared. "Immortality means nothing when you wander alone. When I left, I had nothing, no one. My family had been slaughtered before my eyes. My people were dying. Leaving them was the only way to save them. I asked for nothing in exchange. I knew joining the Brotherhood was a life sentence. Even so, I committed myself to their cause. Then through some miracle, I managed to be in the right place at the right time and found the one soul who can fill the void in my own. Now that I have found her, you cannot take away my only means of protecting her. She needs me." Nord's breathing was ragged, his enraged words dropping to a rough whisper as he concluded, "Almost as much as I need her."

There was no immediate response, and his hands curled into fists at his sides, his chest heaving. Before he could demand an answer, soft lavender light flickered throughout the mist. It was oddly soothing, but the unexpected change made him wary.

When the voice did speak, it was far gentler than he'd ever heard it.

"Then be worthy of her, Warrior. Do not let fear win a second time."

"What is that supposed to mean?"

The mist went dark.

"What the fuck does that mean?" he shouted into the darkness.

"Welcome home, Warrior of Odin."

When Nord came to, he was lying on his back in the snow, his body a catalog of aches. He tried to push himself up, but Finley's hand on his shoulder checked the movement.

"Give it a second. You took a hard fall."

He sought Lina's worried gaze first. "What happened?"

She bit her lip, confusion flickering in her eyes as she reached out and ran her fingers gently down the side of his face. "You don't remember?"

This time, he ignored Finley's protests and sat up, his uninjured hand lifting to cup the back of his head with a low groan. "Just touching the stone."

The others exchanged looks.

"What?" Nord demanded.

"Told you he was acting funny," Quinn muttered.

"Funny?" Nord repeated. "How?"

Lina opened her mouth to reply, then closed it and shook her head, seemingly at a loss.

Nord reached for her, finally noticing the blood coating his hands. A chill that had nothing to do with the cold ran through him. "What the hell happened?"

"You opened the portal, mate."

Nord snapped his head to the gateway, and he grunted with pain as dozens of tiny lights exploded in his periphery. Warm amber light spilled out of the archway where he and Finley had been standing.

"How?" he asked again, tearing his eyes away from the rippling wall of light.

"I didn't actually see what happened. You asked me to check for runes on the second gateway, and then I guess you slit open your hand while my back was turned. Everything happened pretty fast after that. It's sort of hard to make sense of it all, but you, uh . . ." he trailed off.

Quinn picked up the story with her usual finesse. "After groping the stones, you decided you wanted to try your hand at finger painting, and then you were possessed by a demon and flung up into the air while spouting off creepy shit in the demon's voice. Was that really so hard?" she asked, looking between Lina and Finley.

"Quinn," Lina said sharply, glaring at her friend before shaking her head and returning her attention to Nord. "That's not what happened. Not exactly anyway. You did get this weird look on your face while touching the stones, and then like Fin said, you cut open your hand to trace the runes you'd found. I tried to stop you, it didn't seem like you were in control of yourself, but when I touched you, there was this burst of power that sent us both flying."

"You forgot the demon part," Quinn said.

"He wasn't possessed by a demon," Lina insisted with exasperation.

"You don't know that. Have you seen *The Exorcist*?"

"What does that have to do with anything?" Lina asked.

Quinn held up her hands. "I'm just saying, he made a blood offering, and then all of a sudden he was floating and speaking with someone else's voice. That seems like some demonic shit to me."

Instead of refuting her friend's explanation outright again, Lina bit her lip and shifted her eyes back to Nord.

"Lina?" he asked when she still hadn't said anything.

"Well . . . that is sort of what happened."

"So demonic possession is your working theory?" he let out an incredulous laugh. "Fin?" he tried again, looking to his friend to offer a more plausible alternative.

Silver faded from the Guardian's eyes as he dropped his hold on his power. "Not picking up any residual magic to say for sure, but *something* definitely took hold of you."

Nord suppressed a shudder, feeling as though thousands of insects skittered across his skin. "You mentioned I spoke. What did I say?"

"The Warrior has returned," Lina answered, her eyes wide. "Do you know what that means?"

Nord shook his head slowly, the slight movement painful. "No." But as he said it, he couldn't help but feel that he'd heard something similar before.

"I wonder who The Warrior is?" Lina said, chewing her lip.

"The devil," Quinn answered immediately.

"I will remove your mouth," Lina snapped, giving Quinn a warning look. "Knock it off, Satori."

Quinn rolled her eyes but didn't say anything further.

"It obviously refers to Nord," Finley answered, drawing everyone's attention. "This," he continued, circling his finger around, "is all connected."

"You don't think the same thing would have happened if someone else tried to open the gateway years ago?" Lina asked.

Finley shrugged. "Hard to say, but it seems unlikely. Nord's blood is what triggered it, only makes sense that everything ties back to him."

Nord frowned, not liking his friend's assessment but unable to deny it had a certain ring of truth to it.

"Well, whatever the case may be," he said with a groan as he pushed himself to his feet. "The gateway is open, which is all that matters right now. We've wasted enough time—"

"Just a second," Finley said. "We don't know what we're going to find in there. Let me get you healed up first."

"You really think we might be walking into something dangerous?" Lina asked.

"Isn't that our MO?" Quinn replied.

Lina frowned. "I just thought, since only someone connected to them could open the gateway, they'd—"

"What? Welcome us with open arms?" Quinn asked. "Would you?"

"I guess not . . ." Lina said, giving the rippling portal a wary once-over.

Healed once more, Nord reached out and grasped Lina's hand with his. "Whatever's waiting for us on the other side, we'll face it together, like everything else."

She threaded her fingers through his, her expression grim but determined. "Then they don't stand a chance."

CHAPTER 7
LINA

She didn't take her first full breath until they'd been traveling a good forty minutes. Quinn and Finley had her half expecting bullets or axes to come flying their way as soon as they set foot on the other side of the portal, but so far, it had been entirely uneventful.

The further they walked without issue, the more Lina relaxed and began to appreciate the reality of where she was. At first glance, Novasgard didn't seem to be that much different from Earth. There was no red sky or extra moons hanging on the horizon. But then Nord had mentioned it was chosen for its similarity to his homeland, so she hadn't really expected it to feel like something out of a sci-fi movie.

What it did have was a sparkling blue ocean, soaring mountains, and a lush forest. It reminded her of the Pacific Northwest, not that she'd ever been there personally, but she'd seen enough pictures to recognize the landscape.

It was also clearly not the dead of winter. Or, if it was, winter here was nothing like the snowy wonderland they'd just left.

Already, they'd peeled off their heavy coats and shed their scarves and gloves.

"How much farther will it be before we find signs of life?" Quinn asked.

It was the first time any of them had spoken above a hushed whisper, and the eruption of activity in the nearby trees as a result of her raised voice had Lina reaching for her power.

Instead of finding herself surrounded by a group of scouts with weapons aimed at their chests, the noise was the result of dozens of big black birds taking flight. Their annoyed squawking told Lina they weren't exactly fans of their peace being interrupted.

Head tilted up at the sky, she noticed when the largest of the birds circled back around and swooped low. She couldn't shake the feeling it was looking straight at her.

"Sorry about that," she muttered. "We're just looking for a safe place to hide. Didn't mean to disturb you."

"Talking to wildlife now?" Quinn asked.

"Never know when we're going to need friends." Lina didn't look away from the bird, her mouth going dry as she realized just how large it was.

"And so you're trying to win over a flock of ravens?"

"Those are no ravens," Nord said softly, coming to stand beside Lina, his hand resting protectively at the base of her spine.

"What are they?" Lina asked.

Nord shook his head.

"Well, they're big black birds, so ravens will just have to do for now," Quinn said, but even her bravado seemed to dwindle as the bird loomed closer, the shadow it cast on the ground swallowing up all four of them. "Fuck, he's a big one. I think one of us could climb on his back and take him for a ride."

"Let's not go trying that, 'kay?" Lina asked.

Quinn nodded her agreement.

Finley moved in close to Nord, his voice pitched low. "Think we've been spotted?"

"Without a doubt," Nord replied, his eyes still tracking the bird who was now flying in the opposite direction.

"Best we keep moving then."

"Wait," Quinn said, stumbling a little as she rushed to grab Finley's arm and stop him. "You think those birds are off to report our whereabouts to the humans or something?"

"Wouldn't be the craziest thing that's happened recently," Finley said.

Quinn paled. "I was prepared for Vikings, not shifters."

"Trust me," Nord said, "you weren't prepared for Vikings either."

"I doubt we're dealing with shifters," Finley added.

"If not shifters, then what?"

Finley gave Quinn a long look but didn't answer. "Come on," he said instead. "Let's go."

"Shit," Quinn said under her breath, her eyes lifting to meet Lina's. "It's always something, isn't it?"

Lina gave Quinn an apologetic smile. "At least things aren't boring."

Quinn tucked her arm in Lina's as they moved to close the growing gap between them and the men. "Right about now, I think I'd love me a little boring."

As she readjusted the cane she'd hung from one of her belt loops, Lina couldn't help but agree. Even so, she found herself saying, "But we weren't made for boring, Satori."

"I hate it when you're right," Quinn groaned.

The conversation died down after that, the four of them walking along the edge of the forest, following it to where the land met the sea.

"I didn't realize we were up so high," Lina said, her gaze raking over the series of jagged cliffs that started across the stretch of water and curved around in an elongated S shape, tapering off somewhere behind them. She squinted. "Is that a waterfall?"

It was hard to make out from this vantage, the actual cascade of water predominately falling over the other side of the sheer glossy black and gray cliff face. But the billowing sea spray at the base of the cliffs on the northern curve of the S seemed to indicate that it very much was.

"It's beautiful," Quinn murmured, still holding onto Lina's arm.

"It really is," Lina agreed.

She should have known better than to be lured into a false sense of security by the beauty of her surroundings.

Nord was the first to hear them approach, spinning around so fast the dirt beneath his feet flew up and over the edge of the cliff. It was then Lina realized just how precariously they were positioned. One wrong step, and they would be the ones going over. Whoever followed them here must have been counting on it.

Score one for the home team.

Finley was next, his hands moving to his lower back as if to unholster his gun, but a slight shake of Nord's head had Finley checking the movement.

Guess they weren't going to pull out any of their weapons. Yet.

Lina and Quinn were slower to turn. Heart hammering in her chest and adrenaline surging through her veins, Lina braced herself for the worst. Though she wasn't sure what she was expecting to find, four men and two women decked out in surprisingly modern-looking clothes holding staves, a couple notched crossbows, and one fierce-looking black bird sitting atop one of their shoulders wasn't it.

It was hard to tell which of the six was in charge, staggered as they were, but Lina's eyes kept going back to the man with the bird even though he stood in the back and off to the side. His arms were crossed over his heavily muscled chest, his loose black hair with its small braids and silver beads brushing his shoulders. His sharp jaw was coated in thick stubble. His skin was weathered, one eye bisected by a thick scar, its color a cloudy white. The other was a shocking emerald color. She caught a hint of dark ink that trailed up the sleeves of his olive-green shirt. There wasn't a weapon in sight unless she counted the bird . . . which eyeing those wicked-looking claws and pointed beak, she definitely did.

Since they didn't seem inclined to talk, Lina did.

"Uh, hey there."

Six sets of eyes shot her way, and Lina felt the icy trickle of sweat roll down her spine.

She was arguably the strongest animagi still in existence, but damn if these six didn't make her want to use Nord like a human shield.

The woman in the front row gave Lina a blatant once-over. The look in her eyes once she was finished made it clear she wasn't impressed with what she found. Lina bristled, fighting the urge to prove just why she shouldn't be underestimated. But a keen sense of self-preservation kept her from following through on the impulse.

This was not a woman she wanted to fuck with unless she absolutely had no other choice. To start, she had a body made for battle and was currently aiming a crossbow at Lina's forehead. She was ripped, her muscles prominent but not in a bulky way. There was a network of scars that ran along her exposed ebony skin, which she seemed to showcase with her intricate sleeve of tattoos rather than conceal. As if they were badges of honor.

Then there was the matter of the sheer badassery she sported like a fucking mantle. She wore her long hair in a series of interconnected braids pulled back in a thick ponytail. There was a tiny silver ring in her nose and more running along the curve of her ears. She also had one dangling earring in her right lobe, the curved blade of the dagger hanging there looking real enough that she could pull it out and hurl it in one easy throw.

Her lips were curled up in a taunting smile, as if she could easily read Lina's thoughts and her reticence to act.

"You trespass on sacred land. Give us one reason we shouldn't kill you where you stand."

Lina blinked, thrown off by the woman's use of perfect English with its soft British accent. It wasn't like she was expecting to hear them still speaking in Old Norse—she hadn't given it much thought one way or the other—but stumbling across something so familiar when she'd been prepared to face anything but was a bit of a mindfuck.

At a complete loss for words, she merely pointed at Nord, like the sight of him alone was answer enough. The woman dragged her gaze to him, though her weapon remained trained on Lina. This time she seemed much more impressed after her perusal.

"Well?" she demanded.

"We came through the gateway," Nord answered.

The woman's expression didn't change, but the others shifted around her. All except for the man with the bird. The only change there was a slight narrowing of his eyes.

"Impossible," she scoffed.

"And yet here we are," Finley said.

She gave him a downward flick of her eyes and a condescending, "Hmmm."

"We seek sanctuary," Nord said, drawing her attention back to him.

"What makes you think we're inclined to provide it when you have no right to be here in the first place?"

Nord let out a soft snarl at that. "I have every right to be here."

The woman tilted her head, studying him carefully. "The gateway has lain dormant for centuries."

Quinn shifted at her side. Lina shot her a questioning glance, wondering what about the woman's words caused Quinn to react, but her friend ignored her and kept her gaze focused on Bird Man.

"See for yourself," Nord offered.

She stared at him for a long moment before jutting her head to the side and sending the other female and two of the men running off in the direction of the gateway.

Lina started to relax now that they were no longer outnumbered.

The woman smirked, as if she'd noticed and thought that incredibly foolish.

Fed up with the woman's attitude, justified or not, Lina blurted, "The fact that we even know about the gateway at all should be enough to lend our explanation credibility. Especially if it's been all but forgotten for as long as you claim."

She shrugged. "Or you read about it in some history book. Just because you utter pretty words doesn't mean what you say is anything of value."

Lina's temper spiked, and she took a step forward. "Listen—"

Quinn stopped her with a hand on the chest, but the damage was already done. With a single step, Lina had shattered their fragile peace, and the trio reacted immediately.

The woman fired her bolt, the bird dove with a piercing screech, and the man she'd mostly ignored until now slammed down his gnarled wooden staff with a flash of violet light and an earthshaking boom.

The ground rolled, and Lina fought to keep her balance, taking a few staggering steps forward to ensure she was far away from the edge of the cliff if any of it started to give way. Beside her, Quinn let out a startled yelp as Finley tackled her, sending them both sprawling onto the ground, Finley landing in such a way that his body rested protectively over hers.

Before Lina could even worry about the projectile heading straight for her, Nord had already negated the threat. She looked up in time to witness him plucking the bolt out of the air and snapping it in his hands like it was a toothpick. He flung the splinters to the side and faced off with Bird Man.

"Call off your bird."

The man didn't budge as the bird continued its low circles above Lina's head.

"Call. Off. Your. Bird," Nord demanded again, his voice a dark, dangerous growl.

"Or what?" the man asked, his voice clipped and every bit as dangerous as Nord's.

"I'll rip its fucking head off and feed it to you."

The bird let out an enraged caw and dove for Nord.

Done feeling like a bystander, Lina called up a mighty wind that sent the bird veering off course.

"What are you?" the man growled as his bird fought against her unnatural gusts.

"The one you should be worried about right now is me," Nord said, answering before she could. "I gave you two chances—two more than I usually give—out of respect for our shared bloodlines, but you failed to obey."

Lina knew the second Nord dropped control and let the berserker take over. His entire body seemed to swell with the release of his rage, his muscles bulging, his face taking on a feral cast. Even his eyes changed. Perhaps she'd never noticed before because his Guardian power had masked it, but the ice blue was now a bottomless black.

The crossbow fell, forgotten from the woman's limp fingers. "Stop!"

It was not immediately obvious who the order was for, but she was not the only one in their ranks that appeared rattled. The man with the staff fell to one knee, and Bird Man dropped his aggressive stance.

Nord's nostrils flared, and a muscle pulsed in his jaw. He was primed for a fight and looked pissed to miss out on his chance to shed blood.

The woman held up her hands in the universal sign of surrender. "We know what you are, berserker, though your kind exists only amongst our legends now. It is not within my power to grant you and your friends sanctuary, but I will take you to the one who can."

With visible effort, Nord regained the hold on his rage. Given the last forty-eight hours, Lina knew it was a tenuous hold at best. The fact that his eyes were still more black than blue confirmed it.

She waited an extra second to undo her windstorm. A disgruntled-looking bird flew back to his master and landed on his shoulder with practiced ease. There he shook out his feathers and pointedly glared at Lina. The intelligence in that gaze unnerved her, so she shifted her attention to the commotion going on beside her.

Quinn jabbed Finley in the ribs with the tip of her finger. "You can get off me now."

Finley pushed up and held himself in the plank position, his face hovering just over hers. "I think what you meant to say was 'thank you' so, you're welcome."

Quinn scowled up at him. "Thanks for what? Smothering me half to death and ruining my shirt?"

One side of Finley's mouth quirked up. "We'll just consider that even for the lipstick you left in mine."

She flushed a bright pink before giving his chest a shove. "Off. Now."

Finley's smile stretched, but he got to his feet and even offered Quinn a hand, which she begrudgingly accepted.

Since those two were looking after each other, Lina went to Nord.

"You okay?" she asked, resting her hand lightly on his shoulder blade.

He was rigid beneath her touch but gave her a terse nod. She was about to dig deeper, but she could feel the curious stares of the others on them and knew that Nord wouldn't reveal anything until they were alone.

"So," Lina said, turning to give the woman a tight smile, "what should we call you now that we're all good friends?"

"I'm Strega," she answered. Then she gestured to Bird Man. "This is Søren, and that's Arrick."

Lina nodded to each of them in kind. "I'm Lina, that's Quinn and Finley. And this is—"

Nord cut her off, looking like he'd rather be anywhere else in that exact moment. "You might know me as Gunnar. Gunnar Bloodaxe."

If they were stunned before, they were absolutely beside themselves now.

Lina exchanged confused glances with Quinn and Finley, wondering why a mere name would turn these previously stone-cold warriors starstruck. She'd known Nord's father had led a tribe, but just how famous was Nord in his own right that his name alone could evoke such a reaction after all these years?

Strega was the first to recover. "Um. Well, I . . ." she fumbled in her search for words, looking thoroughly awestruck. "Welcome home, warrior."

Nord nodded, looking pained.

Arrick was standing again but leaning heavily on his staff, his entire body quaking. He couldn't manage more than a deep bow.

Søren held Nord's gaze for a long, drawn-out moment, then shocked the hell out of Lina when he lifted his fist to his chest and bowed. "Welcome home, Warrior of Odin."

"Told you," Finley muttered so softly Lina barely caught the words. "It was always about him."

CHAPTER 8
NORD

He could feel the others' curious gazes crawling over him, demanding answers to questions he had no desire to answer.

Who are you?

Where have you been?

Why now?

Gunnar may as well be another person entirely for how far in the past Nord buried that part of himself. Picking up the mantle again now felt like a snake attempting to reattach the skin it already shed. Futile. Absurd. Utterly unnatural.

There was no going back, yet here he was, making the attempt anyway because this is who they needed him to be. Who she needed him to be.

Gunnar could keep Lina safe. Nord could not. The choice made itself.

He sighed inwardly, hating the way a name alone could change the way people determined his worth. He vastly preferred the antagonistic greeting they'd been given to this undeserved deference. That was at least honest. If they'd seen it through and clashed on the battlefield, when their opinions shifted from averse to respectful, it would have been earned.

Nord looked up as Søren's bird flew down through the trees and landed back on his master's shoulder.

"Your bird have a name?"

"Yup."

Nord bit back a smile, relieved that not everyone was going out of their way to kiss his ass.

"Astrid left eight days past to attend the elder's gathering and renew the accords. She should return any day now. You're of course welcome to stay as our guests until she can meet with you." Strega hadn't stopped speaking since they'd left the cliffs.

He'd mostly ignored her steady stream of chatter since it was little more than useless drivel, but he keyed in now.

"Astrid. She's your leader?"

Strega nodded. "Yes. She's what you might consider our jarl, though we got rid of those antiquated titles a long time ago. We chose her as our leader and look to her to make decisions on our behalf."

"Sort of like an advisor?" Lina asked.

"It's a little more involved than that, but essentially, yes. If there's not a clear consensus among us, Astrid is the deciding vote. She's also our mediator, judge, mother, protector, and war chief. Pretty much our go-to in all things."

"You mentioned accords," Finley said, joining the conversation. "So there are more people here than just your community."

"Of course. We were not this land's first inhabitants. Things were . . ." Strega seemed to be choosing her next words with care. ". . . bloody, for a long time when the first of us arrived. But our ancestors were tired of war. So for perhaps the first time, they sought peace through diplomacy instead of might. We've flourished ever since."

Nord frowned, wondering how many more of his friends had

been put in the ground because the peaceful escape they'd hoped for had ended up being more of the same.

"But once the accords were signed, trade opened and alliances were forged. We became the protectors of the land and its people, in exchange they offered—"

Søren loudly cleared his throat.

Strega swallowed whatever she'd been about to say and tossed an apologetic smile over her shoulder. "Perhaps some things are best left to discuss after Astrid has made her decision."

Nord could appreciate their caution, though it only made him more curious about what they were attempting to hide. He was willing to bet the orb filled with crackling purple light in Arrick's staff had something to do with it.

"It's not much further. Just around this bend, and we'll reach the main gate," Strega announced.

"Apologies if this is an intrusive question, but won't the rest of your party wonder where you've run off to?" Finley asked.

Strega shook her head. "We have ways of communicating with them."

Nord's eyes returned to the bird perched on Søren, noting as he did that Finley's had done the same. They caught each other's gaze and exchanged knowing looks. Her answer had been intentionally vague, but it confirmed what they'd already suspected.

"Curiouser and curiouser," came Finley's voice in his mind.

The time for proper answers would come. For now, they just needed a place to rest without worry they'd be found. A hot meal wouldn't go amiss either. After a full day's travel on foot and a night without sleep, they were running on fumes.

It seemed to be affecting Quinn the most, she hadn't spoken at all since Strega took over as their guide, but Lina wasn't faring much better. He slowed his pace so that she could catch up to him.

"Want a ride?" he asked.

She looked up at him with a startled blink.

He chuckled as her cheeks flooded with color. "Not that kind of ride." He pointed to his back. "I can carry you the rest of the way if you want. Give your feet a break?"

He couldn't decide if she looked disappointed or relieved by his clarification.

"It's probably not the best idea to appear weak in front of these guys, but my feet and I appreciate the offer."

"Anyone foolish enough to assume you were weak wouldn't live long enough to regret it," he told her, holding out his hand.

She accepted it with a little laugh. "I think you're overestimating my street cred."

"No, I've just seen what you can do."

"Pretty sure you're just biased."

"When it comes to you? Definitely. But that doesn't make my assessment any less true."

A smile blossomed across her face, sending longing spiraling through him like a hurricane. Not just longing for her, though the fact that she had no idea how amazing she was only made her more irresistible. It was longing for a life that would always be just out of reach. One free from responsibility and obligation where the consequences of being selfish wouldn't result in someone else's death.

He was beyond tempted to say fuck it all, toss her over his shoulder, and just keep running until they were the only two beings left for miles. He couldn't imagine a more perfect life than one spent by her side, losing themselves in each other. But he wasn't the kind of man that could shirk his duty. If he had been, he wouldn't be the man she needed nor one worthy of her love.

So here they'd stay, no matter how desperately he wished it could be otherwise.

Completely unaware of the direction his thoughts had taken, Lina tucked a piece of hair behind her ear and let out a soft snort of amusement. Then she wrapped her other hand over his inner elbow and rested her head against his shoulder.

"You know, I never thought I'd say it, but that hellish endurance training of yours is definitely coming in handy right about now.

Pretty sure I would have passed out beneath a tree a few hours ago without it."

He let out a surprised huff of laughter. "I wouldn't have allowed that to happen."

"Oh? You think you could have forced me on by sheer will alone?"

"No," he murmured as he lifted his free hand and curled it around the right side of her face. Pressing her closer to him, he leaned down and brushed his lips over the crown of her head. "I'd just never leave you behind."

He heard the slight hitch of her breath, then the soft sigh that told him how his words affected her. There was a beat of silence before her low and slightly husky reply, "It's the same for me, you know. Even though you tried to force me to." Her fingers spasmed around his arm. "You and me, we're a package deal."

Still unable to see her face, he took his cues from what he heard in her voice. Right now, it sounded like a fight for control of her emotions, so instead of telling her how the sight of her bursting into that holding cell looking like an avenging angel had filled his heart near to bursting, he opted for something lighter.

"I think you proved that well enough yesterday. It's not every day someone breaks into a top-secret facility for me. Actually, I'm pretty sure that's the first and only time I've been on the receiving end of a rescue. Usually, it's the other way around."

"Was that really just yesterday? It feels like a lifetime ago."

"I owe you a proper thank-you for saving my life once things calm down."

"I'm going to hold you to that, berserker. Lord knows I need something good to look forward to."

He was half a second away from leaning down and whispering all the things she could look forward to when the gate came into view. It appeared to be carved from the mountain itself, the gate's obsidian stone glossy and reflective, stretching up a good sixty feet and easily as long.

"Holy shit," Lina whispered, tipping her head back to take in the towering gate with its massive rune placed in the center.

As they watched, Strega began muttering under her breath, and the rune blazed to life. He lifted a hand to shield his eyes from the blinding intensity, but the light quickly faded. As it did, the stone wall vanished and revealed the hidden city.

Nord sucked in a shocked breath at his first real glimpse of his people. It was as Strega had said. They'd flourished.

Finley's voice sounded in his mind. *"Looks like things have changed since you left."*

That was one way to put it.

Gone were the wattle and daub longhouses of his past. In their place were sprawling wood and black stone buildings overlooking a glittering sea with a long dock and countless ships. The ships, at least, felt familiar, though even their construction had evolved into sleeker, more modern vessels. There was very little of his heritage to be found, and yet he could feel its influence.

It wasn't exactly like coming home, but it was the next best thing.

"Welcome to Novasgard," Strega said. "Let me show you where you'll be staying."

CHAPTER 9
LINA

"Someone will come for you in the morning. Until then, make yourselves at home. Everything you need for the night has been supplied. Rest well."

With that, Strega waved her palm along the outer wall, and the door to their suite reformed the same way the gate to the city had.

"What if we . . ." Lina started, but the woman was already gone. "Well then."

"Why do I get the feeling she just locked us up for the night?" Quinn asked. "Albeit in a rather nice prison."

Lina cast her eyes around the spacious suite. Their accommodations were undeniably fine. "Because she did?"

After Søren and Arrick left them without so much as a backward glance, Strega had escorted them here. The building itself was one of the taller ones they'd come across, with their room located on its top floor. During her brief walkthrough, Strega had pointed out a rather modern-looking kitchen, two bedrooms with separate bathrooms, and the main room with its long table and sitting area, which they were currently standing in.

The suite and its furnishings invited comfort, despite its lack of personal touches. Everything was decorated in neutral shades with glossy black accents that encouraged a person to sit back and relax. If it was a prison, it didn't look like one Lina had ever seen. Rather, it had the feel of an upscale hotel.

A hotel they couldn't currently leave.

"She could have at least showed us how to work the shower before she took off," Quinn muttered.

Lina's stomach growled. "Or the kitchen appliances."

Quinn shrugged. "Who needs appliances when we have you?"

Finley lifted the lid on what Lina assumed was some sort of refrigerator. There was a rustling as he shuffled the contents around. "This thing is stocked. We'll be fine. Between the four—" His eyes shifted to Quinn and his lips curled in a teasing smile. "—three of us, we'll figure it out."

Quinn scowled at him but didn't seem to have the energy for one of their usual verbal sparring matches. "Great, then I'm going to take a shower. I'll expect you three very competent adults to have the food situation sorted by the time I get out."

"Good luck," Lina called as Quinn walked off, dragging one of the now battered-looking suitcases behind her.

"Guess she's claiming that room, so I'll be in the other."

Nord gave Finley an arch look, his arms crossed over his chest.

"For fuck's sake," Finley groaned. "Why am I always the one on the floor or the couch?"

Nord clapped him on the shoulder. "Best get used to it, brother."

"I'm sure if you asked nicely, she'd let you share the bed," Lina offered.

"When does the straightforward approach *ever* work with her?" Finley asked.

"Fair point. She does love her hoops."

Finley sighed and started rummaging through the cooler. "I think she's got the right of it, though. Looks like we're locked in for the night. Might as well regroup best we can. No telling what's in store tomorrow." His eyes glowed as he accessed his power and inspected the various appliances. "A few tweaks ought to do the trick. Looks like the power source is unique, but the concepts are familiar."

Glad that at least one of them knew what to do in the kitchen, Lina left Finley to it and turned to Nord.

"Do you think this Astrid will be inclined to help us?"

"Not us," Finley interjected. "*Gunnar.* You saw how the others reacted when they learned who he was. I don't think the lady will have a choice."

"Is that true?" Lina asked, trying to keep her voice carefully neutral. She was beyond curious about Nord's past but didn't want to pry if he wasn't ready to discuss it.

Nord dipped his chin in a tight nod but kept his attention laser-focused on pulling items out of the other bags and sorting them into piles.

Yup. He's definitely not ready to open that can of worms.

Lina felt an answering pang of sympathy. It was no easy feat coming face-to-face with your past. She should know . . . she was sort of the expert.

With Finley in charge of dinner and Nord with his busy work, Lina glanced around, searching for something she could use to keep herself occupied. Not finding anything, she sank down in one of the chairs and let out a low groan. Her body ached. They'd woken with the dawn, and she knew they'd walked for hours before getting through the gateway, and then another several hours after. There was no telling what time it actually was, though, or if time even worked the same in this realm. The sun had just started its descent in Novasgard when Strega dropped them off. Best she could tell, it was early evening here, although her body felt like it was well past midnight.

Nord's gaze caught hers from across the table. "I think I saw a tub in there."

While a soak sounded great for her worn-out body, the idea of being alone with her thoughts was anything but. The quiet moments were the hardest to get through, because there was only one direction her mind wanted to go and nothing to help distract her.

She eyed the cane she'd set against the wall and felt her heart twist in her chest. Closing her eyes against the wave of sorrow, she took a ragged breath and tried to stay in the present.

"Maybe later."

His eyes searched hers, likely reading everything she was feeling in that single, piercing look. His expression softened, and he walked around the table to her.

"What can I do?"

She swallowed and shook her head while attempting a reassuring smile.

Nord took a seat in the chair next to hers and captured her hand with his own. "You sure?"

God, this man . . . What did I ever do to deserve him?

Lina was pretty confident the answer to that question was nothing—unless being brutally murdered in her first lifetime set her up to win the karmic lottery the second time around. Nord was the real-life embodiment of the dashing prince girls dreamt about when picturing their happily ever afters. Though his armor was blood-spattered, he wielded an ax instead of a sword, and she was pretty sure he wasn't hiding a valiant steed anywhere.

Which was perfectly fine as far as she was concerned. She'd take a 'rough around the edges' prince to a 'pretty but useless' one every time.

Nord was everything she could have ever asked for but never truly believed existed. A man as fiercely protective of her heart as he was the rest of her, with the body of a god and all the sinful talents of the devil. She wouldn't change a thing about him. Especially now that she knew just what he was capable of in the bedroom. He was the man of her dreams . . . the sweet *and* filthy ones.

Her expression must have reflected her thoughts because he tilted his head to the side, his eyes narrowing with interest while his lips quirked with amusement. "Seems like you thought of something you'd like me to do for you, Kærasta."

She fought hard to keep her reply breezy. "I was just remembering what a great distraction you make."

His gaze turned heated, and his voice dropped to a low, sexy whisper. "You know I love to *distract* you. Frequently and with great abandon."

Lina squirmed in her seat, feeling her cheeks pinken.

"Shall I get started?"

Liquid heat spiraled through her at the offer, but she couldn't resist teasing him. "Maybe later."

His grin was slow and deliciously wicked as he lifted her hand to his mouth and feathered a kiss across her knuckles. "I don't know, a distraction sounds pretty good right now. Sure I can't persuade you to reconsider?"

"I'm sure you probably could . . ." she replied, more than a little breathless as he unfurled her hand and pressed a kiss against the inside of her index finger and then took the tip into his mouth and sucked hard before swirling his tongue around.

Her body reacted instantly as she recalled the other times—and places—he'd used the same toe-curling trick. She pressed her thighs together in an attempt to relieve the growing ache, less than a hairsbreadth away from caving when Finley cleared his throat.

"Oh, come on. I'm standing *right* here."

"Go stand somewhere else," Nord shot back, his eyes never leaving hers as he took another of her fingers in his mouth.

"You're the two with the fancy room. Besides, it might be a bit difficult to finish dinner without"—Finley gestured to the containers of food and cookware he'd pulled out—"you know, dinner."

"We'll manage just fi—" Nord started, right as Lina's stomach let out another rumble. He sat back with a laugh. "On second thought, maybe you should hurry up."

Finley snickered. "On it."

When his back was turned to them once more, Lina fanned her face. "I was right. Excellent distraction."

Nord winked, his eyes glowing with an unspoken promise she had no trouble interpreting as all the ways he was planning on distracting her once they were alone.

Yup. Definitely my kind of prince.

Finley was just setting out dinner when Quinn sauntered back in the room, wearing a pair of high-waisted pants that were too thick to be leggings but not quite sweats and a creamy cable-knit sweater that fell off one shoulder. Her hair was still wet, but tied up in a bun, and she was carrying a familiar set of envelopes.

"Where'd you get the clothes?" Lina asked, pretty sure the outfit wasn't something Quinn scavenged from her uncle's place.

"The closet's stocked," she said with a shrug. "I didn't look at everything in there, but from what I could tell, there seemed to be something for just about every occasion."

"And they just so happen to be in your size?" Finley asked.

"More or less," she replied.

Nord and Finley exchanged a glance, as if that was a juicy piece of gossip. As far as Lina was concerned, a closet full of clothes was the least of their worries.

"Here," Quinn said, taking a seat at the head of the table and tossing the envelopes into the center. "Wasn't sure if you wanted these."

Lina reached out to collect them out of habit but faltered before her hand made contact. As badly as she wanted to know about the contents, she just couldn't bring herself to face them yet.

"Thanks," she said, realizing all eyes were on her. She picked them up and set them beside her elbow on the table.

"You're not going to open them?" Quinn asked.

"We're about to eat," Lina said.

"So? Aren't you curious?"

"Of course I am . . ." She hesitated and blew out a heavy breath before admitting, "I'm just not ready."

Quinn's expression twisted, and Nord reached out and brushed the backs of his fingers against her arm in silent support. As always, Finley handled the sudden tension in the room with all the finesse of a stampede of elephants.

He plunked a glass of what looked like wine in front of her, made a face, took it back, and then set the open bottle down instead.

"What's this for?"

"Courage," he said, taking the last seat at the table. Without waiting for anybody else, he ripped off a hunk of crusty bread and shoved it in his mouth. Still chewing, he loaded his plate with heaping scoops of the seafood and pasta dish he'd created. He was on his second large forkful when he finally realized the others were all staring at him. "What?"

Nord shook his head and tossed Lina a smile. "And he calls me the barbarian."

Lina's shoulders shook with quiet laughter.

"Hot," Quinn deadpanned, looking equal parts impressed and disgusted.

He flashed her one of his signature grins. "What can I say? I'm a man of impressive appetites."

"What you are is a pig," she replied, making a smaller plate for herself and taking a delicate bite. Then she let out a low moan and took a second, much larger one. "Holy shit, that's good."

Finley stared at her as if entranced and then roughly cleared his throat.

Lina pushed the bottle he'd set in front of her toward him with a finger. "Seems like you might need this more than me."

He accepted the bottle with a grin and took a deep swig. He eyed it appreciatively as he set it back down. "Mmm. Can't remember the last time I had a proper bottle of mead."

Nord's brows shot up with interest, and he snatched the glass Finley had first set in front of her, draining it entirely.

"Good?" she teased.

"Nectar of the gods," he replied, licking his lips and reaching eagerly for the bottle.

"Hey," she said, dragging it out of his reach. "At least let me try it before you hog it all."

"Don't worry, I spied a whole crate of them in there," Finley said.

Curious what all the fuss was about, Lina lifted the bottle to her lips and took a tentative sip. A familiar warmth spread out from her chest as a honey and clove flavor exploded on her tongue. "Oh, yum. I get it now."

Nord smirked and plucked the bottle from her fingers, draining it.

Quinn watched them all with amusement but was too busy cleaning her plate to join in.

Finley stood to grab another bottle, and Lina set to work loading her plate and digging in. The tension in the room had lifted as the delicious food—not to mention potent alcohol—took over, replacing it with a much more relaxed atmosphere. It wasn't long before they were all settled back in their chairs, empty plates shoved away from them, looking far more content than they had in days. Thankfully, the mood held as the conversation shifted from light chitchat back to their current predicament.

"So what happens after you speak with Astrid? Are we planning to stay here indefinitely?" Quinn asked.

"Even if that was an option," Lina said, jumping in before Nord could answer, "we can't hide here forever. We're not running away; we're buying ourselves time. There's too much we left unfinished back home."

Nord's expression was warm with approval, while Quinn and Finley nodded their agreement.

"Assuming Astrid gives us the time we need, what piece of unfinished business were you looking to deal with first?" Finley asked with a curious tilt of his head.

Lina's mouth dipped in a small frown as she considered the shit-show they'd have on their hands as soon as they returned. She wasn't exactly looking forward to a run-in with the Brotherhood or the Drakes and the rest of the Mobius Council. Neither was a fight they'd easily win. While they might be powerful, there were only four of them. Their enemies could make up what they lacked in magic—not that they were slouches in that department by any means—with sheer numbers.

"I have no idea," Lina admitted, letting her hands fall into her lap. "There's not exactly a good option here."

"Not to mention Crombie's going to come to collect on your promise sooner rather than later—" Quinn started, breaking off at Lina's stricken expression and frantic head shaking.

She'd almost forgotten she was bloodsworn to the fae douche bucket. Might as well add a demanding ex-prince to the list of assholes she'd have to deal with.

"What promise?" Nord asked, his eyes narrowing dangerously as he leveled them on Lina. "Does this have anything to do with why he helped you free me?"

Her mouth went dry, and she took a bracing sip of mead to help her stall. She really thought she'd have more time to figure out how to explain what happened in a way that would piss him off the least.

"Lina . . ." he said, his patience slipping.

"Well, you see . . ."

"Tell me," Nord demanded, likely conjuring up far worse things in his mind than what had actually occurred.

Lina blew out a breath. "In exchange for helping us break through the wards and help get you out, Crombie made me promise to steal something from the Mobius Council in return."

"He didn't just make her promise, mate. The piece of shit blood-swore her."

Lina glared at Finley. *Just go and make it worse, why don't you.*

"And you *let* her?" Nord snarled.

"Hey, I tried, but you know how she is," Finley said, lifting his hands in surrender.

"For the record, I don't need anybody to 'let me' do anything," she snapped. "Not that I have to explain myself, but I didn't have much time, and I had even fewer options, so you can just take your objections and shove them up your ass."

"Amen, sister," Quinn said, holding up her hand like she was giving Lina a long-distance high five. When Lina failed to return the gesture, Quinn shrugged and took a sip of her drink.

Nord's eyes glittered with challenge, but Lina refused to back down. Instead, she jerked her chin up slightly and held his intense gaze.

"Just because you don't like the outcome, that doesn't change the position we were in. Don't act like you wouldn't have done the same exact thing if it was my life on the line instead of yours," she added for good measure as she pointed at him. Then, still riding the high of her frustration, she shot a dark look at Finley and Quinn. "And you two have giant fucking mouths. Would it have killed you to stay out of it?"

"Probably," Quinn said with a considering nod.

"Definitely," Finley said with an unrepentant grin. "When you do stupid things, you deserve the consequences."

"I'm going to remember you said that," she promised.

Nord ignored their side conversation, his eyes still leveled on her as he asked, "Do you have any idea what you've done?"

"Of course I do," she replied hotly.

Sort of.

"I don't think you do," Nord said, leaning forward as his voice dropped. "That bastard can find you, anywhere, anytime he wants. The longer you go without fulfilling your promise to him, the greater his hold on you will be. You shouldn't be worried that he'll come to collect. You should be worried that he *won't*."

"Why do you say that?" Lina asked, trying to hide the tremor his words caused by clasping her hands together.

"Because eventually, you'll become his damned slave. He'll be able to manipulate you as if you were little more than a puppet on a string, and you'll be helpless to do anything but yield to his whims. We need to find out what he wants and give it to him as soon as possible. It's the only way to void his claim on you."

"So . . . that should be a priority then?" Lina asked, trying for lighthearted and failing miserably.

Nord's voice dropped further until it was little more than a growl. "The only one who should ever hold any claim over you, Kærasta, is me. So yeah, I'd say it's a fucking priority."

A sharp thrill ran through her at the words. She sort of loved the whole possessive alpha male thing he had going on right now. Not that he'd appreciate her saying so.

"Right then. And should we focus on him before or after we deal with The Director and Mikel Drake? Because I'm pretty sure they aren't the kind of guys willing to politely line up and wait their turn."

Just like that, the mood plummeted. To be fair, it had started dropping with Quinn's mention of Crombie, but Lina's words wrung out every last bit of lighthearted fun they'd managed to steal.

"We're going to need an army to deal with everyone coming after us," Quinn muttered.

"You're not wrong," Finley said.

"Do you know where we can get one of those? Is there a store or website I can order one from? Mercenaries-R-Us, maybe?" Lina asked bitterly.

"MurderSquad.com?" Quinn offered.

Lina huffed out a laugh, and even Finley cracked a smile, but Nord's expression remained shuttered, his thoughts clearly troubled.

She reached out and rested her hand on top of his. "I know things seem pretty impossible right now. And I don't think any of us were under the impression we were going to find a solution overnight. But between the four of us, we'll figure something out. Quinn and I know the ins and outs of the Council, and you two know everything there is to know about the Brotherhood. It's not like we're walking into this blind. I'm sure we'll think of a way to best exploit their weaknesses—"

"What weaknesses?" Finley said under his breath. "The Brotherhood has centuries of experience to draw on."

Her eyes snapped to his. "We bested them once already. Are you saying it can't happen again?"

"The Director won't make the same mistake twice," he warned her.

Lina glanced at Nord, but his far-off gaze and clenched jaw told her he was lost to dark thoughts. She wasn't going to find any help from his corner, not right now. With a shrug, she turned her attention back to Finley and said, "So we come up with something he won't expect."

Finley chuckled darkly. "I appreciate your optimism, love, but there's a reason the Brotherhood is the governing power of every world they come across. They're unstoppable."

"That," Lina said firmly, unsure where her certainty came from, but knowing in her bones she was right, "that right there is why we're going to win. You Guardians are too damn arrogant to consider the fact that no one is untouchable—not even your precious Brotherhood. That's the weakness that will be their downfall."

"Lina," he said, shaking his head, "this is what they do."

She cocked a brow. "Haven't you learned by now not to underestimate me?"

"I don't underestimate you; I've seen what you can do, but the reality is—"

"You want to talk about reality, Fin? Reality is my birthright. It's mine to control. *Mine.* I can change it into anything I want."

Finley pressed his lips together, seeming to choose his next words with care. Eventually, he blew out a breath and said softly, "So can they."

"Not like me."

"Lina," Quinn said, her voice gentle. "You're still only one person. Maybe if we had the Codex and knew how to access the full potential of your power like Alistair wanted, then that would be enough, but as it stands . . ." she trailed off, her expression apologetic.

An uncomfortable weight settled in Lina's chest, and she dropped her eyes to the table in front of her. What else could she say to make them believe her—believe *in* her?

Why don't they understand that we have to win? No matter how badly the odds are stacked against us, losing is not an option. To lose means we die, and I'm not ready to face death. Not again.

Her head shot up as the words she needed came to her. Squeezing her hands together in a tight fist, she met each of their eyes as she said, "Maybe we'll be outmatched no matter what we do. But at the end of the day, they're fighting because it's their job. We're fighting for our lives. And that . . . it changes everything."

CHAPTER 10
NORD

He'd lingered at the table after Lina had said good night, waging a losing battle as he fought for calm. The only reason the berserker wasn't demanding bloodshed was because the object of his fury was another world away. But that didn't mean the beast would let the matter lie either. He was howling with the need to possess and dominate.

When Nord stood, his mask was firmly in place, but it would take little more than a word for it to crumble. He hoped, for both his and Lina's sake, that his belief in the strength of their bond wasn't misplaced.

He left Quinn and Finley without a word, his footsteps soundless as he padded down the hallway and crossed the threshold to join Lina in their temporary bedroom. She faced away from him, her movements jerky as she kicked off her boots and socks, shed her pants, and then straightened to peel off her long-sleeved shirt.

He watched her for a moment, appreciating the way the light from the hallway behind him caught her hair and made it glow like starlight even as the rest of her was mostly bathed in shadow. A poet he was not, but he couldn't help but find the description an apt one. If he was the darkness, then Lina was the star. From the moment he'd met her, she'd cast away his shadows and surrounded him with the beauty of her light. And he knew, as long as she was there to light the way, he'd never be lost again.

"Want some help?"

She froze for half a second, her arms bent awkwardly in the air as she shot him a sheepish grin over her shoulder. "Pretty sure I know what I'm doing."

He slowly swept his eyes down her body, noting the shiver it caused as his eyes returned to hers. "It's more fun to get naked with a friend."

He caught her soft inhale before she arched a brow.

She tossed her shirt on the floor as she turned to face him with her hands on her hips. "Is that what we are? Friends?"

Lust punched through him at the sight of her standing there, challenge shining out of her eyes and echoed in her stance. The berserker growled with pleasure, eager to take her up on her offer.

Nord pretended to consider the question as he stepped further into the room, hooking his foot around the door to kick it closed behind him. "I'd like to think so," he said, fighting against a smile as her brows pinched together in a frown. "But it's hardly the only title I'd give you," he added before she could give voice to the question she was clearly preparing to launch at him.

Using the tip of one boot, he stepped on the back of the other and slid it off. As he'd expected, her eyes dropped, checking the movement.

"Oh?" she asked, pulling her gaze back to his face.

Nord nodded, making short work of his other boot before he reached for the back of his shirt and pulled it up and over his head.

Lina blinked in a distracted fashion as he continued to move toward her, his hands dropping to his waistband. Seeing how badly she wanted him stoked the flames of his own desire. He'd been hard for her before ever stepping foot in the room, but as she continued to stare with that hungry gaze, he found himself straining against his pants, aching to feel her repeat those fevered sweeps with her hands. Or her mouth.

Her tongue darted out to wet her lips. "Such as?"

"Charge . . . purpose . . ." he started to list while his fingers worked at his button.

Lina swallowed when he started to drag his zipper down, drawing the task out when she bit down on her bottom lip.

There was less than a foot separating them as he hooked his thumbs beneath the denim and shoved the material down, easily stepping out of the pooling fabric and closing the distance.

"Lover," he added, trailing his fingertips down one of her arms and watching her skin pebble in response. He repeated the caress on the other arm, loving every hitch of her breath. "Partner."

Her breath caught as he curled a finger beneath her chin and lifted it until her eyes met his. "Equal."

Her gaze seared him as he dipped his head, halting the movement so that his lips hovered over hers.

"Nord," she protested.

This time he couldn't fight his grin. They were so close that his lips brushed over hers as he whispered the last word on his list.

"Mine," he declared, lowering his mouth and claiming hers in a searing kiss.

She swayed into him, her fingertips digging into his skin as she clutched his shoulders, and she fought to keep her balance. One of his arms curled around her hips, anchoring her as he pulled her body flush against him.

The kiss was equal parts branding and punishment—though he wasn't sure which one of them was being punished. Ever since he'd learned the price Crombie extracted for his service, he'd been teetering on the edge of his bloodlust. The need to prove that Lina belonged to him, to stake his claim, had overwhelmed him. All he could think about was sliding into her sweet heat until she filled the night with cries that were for him alone. He needed to be inside of her more than his next breath.

Nord's lips were relentless as they moved over hers, reclaiming what was his. It wasn't until she opened to him, her tongue eagerly welcoming his, that the fist clenched around his heart finally started to loosen its grip.

Even so, it wasn't quite enough to sate the beast within. He pulled back, his forehead dropping to hers as he wondered if he dared ask for what his very nature demanded.

Her breath washed over him in shallow pants, her cheeks flushed as she caught his gaze. "And here I was thinking you were mad at me," she laughed, her grin impish though her eyes were searching.

"You?" he asked as his hand fisted in her hair and tugged it further back. "Never."

She ran her fingers down his cheek, a crease forming between her brows. "Then why does it feel like you're angry?"

"Not angry, Kærasta, fucking enraged."

Understanding dawned in her eyes, and her throat bobbed, but she didn't step away. If anything, she pressed closer.

He drew his hand down her back, his palm molding itself to her curves as he admitted, "But not with you. Never with you. It's that fae bastard who constantly tries to take what is mine that set me off." His voice dropped, his whisper agonized. "You should never have to put yourself in danger because of me."

"I won't apologize for doing what I had to," she said, her chin lifting defiantly.

"I'd never ask you to."

"Why do I sense a but coming?"

He let out a humorless laugh, surprised that she could sense what he was trying to dance so carefully around. He should have known better. The woman saw straight through him. "Because I'm not the one in control right now."

She tilted her head. "You seem in control to me."

It only seemed that way because the berserker wouldn't get what he needed by force. Otherwise she'd already be bent over the bed with her legs spread and her ass in the air. It was nowhere near that simple. No, to satisfy the beast and stave off a full-blown rampage, he needed her to give in to him, willingly and without question.

A desperate growl sounded low in his throat, and he knew the instant she saw the flicker of the berserker in his eyes because her breath left her in a low whoosh.

"Oh."

"Fuck," he groaned, the need to dominate at war with the need to protect.

Lina lifted a hand, curling it around his face. "Tell me what you need."

If it had been anything but an order, he might have been able to resist. But the proof that she wasn't scared, even knowing what drove him, gave Nord the courage to give in.

"Do you trust me?" he asked.

Her eyes hooded and her cheeks darkened. "You know I do."

"Then get on your knees."

She obeyed immediately, her gaze never leaving his. Her eyes flared, but it was not disgust he saw shining back at him. It was desire, as potent as his own.

"Take me in your mouth."

She licked her lips as her eyes dropped. His cock throbbed in response, swelling further under her intense regard. Her hands trembled as they lifted to free him from his boxer briefs, but he knew it was anticipation rather than fear coursing through her. She took him in her hand as soon as he sprang free, and the satin glide of her hand had him fighting the urge to start thrusting. It was damn near impossible to make himself remain still, and that was before she repeated the motion by sliding her tongue along the bottom of his shaft from base to tip and then wrapping her lips around him.

"All of me."

She moaned around him, the sound reverberating straight

through his cock and settling at the base of his spine. He bit back his own moan as he watched her slide her mouth down, taking him straight to the root while she reached up and grasped his balls.

Almost of its own accord, his hand snaked out to pull her hair to one side and hold the golden strands in his fist so he could watch as she worked him, her cheeks hollowing with each delicious pull. He practically shook with the need to take over, to tug her head back and thrust fast and deep, but he managed to resist the urge.

Barely.

As she pulled back again, she flattened her tongue beneath him before wrapping it around the tip and sinking back down.

"Fuck, yes," he growled, his head falling back as she continued to suck him.

As good as it felt, it wasn't enough. The beast required further proof of her submission. He needed to know without a doubt that he fucking owned her.

"Touch yourself."

Lina's free hand moved between her legs, her wanton moans building as she worked them both into a frenzy.

It still. Wasn't. Enough.

"Stop."

Her eyes shot open, a silent plea in their depths.

Not yet, my queen.

"Get on the bed."

She scrambled up, her skin flushed with unfulfilled desire. She started to crawl to the center of the bed, but he stopped her with a hand on her ankle, tugging her back. He ran his other hand down her back, pressing her chest into the thick blanket and lifting her hips higher, giving him a perfect view of her slick arousal.

"Touch me," she begged, her legs trembling.

"I am touching you."

"You know what I mean."

"Not yet."

Lina whimpered, grasping the blanket on either side of her. He let his eyes continue with their greedy perusal, loving the way her body responded to just a look. As he drank her in, an idea took shape.

Yes.

Nord wasn't sure the voice was his or his berserker, but in this, they were in absolute agreement.

His eyes lifted to find her hooded gaze focused on him. He ran a single finger along her slippery folds, the tip of his finger slipping in before moving past the area she so desperately craved for him to fill.

"Tell me something, Kærasta."

"Okay . . ." she replied, sounding like she'd only half heard him.

He leaned over until his mouth was at her ear. "Has anyone ever taken you here?" His words were accompanied by the slide of his thumb before he pressed in, highlighting exactly what he was talking about.

"N-no," she breathed, her breath coming out is a pleasured gasp.

"Good, then I'll be the first *and* the last."

She'd been ready for him before, but his words took hold of her, making her writhe desperately beneath him.

"Please," she begged.

"Would you like that?"

"Yes, God, please."

"I need you to do something for me first."

"Anything."

He whispered what he wanted her to do, and her eyes went wide before she stuttered out a laugh. "You want me to use my magic *now*?"

"Trust me, you're going to thank me after."

She took a deep breath and made to sit up, but he kept her in place with the press of his hand against her back.

"I didn't tell you that you could move."

She gave him an exasperated look, but he slid his finger along her seam again, and she shuddered beneath the touch.

"Focus," he warned her, a small smile playing at his mouth as he continued to tease her with his fingers.

Once again, Lina did as she was told, but he could tell she was struggling to keep her mind on her task because it was almost a minute before the small bottle appeared beside them on the bed.

"Good girl," he murmured, pressing a kiss to the nape of her neck as he snagged the bottle and stood.

Lina watched him over her shoulder, her back rising and falling with her ragged breaths. "Aren't you going to . . ."

"Not yet. I have to make sure you're ready first."

"I'm ready," she rushed to assure him.

He knew his answering smile was pure beast as he flicked open the lid and squeezed the clear liquid out. "You're not," he said as he coated his fingers and then dropped the bottle back onto the bed and met her gaze. "But you will be."

Wrapping his arm around the front of her, he worked at the swollen bundle of nerves there, building her climax. She bucked against him, chasing it. Just as she was about to fall off the edge, he slid the first slick finger into her.

Lina buried her face in the blanket and let out a muffled groan as she arched her back in a demand for more. He couldn't deny her. She came almost immediately, her body spasming with the intensity of her climax.

He could have found his own release from the beauty of hers alone.

"Jesus. Fuck. Wow," she gasped.

"Now you're ready."

She grinned, her eyes glowing, her cheeks flushed, and strands of her hair stuck to her face and neck. "Finally."

She watched as he worked more of the silky liquid onto his shaft, her lips parted, her gaze hot. "I love watching you do that," she admitted when she realized he'd caught her staring.

"Stroke myself?" he asked, slowing down the movement of his hand to draw it out for her.

She bit her lip and nodded. "I used to fantasize about walking in on you in the shower and catching you."

"Really?"

Her grin was pure siren. "I mean, you weren't giving me the real thing. What else was I supposed to do?"

"And what else did you do during these fantasies of yours?"

"Nothing."

"You didn't touch yourself the way you wished I would?"

"I didn't want to settle. It was you—all of you—or nothing at all."

Nord's heart thumped wildly in his chest, and the fist that had held him prisoner in its grasp lost the last of its hold. She was his. Utterly. Relief washed through him, but it was short-lived as the hot flare of desire reasserted itself.

He might have gotten what he needed, but they were far from done. As he positioned himself, he caught her gaze once more.

"Tell me if you need me to stop," he ordered.

"I never want you to stop."

He huffed out a laugh, but stars were already exploding behind his eyes as he started to press himself in one delicious inch at a time. Lina gasped, her body tensing momentarily before she relaxed and pressed back, urging him on. She was so damned tight he could hardly draw in a breath around the pleasure. His hands fell to the plump globes of her ass, and he kneaded the muscles, spreading them wide as he slid deeper.

Lina arched back, trying to take more of him.

Nord let out a hiss as ripples of pleasure exploded along his skin. He was so fucking close and they'd just started.

"More," she demanded, proving once again that while he was the one fucking her, she was the one in control.

And just as she had when he was the one issuing orders, he obeyed, filling her in one long thrust that left them both shaking.

"No one told me it would feel this good," she moaned.

"Just wait. It gets better."

He drew out, his hand moving to the apex of her thighs and

circling as he slid back in. Lina clenched around him as she let out another throaty groan. "So fucking good," she panted.

Nord moved in earnest then, Lina trembling each time he pulled out and drove back in. Her breathing grew shallow, her skin flushed with desire. Watching her get lost in her pleasure, pleasure he gave her, stoked his own. He could feel the wave of his climax cresting.

He moved his fingers over her, pinching the tight bundle of nerves the way he knew she loved. Lina gasped, her body quaking as he continued his tender assault. She lasted only a few more thrusts before she came with a long, drawn-out moan.

Nord was right behind her. He came with a roar, his chest pressed to her back and his arms curling around her as he pulled them sideways. They were both panting, sweaty, and still mostly lost in the high of their climax as he pressed his lips to her damp skin, peppering it with kisses.

"You okay?"

"Mmm," she hummed.

He smiled, his berserker's relentless need now replaced with bone-deep satisfaction.

"Don't move. I'll be right back."

She murmured inaudibly as he stood. Heading to the bathroom, he cleaned himself and grabbed a washcloth that he dampened with warm water. Returning to the room, he took care of Lina and then rejoined her on the bed.

She rolled in his arms, turning so that they were face-to-face. He could tell that it was a struggle for her to open her eyes.

"I think I went blind there for a second," she mumbled. "And I *definitely* forgot my name." Her smile stretched further. "But not even the most earth-shattering orgasm in the history of all orgasms could make me forget you calling me yours."

He chuckled, hugging her tighter and kissing her. "I love you, Lina," he breathed against her lips. "And you are mine. Always."

The simple declaration didn't come anywhere near close to

explaining the depth of what he felt for her or what she meant to him, but it was the best he could manage in the moment.

Her blissed-out smile told him she didn't care.

"Ah, Lina . . . that was it," she teased, before snuggling back into him. "And we both know I love you more," she added, her eyes closed, her breaths slowing as they got deeper.

Nord cradled her against him, his fingers roaming through her hair and down her back. *I really fucking doubt that.*

CHAPTER 11
LINA

She slept so hard she didn't even realize Nord had picked her up and tucked her beneath the covers at some point during the night. Though, after a few sleepless days and a climax that exploded through her like a damn supernova, it only made sense that her body might demand time to recover.

Lina wasn't complaining. She just spent the night wrapped in the arms of the man she loved beyond all reason, without a single dream to disturb her hard-fought peace. Reality was impossible to ignore once the sun rose, especially with whoever was pounding on the door.

"Go away," she growled into her pillow—a pillow that was comprised of hard muscles encased in smooth skin and currently rumbling beneath her.

"I don't think they can hear you. The knocks are coming from the front door."

She blinked sleepily at him. "But they're so loud."

"Probably because we've been ignoring them for the last ten minutes."

Wow. I really have been out of it.

"Why haven't you told them to fuck off?"

He lifted one of his shoulders in a shrug. "I thought Fin would deal with it. Besides, I didn't want to leave you."

Her insides turned into something resembling marshmallow fluff as a smile stretched across her face. "Because you looooove me?" she teased, expecting him to roll his eyes and play it off.

But he didn't.

Instead, he took her chin between his thumb and index finger and tilted her face so that she was staring straight into his eyes.

"So fucking much it consumes me, Kærasta." He took her hand and pressed it against the wall of his chest so that when he spoke, his words vibrated beneath her palm along with the steady thump of his heart. "The only reason this heart beats is for you."

Eyes suddenly wet with tears, Lina blinked a few times. "Well, shit."

He grinned at her before leaning forward and capturing her lips with his own. "Never doubt my love for you, Lina. It's the compass that guides every path I walk."

Too moved by his heartfelt declarations to return them with her own, Lina settled for the far less romantic, "Well, aren't you Shakespeare this morning?"

He laughed. "I just thought you should know."

Lina buried her face against him, wrapping her arms around him and holding him tight. "It's the same for me," she whispered.

Nord kissed the top of her head. "I know."

The next round of knocking thundered against the door. Nord sighed. "It's probably best we get up and deal with whoever is out there. Doesn't seem like they're going to give up anytime soon."

"You're probably right," she agreed, not budging an inch.

It was with a reluctant sigh that Nord finally untangled himself from her arms, running his hand possessively over her back and leaning down for one last kiss before he swung his legs over the side of the bed and stood.

Lina didn't even try to pretend that she wasn't shamelessly

ogling him. She let out a low, appreciative whistle that had him smirking at her over his shoulder as he moved into the bathroom.

By the time the water shut off, she was perched on the end of the bed, the sheet draped around her and a sign she'd conjured held up over her head.

"Ten out of ten," she declared loudly, her eyes boldly roaming over his body. "Even the Russian judge agreed."

Nord laughed, shaking his head as he moved across the room and located some clothes that appeared to be in his size hanging in the large freestanding armoire. Lina watched as he got dressed, a hot flicker of desire fluttering through her. No matter how many times she had him, it would never be enough. When it came to Nord, she was insatiable.

He pulled up a pair of fitted black pants and then shrugged on a dark gray shirt. Lina eyed the clothes with a curious frown.

"What are the odds they'd just so happen to have clothes in our exact sizes?" she wondered out loud. Then, upon closer inspection, she added, "And don't those look almost too similar to the styles back home to be a coincidence?"

It was something that had been niggling in the back of her brain since they ran into Strega and the others, but until now, there'd been far more important things to worry about than how a group who'd seemingly been cut off from their world mirrored it so closely. To be fair, pants were pants, and a shirt was a shirt, but the textured fabric closely resembled denim, and the shirt matched the popular Henley style right down to its buttons. Even their lodgings and its furnishings had an aura of familiarity about them.

Nord glanced down as he smoothed a hand over the front of his shirt. His brows pulled together as he glanced back at the armoire. "Good question."

"Do you think it's some kind of magic?" she asked as she padded over to flip through the rack for herself.

Nord's frustrated exhale beside her was Lina's only indication that he'd instinctively tried to use his old Guardian abilities to check.

"It's a possibility," he finally answered.

"You sound uncertain," she said, glancing over at him.

"My people didn't have access to the kind of magic required for something this elaborate."

Lina nodded, understanding his unspoken concern. *If it was magic, where'd it come from?*

"I don't believe we're in any harm, but we should keep our eyes open."

"Agreed," she said, selecting a black tank top, a pair of pants similar to the ones Nord was wearing, and a tan moto-style jacket with reinforced elbows.

"For the love of all that's good and holy," Finley thundered as the latest round of knocking started up again. "Take a fucking hint."

"I think time's officially up," Nord said.

Lina nodded. "You go. I'll be right out."

He pressed a hot kiss to her lips and swatted her on the ass before heading to the door. "Hurry up."

"Sir, yes, sir," she said, saluting him with the hand not clutching her clothes.

He paused by the door, his eyes glittering.

"What?" she asked as a wave of heat slammed through her.

Nord gave her an enigmatic smile. "You'll see."

Lina let out a breath she hadn't been aware of holding when the door closed behind him with a soft click. She had absolutely no idea what just happened, but she was certain she was going to enjoy finding out. She'd come to learn that anything that put *that* look on his face was bound to end in multiple orgasms.

Lina turned back to the dresser, confident she'd discover fresh undergarments waiting for her if she looked, but there was something about the idea of putting on underwear that might have belonged to someone else that wigged her out. Instead, she used her magic to create a clean pair and then finished dressing quickly. She'd just tugged her boots back on when the sound of raised voices cut through her soft humming.

"Shit," she muttered, using magic to take care of the laces as she raced out of the room.

Quinn's towel-clad head peeked around a door at the end of the hall. "Is it safe?" she stage-whispered loudly.

Lina shrugged, moving toward the sound of the voices.

"Holler when you know," Quinn called.

Giving her a thumbs-up, Lina quietly moved into the living room, not wanting to draw unnecessary attention to herself. She needn't have worried; the three men facing off at the door were far too focused on each other to notice her entrance.

The sheer aggression pumping through the room caught her off guard. She took a step back, more out of an innate sense of self-preservation than any genuine fear.

What the hell happened?

Nord couldn't have left her more than a few minutes ago. And he'd been in a great mood when he had, so how had things escalated so quickly?

Her eyes fell on the glowering man standing in the doorway. Søren looked every bit as menacing this morning as he had yesterday. Even with his hair pulled back in a glorious man bun and without his massive raven.

"She asked for you specifically."

Nord shrugged. "Then she can keep waiting as far as I'm concerned. I already told you, I'm not going anywhere without the rest of my friends. The outcome of this meeting affects all of us. It's only fair they're present to take part."

Søren growled low in his throat. "I will not allow you to disrespect Astrid by leaving her waiting."

Oh buddy, bad move. No one can out-badass a berserker. You'd have better luck intimidating a corpse.

Nord crossed his arms, his muscles seeming to swell as black shot through his eyes. "And I will not allow her to disrespect my companions by refusing to meet them before she makes her decision."

Lina's heart nearly burst with pride as she eyed him. So many men would have left without a second thought, but not Nord. He knew it was important for all of them to stand together, to prove that he considered them his equals. And if he was as important to these people as she was coming to believe he was, then that was a hell of a declaration for him to make.

Søren eyed Nord, and for a second, Lina thought he was foolishly going to push the issue, but instead he sighed heavily. "Fine. But we leave now."

Nord caught her eye, checking to make sure she was ready to go and signaling to her he'd been aware of her presence the entire time. Then he looked back to Søren and waved an arm. "Lead the way."

"Uh, Quinn?" Lina called.

"All clear?" Quinn asked, still towel-drying her hair as she walked into the hallway.

"You might want to put some shoes on. Looks like we've been summoned."

Søren's tour of the city left little room for sightseeing. He walked fast, his long strides almost requiring Lina to jog to keep up. As he led them to the woman who'd decide their fate, he wove through fishermen coming in with their morning hauls, curious townsfolk looking for a glimpse at the newcomers, and buildings that all seemed to blend together as they blurred past.

"I'm starting to get the feeling Scarface doesn't want us to be able to find our way back on our own," Quinn whispered as he took another seemingly random turn.

"Too bad for him you have perfect recall," Lina replied with a smirk.

Quinn's eyes lit up with quiet laughter. "What can I say? The job comes with perks."

Lina chuckled, but it faded fast as Søren angled them to a door set within the stone of the mountain itself. He waved his hand over an invisible panel, and the door slid open without a sound.

Nord gave her a significant look over his shoulder as he wordlessly followed Søren inside. Lina knew now was hardly the time to play twenty questions, but she couldn't help but wonder once again where their magic came from. Especially since it was becoming apparent that it was an integral part of their city setup.

She braced herself for the oppressive feeling that usually accompanied being beneath the earth, but she was pleasantly surprised by an open, airy feel to the space as they filed in behind their guide.

The main walls were bare obsidian stone, but the stone that once filled the space had all been cleared away. In its place there was a towering ceiling, several impressive sculptures and other works of art, scattered benches, one curving window that looked out into the marina below, and a single chair that was more akin to a throne with its velvet cushion and intricate antler details.

Lina's eyes caught on a sculpture that hung suspended from the middle of the room. It was massive, carved to look like the skeleton of a snarling horned beast mid-flight. Then her brows furrowed as she moved closer and realized it was not a sculpture at all, but rather a meticulously reconstructed fossil.

"This place is like a museum," she breathed, wandering over to a display of perfectly preserved weapons, her hand reaching out instinctively.

"Glad to see you appreciate the accomplishments of my people," a woman's voice sounded from the back corner of the room as she entered from a door Lina hadn't noticed.

Lina could only assume this was the mysterious Astrid as she snatched her hand back, feeling like a child caught with the cookie jar as she spun around. "They're lovely," she managed, trying to calm the guilty race of her heart.

From somewhere behind her, Quinn snickered.

Astrid's expression was unreadable, but her blue eyes seemed to dance with amusement as she walked with the confident swagger of a woman who knew she was the biggest threat in the room.

Lina relaxed infinitesimally because *she* knew that wasn't true—Nord held that title hands down. But also, there was something kindred about the Novasgardian leader. Like if they'd met for the first time at a bar over drinks, they'd find they had a shocking number of things in common.

As she moved further into the light, Lina got her first unimpeded look at her.

Astrid was a striking woman. She could easily understand why she'd been chosen to lead. She appeared to be in her mid-forties, was easily over six-feet tall, well-built, and exuded an unflappable confidence. Her skin was sun-kissed, her face free of makeup, and her light blonde hair cut short at the sides and long on top, with a sweep of it falling over her broad forehead.

Lina immediately noted the similarity to Nord's haircut and couldn't help but think the two could be related. Though it was the other, less tangible, similarity that really drove the thought home: while neither held a weapon, they were both clearly seasoned warriors.

She was impressed despite herself. This was a woman with stories to tell, and Lina found herself eager to hear them.

Astrid came to a stop once she was in front of the throne, though she did not sit. She stood in front of it, her hands clasped behind her back.

"My scouts tell me that one of our fabled berserkers has returned. And a Bloodaxe, at that."

"They spoke true," Nord said, moving so that he was standing about ten feet away from her, with the rest of them loosely lined up on either side.

Interest flared in her eyes. "Why should I believe you?"

"Would you like a demonstration?" Nord asked, an unmistakable edge to the question.

Astrid's head cocked. "That won't be necessary. But I find I must insist on an explanation as to why it took you so long to return."

Lina shifted her gaze to Nord's profile, noting the tense set of his jaw and slight tightening around his eyes.

"I take it you know my history," he started somewhat vaguely.

Astrid nodded once.

"Then it should come as no surprise that my place with the Guardians kept me away from our home for decades. By the time I returned, I didn't think there would be any left who would welcome me."

Lina's heart twisted in her chest, and it took everything in her to keep from reaching for his hand.

"And you?" Astrid asked, unexpectedly pinning Lina with her stare. "Why are you here?"

"Refuge, my lady." Lina blushed as soon as the honorific left her lips. She had absolutely no idea why she said it, only that Astrid seemed to demand it with her sheer presence.

Astrid's lips lifted in the barest hint of a smile. "From?"

Lina snorted. "This might go faster if I were to tell you what wasn't on that list."

"I see," Astrid murmured, her eyes gliding over Quinn and Finley in turn. "You four seem like a capable group, especially if the tales of a berserker's prowess in battle are to be believed. Surely a foe does not exist that you cannot easily beat on your own."

"Perhaps if it was a single foe we faced, but our enemies are numerous and our time short," Nord answered.

"How is it you've come to have so many enemies?"

Lina cleared her throat. "That's my fault."

Nord's eyes cut to hers. "It is not."

She shrugged. "I mean . . . it kinda is."

"Not the time, kids," Quinn said in a low voice.

"You," Astrid said, her attention snapping to Finley. "Explain."

"Me?" he asked, clearly surprised to find himself under fire.

Astrid blinked by way of an answer.

"Well, Lina isn't exactly wrong—"

Nord growled, and Finley shrugged.

"Sorry, mate, but it's true. Everything started when she blew into our lives. Not that it's a bad thing, love," he added, grinning at her.

Lina returned his smile, letting him know she wasn't offended by the assessment.

Finley scratched the back of his neck and continued. "Well, you see, Lina was murdered by her ex-fiancé."

"And yet here she stands unharmed," Astrid replied, her tone dry though her eyebrows had lifted.

"It's a long story, but the short of it is, we tracked him down and repaid the favor. His father didn't like that, so he killed Lina's uncle and made it pretty clear we're next on his hit list."

"Is that all?" Astrid asked dryly.

"Not quite. You see, while that was all going on, Nord and I sort of, definitely, pissed off the Brotherhood. Well, that was mostly Nord's fault. He chose Lina over them, and well . . . the Director's not the sort of man to let that slide."

Astrid pressed her lips together. "So you have the Brotherhood and the family of your scorned lover after you?"

"Don't forget the shithead fae prince," Quinn added.

"What's your part in all this?" Astrid asked, her attention snapping to Quinn.

Lina felt Quinn tense beside her and just barely heard her curse beneath her breath before answering the question.

"I'm the one that brought Lina back. And . . . I may also be partially responsible for pissing off said shithead to begin with. Fae don't tend to be fans of blackmail," she added with a dark smile.

"Well," Astrid said after a moment. "I suppose I can see why you need sanctuary. But I still cannot help but wonder why I should help you. It was your choices collectively that led your enemies to your doorstep. It is your responsibility to handle them, is it not?"

"Usually, I would agree with you. But we are not equipped to deal with them all at once. What we need is time, a safe place to stay, and allies," Nord answered.

Lina's eyes flew wide. She hadn't realized he was planning on asking for their help. Though . . . with all their talk of armies the night before, it was a perfect solution.

Astrid didn't agree. Lina couldn't put her finger on how exactly she knew that, but there was a definite change in the air and a sudden frostiness to her words.

"You turned your back on your people once, berserker. Why should they come to your aid now?"

Lina braced herself, sure that the words would bring Nord to the very edge of his control. But despite color rising in his cheeks and the wild pulsing of a vein in his neck, he kept his voice steady and his words measured.

"Just because the deal I struck required me to leave does not mean I turned my back on my people. Everything I did, I did to save you. Your continued existence proves that I made the right choice, and I would do it again without question."

Astrid's expression did not alter, leaving no hint to what her thoughts were about Nord's explanation. For her part, Lina was once again fighting the urge to close the distance between her and Nord as her opinion of the woman shifted. She couldn't stand the idea of him being shamed for his past. Not after he'd proven time and again, just how far he would go to protect the people he loved. There wasn't a dishonorable bone in his body, and it pissed her right the fuck off that this woman dared to suggest otherwise.

Before Lina could defend him, Astrid spoke again.

"I will not risk my people's lives for one who is not worthy."

Lina's teeth clenched. *Who the hell does this chick think she is? How dare she judge us? She doesn't even know us.*

Nord, however, seemed to understand where Astrid was coming from. Lina fought against a confused frown as he nodded his agreement.

"Of course. It is only right that we prove ourselves to you before you should extend your assistance."

There was a long stretch of silence, and then Astrid dipped her head in a slight nod. "Very well, we shall hold a hunt in three days' time. If you prove yourselves worthy, then I shall consider your request."

A bubble of laughter caught in Lina's chest. Considering was a far cry from agreeing, but it was something. Maybe, just maybe, things were starting to turn around for them after all. Then the rest of her words sank in.

"Wait. What kind of hunt?"

"Wyvern, of course."

"Of course," Lina replied, her voice hollow as a dull ringing sounded in her ears. *How the fuck are we supposed to hunt a wyvern?* She didn't even know what a wyvern was.

She shot Quinn a worried glance. Her friend returned it with a stricken one of her own. If Lina was freaking out, she could only imagine what Quinn was feeling right now. At least Lina's powers lent themselves to battle, but Quinn was the furthest thing from a fighter, and not even her magic could help her become one.

Unaware of the tumult her words had caused, Astrid continued speaking. "In the meantime, I consider you my personal guests. Please, make yourselves at home. Søren, why don't you give my guests a proper tour of the city?"

Lina couldn't help but laugh at the put-out look on his face.

But all Søren said was, "Of course."

He turned to escort them back out, but before they made it more than a few steps, Astrid's voice rang out once more. "Bloodaxe, a word, if you will."

Nord faltered, looking torn.

"It's okay," Lina whispered, giving his arm a brief squeeze. "Join us when you're finished."

He stared down at her for a long second before nodding and

bringing his lips to hers in a brief kiss. "Don't go far and stay close to Fin until I get back. This won't take long."

"Don't worry about me. I promise not to almost die while we're apart," she teased.

"Lina," he groaned, but he was smiling.

"I know that's what you're worried about."

"Given recent events, can you blame me?"

"No, but I have a feeling we're in the clear. At least for a little while."

Nord chuffed out a laugh, his finger brushing the underside of her chin. "Go, and at least try to behave."

Lina made a face as she started walking backward toward the exit. "Where's the fun in that?"

CHAPTER 12
NORD

As soon as the footsteps faded, Astrid faced him, her lips pursed and her eyes hard as she gave him a thorough once-over. Nord took her blatant perusal of him as permission to do the same.

He couldn't help but notice that she bore a striking resemblance to the legendary shield maiden Brynhild. The similarity was so great, in fact, that it could only mean Astrid was a descendant. Not only was Brynhild her grandmother—many times removed—but she also happened to be his mother's sister.

An unfamiliar feeling ran through him at the realization that he was face-to-face with a blood relative for the first time in centuries.

"Shall I call you cousin?" he asked with a wry twist of his lips.

Her eyes snapped to his. "Astrid will do. The only family I recognize live within the city gates."

Nord allowed the words to cut through him, accepting them as his due even as part of him yearned for acceptance. It had been a long time since he'd had family ties by blood, even diluted blood. Still, he couldn't blame her. His people were nothing if not loyal. To them, his actions would be unfathomable.

"Fair enough." But then, since he was tired of being a pawn in other people's power plays, he added, "Cousin."

Her brow lifted as silence stretched uncomfortably between them. Nord refused to be the one to break it. She called this meeting; let her be the first to lay her cards on the table.

"It would seem your history is repeating itself," she eventually said.

"How so?"

"Well, you turned your back on the group you swore allegiance to. Only this time, they hunt you for breaking your vow."

Nord ground his teeth together so hard he could hear it. "That's not what happened."

"Isn't it, though?" she mused with a knowing smirk. "Seems to be the long and short of it so far as I can tell."

"Well, you're wrong."

"Last time, you at least could claim you were looking out for the well-being of your clan, but this time you broke your word for what, a hot piece of ass?"

A growl slipped out as the berserker tried to slip free of Nord's hold. "Cousin or no, I'd tread very carefully if I were you."

A satisfied look crossed Astrid's face and her posture relaxed from her rigid pose as she crossed her arms and sank some of her weight into her hip. "There it is. I wasn't sure I believed—"

Nord let out a snort of exasperation. "You're baiting me intentionally? Are you insane?"

"No," she said with a small smile. "Just curious. You would be too if you were confronted with a living myth."

"The berserkers are hardly myths."

"Perhaps not to you, but since fleeing to Novasgard, the Allfather has not seen fit to bless us with a single one. So, you'll have to forgive me. You're a bit of a novelty."

He took a second to process that. If what she claimed was true, he was the last of his kind. Even though he'd had a long time to come to terms with the possibility, he couldn't quite ignore the heavy ache the reality of it caused. Shoving the unwanted feeling aside, he replied, "Well, surely you've heard of our tempers."

"Obviously."

"Then perhaps it would be best if you do not go out of your way to provoke me."

"Oh?"

"I could rip your heart out, and it'd still be beating in my palm before either you or it realized you were dead."

Her lips tilted in a wintry smile as her chin lifted defiantly. "I'd love to see you try."

"Trust me, cousin. You wouldn't."

She grinned then. "I still can't believe it. You, here, after all this time."

"I can hardly believe it myself," he admitted.

"You must love her deeply to risk not only the Brotherhood's wrath, but ours as well," Astrid said suddenly, tilting her head as her eyes searched his face for answers.

Nord didn't bother with a response. His feelings where Lina was concerned were none of her business. And his presence here spoke for itself.

She let out a soft sigh. "Our people have changed greatly since you last walked among us, but some things will never change. No matter how much you love her, if she fails to prove her worth, we will not come to her aid. Not even for one such as you, Gunnar Bloodaxe. Clan above all else, remember?"

Nord's jaw clenched, but he nodded.

"Things would be different, of course, if you were married, and you reclaimed your place in the clan. Then she would be one of us, and her enemies our own, but . . ." Astrid let the word hang, looking very much like an annoying little sister as she smiled and lifted her hands innocently.

A sharp thrill ran through him at the thought. He'd already pledged his life to Lina. For him, there'd never be another. But there was no denying the appeal of formally swearing themselves to each other. He'd given up on the idea of a wife and family long ago. A Guardian had no place in his life for such things. Then again, he was a Guardian no longer . . .

As soon as the flicker of hope took root, he snuffed it out. Lina deserved better than a marriage proposal that stemmed from a need to assure alliances. If the time came for them to take that step together, it would be their decision alone. And it wouldn't be one they made in fear.

"Lina has the spirit of a warrior. I have no doubt she will impress you."

Astrid hummed. "And what of the others?"

"Finley has been a Guardian almost as long as I have. He's worthy in every sense of the word. I've only recently met Quinn, but she's fiercely loyal and shows every sign of possessing the qualities we value above all else."

"You mention nothing of her skills in battle."

Nord couldn't help but smile at the thought of Quinn attempting to heft one of his weapons, let alone use it. "Not all battlefields are the same," he replied eventually.

"Very true," Astrid agreed. "I guess we shall have to wait and see what happens then."

"So it would seem."

Astrid's demeanor was far warmer now than it had been since she joined them. "I didn't expect to like you quite so much."

"Does that mean I've passed your tests?" Nord asked.

"Hardly," she said with a laugh. "But I have every faith you will if you're everything the stories claim you are. I know my son will be eager to hunt alongside you."

"Søren?" he guessed.

Astrid snorted, clearly amused at the thought. "No, though his mother was a close friend of mine. You haven't met Björn yet. He accompanied me during my travels, but you met his wife, Strega, yesterday."

Nord nodded, tucking the information away in case it proved

useful down the line. One never knew when they might need to exploit a relationship. Not that he was planning on exploiting anyone, but still . . . old habits and all that.

Since she was being forthcoming, he decided to press his advantage and see what other information he could dig up. "Well, since you've decided not to kill us outright—"

"Have I?"

"We both know blood would already have been spilled if you believed we were a threat to your clan."

"True." They shared a look of understanding before she gestured for him to continue. "You were saying?"

Nord let his gaze arc across the city below. "How is it that a group of war-ravaged refugees were able to build all this?"

"Tenacity, foresight, and, dare I say, luck," she replied.

He turned back to her. "And magic?"

Her lips pressed together. "If you're expecting me to deny what you've clearly witnessed, you're going to be sorely disappointed. But that doesn't mean I'm ready to reveal all our secrets either."

"That explains a few things. But it doesn't explain how your city shares so many similarities with my world when, for all intents and purposes, you've been sealed away all this time."

After a long searching look, Astrid seemed to come to some sort of decision. "Well, the explanation is really quite simple," she said, clasping her hands together. "We haven't."

Shock rippled through him at the admission, and she huffed out a laugh at his expression.

"Just because no one accessed the gateway from your side doesn't mean that our ancestors forgot of its existence. When the months turned to years and no one ever returned, our people decided to go in search of their own answers. They returned with news, and we learned of our defeat as well as the ways the world had changed. Some of those changes were shocking, while others were . . . exciting. My predecessors believed it was in the best interest of Novasgard to stay apprised as to the goings-on of our homeland. I have to say I agree. And so we've continued the tradition ever since, sending scouts to keep an eye on the place we came from. While they're away, they mingle with society and learn, then return with stories and souvenirs that we share with the rest of the community and turn into prototypes for our own advancements."

She shrugged as if her revelation was of no importance. "Of course, we were not able to replicate everything with our differing resources, but what we could not copy outright, we found ways to modify. And thus, here we are," she said, gesturing to the world outside the window.

Nord was impressed despite himself. Their utilization of the gateway explained all the weird coincidences Lina pointed out: the similar clothes, the amenities in their suite, even the accents. If they had any hope of blending in while on Earth, they'd have to learn and master the primary languages.

His eyes snagged on one of the many ships in the water below, nostalgia filling him at the sight of a knörr setting sail. "I cannot deny you've built something incredible here, but it's nice to see that not everything has changed."

Astrid's eyes glittered as they found the merchant vessel he was studying intently. "Tradition is important. Some things are worth holding on to. Do you sail often?"

He couldn't remember the last time he'd set foot on a boat of any kind, and yet in that moment, he could feel the wind raging in his hair and the spray of the sea on his face. "Not in a very long time."

Even to his ears, the words were filled with a fierce sort of longing.

"Perhaps you and your friends would like to borrow one of our vessels while you're here? Surely the water calls to you. It runs in our blood."

"Perhaps," he replied, knowing even as he said it, he had no intention of taking her up on her offer.

It was not the adventure that he missed, but the men that once rowed beside him. Being here, surrounded by the evidence of his past, dredged up all sorts of memories he'd buried deep within.

But he couldn't afford to let those ghosts roam free. Not with monsters lurking around every corner, waiting for him to drop his guard so they could strike.

Too much was at stake.

And the one thing he would never risk, not even for a chance to feel as though he was sitting beside his father one last time, was Lina.

Nord turned his back on the sparkling water and faced Astrid once more. "Was there anything else you wanted to speak to me about?"

CHAPTER 13
LINA

"I can't believe we're actually going through with this," Lina muttered, drawing her fingers along the body armor Nord had laid out for her with morbid fascination.

All in all, there were four pieces that were supposed to be worn over an accompanying bodysuit. One for the torso, two for the lower half of their arms, and then something that reminded her of a pair of chaps. If chaps were badass and skintight.

Lina was already wearing the fitted one-piece, and she was surprised by how breathable the heavy-duty fabric was. At first glance, it looked like a wetsuit, but now that she was wearing it, it reminded her of the unitards she used to wear to ballet class. She assumed the special material was their version of bulletproof, except it wasn't bullets they were worried about. She wasn't fully convinced it was up to the job.

"Not like they gave us much of a choice, love," Finley pointed out as he strapped himself into his chest piece.

She didn't bother to fight her smile at the sight of him all decked out. She was so used to his perfectly polished 007 persona that it was jarring to see the transformation from playboy to superhero.

Gone were the suit and tie, and in their place the Novasgardian equivalent of tactical gear. All he was missing were a couple of black smudges beneath his eye and some foliage to crawl beneath, and he'd be all set. Or maybe what he really needed was a rubber mask and a cape.

"Do me a favor," she begged with a grin.

His hazel eyes were wary, but his lips were already twisted up. "I know I'm going to regret asking, but what do you need?"

"Can you say, 'I'm Batman' for me in one of those real deep growls?" she asked with a snicker.

Quinn started laughing so hard she snorted.

Finley rolled his eyes, feigning annoyance, but Lina could see that he was fighting against laughing himself.

"Not a fan?" she asked.

"Bruce Wayne's a pretentious twat, and Batman is the worst excuse of a superhero ever. Why would I lower myself to such pathetic standards?"

"Fin, I hate to break it to you, but you're exactly like him."

He gasped in mock outrage. "How dare you."

Lina held up a finger. "One, you have the McMansion. Two, you have the secret underground lair complete with ridiculous robocars. Three, you are the embodiment of the billionaire playboy by day and savior of humankind by night. Four—"

He waved her off with a laugh. "All right, all right. I get your point. But for the record, I am far better than any fictional superman."

"How do you figure?" Quinn asked, finally controlling her laughter enough to join in the conversation.

Finley's eyes shot to hers, his answering smirk slow and more than a little flirtatious. "Because, sweetheart, I don't have to rely on a bunch of pathetic toys to get the job done. And, more importantly, because I'm real."

Quinn raked her gaze over his armor-clad body, her eyes lingering on the taut ridges cut into the armor as she lifted them back to his face. "Are you certain? You kinda look like one of those plastic action figures to me." She tapped a finger to her lips. "And now that I think about it, I'm not entirely convinced you aren't a Ken doll beneath your pants."

Finley scowled. "I'd be happy to prove that I'm not if you'd like to check."

"Nah, I'm good, thanks."

Lina was laughing so hard by this point, she had to force herself to suck in a series of deep breaths before she passed out from a lack of oxygen.

Nord chose that moment to join them, eyeing their varied expressions with interest but staying silent as he walked over to her. Lina gave herself permission to drink in the sight of him with his armor fully donned and his inked muscles on full, tantalizing display. And she knew for a fact there was nothing over-exaggerated about the ridges cut into his chest piece. All he needed was a wind machine and some kind of slo-mo effect, and he'd be straight out of a 1980s dream sequence.

"Why hello there, handsome," she practically purred.

His lips curved up as he reached her. "Why aren't you dressed yet?"

She pointed to various pieces in front of her. "I don't know what I'm supposed to do with any of that. They didn't exactly come with instructions."

"I didn't know you'd require any."

Lina put her hands on her hips. "Do you remember that day you took me shopping? When I got stuck in my bra for twenty minutes? How could you possibly think I'd navigate this any better?"

He grinned. "Let me help you. Here," he murmured, "put your arms up."

Lina obeyed, feeling more than a little ridiculous as he slid the armor over her head and then ran his hands all over it to ensure the fit was correct before tightening the straps that held the front and back together along her right side.

She squirmed as his fingers brushed over her ribs. "Sorry, it tickles," she said when he lifted his brow.

"Almost done," he promised, his breath washing over her neck, making the act of him dressing her far more intimate than it had any right to be. Especially with Quinn and Finley bickering with each other just a few feet away.

True to his word, Nord was finished and moving on to the next piece mere seconds later.

She held her arms out so he could slide the gauntlets on. "Explain to me how something thin enough that you can tickle me through it is supposed to keep me safe from a wyvern that wants to turn me into its afternoon snack?"

"It was crafted with mobility in mind."

"Call me crazy, but maybe it should have been crafted with not getting stabbed by a foot-long tooth in mind."

Ever since Nord had informed her that the skeleton she'd been admiring in the museum was a wyvern, and that it was essentially just a smaller, two-legged version of a dragon, Lina hadn't been able to sleep. He said 'smaller,' but that thing had been huge. And she recalled with almost Quinn-perfect clarity every horn, claw, and tooth it contained. To say she was not looking forward to today's hunt was a gross understatement. Even with a team of experts accompanying them, things could go horribly, horribly wrong. Especially since said experts were really only there to jump in if their group failed Astrid's test.

"You should be more concerned about its tail," he said, in what she assumed was supposed to be a reassuring manner. "It's got a far greater range, so it's more likely you'd be impaled than bitten."

"Not helping," she muttered.

"I won't let anything happen to you," he promised as he helped her into the final piece.

She'd thought it would sit at her hips, like a pair of pants, but they went up over her belly button as an added layer of protection for her lower stomach.

Nord's knuckles grazed against her center as he smoothed the material over her thigh and jerked it another couple of centimeters higher.

"Erm," she managed as her cheeks flamed. "Pretty sure that can't go any higher unless it's supposed to go inside me."

"Hold still," he said with a knowing grin. "A good fit is necessary to ensure no blade—or claw—will tear through your femoral artery."

"Are you sure that's what you're doing? Because it sort of feels like you're trying to give me an up-the-vag armor wedgie."

He laughed as he stood. "All done."

His smile softened as his eyes swept over her, taking in her armored body and the long braid that she'd magicked into resembling one of the styles she'd seen the other women in the city use. The result was both feminine and fierce, and Lina had hoped looking the part might make her feel a bit more prepared for the day ahead.

So far, it wasn't helping much, but she was thankful she made the effort as Nord's heated gaze lifted back to hers.

"Kærasta . . ."

Before he could finish whatever he wanted to say, Quinn's voice cut through the moment.

"So, listen . . . I figure there's about a fifty-fifty chance I die today. You're my porn buddy. Don't forget. Top bedside drawer. And the chest under the bed. And the purple case in the closet."

"I'm sorry, what did you just call her?" Finley asked, his eyes darting between Quinn and Lina.

"My porn buddy. You know, the person who makes sure to sanitize your house of anything you wouldn't want your family to find after you die," Quinn explained.

Finley's brows lifted, his interest unmistakable. "You don't say. And what sorts of things do you need to hide, Satori?"

Quinn's answering smile was pure sex. "I'll make you a deal, Batman. We get through this alive, and you and I can play show and tell."

Lina wasn't sure who was more surprised by Quinn's offer, her or Finley.

"That a promise?" he asked, his eyes locked on hers.

Quinn lifted one shoulder in a careless shrug. "Consider it your motivation."

"Consider me motivated."

"Well, I'm glad you two got that settled," Lina said with a laugh, "but you don't need to worry, Quinn. The only thing dying today is that wyvern."

Despite her own doubts, it was a lot easier to feel confident with Nord at her side. The man was born for this. She trusted he would get them through in one piece.

Finley clapped his hands and rubbed them together. "Right. Everyone ready to go?"

Lina bit her cheek to keep from laughing. Finley was suddenly as eager as a puppy and almost as adorable because of it.

"One last thing," Nord said, moving over to a cloth-covered bundle she hadn't noticed laying on the counter. He unwrapped it, and Lina's eyes widened at the sight of the small arsenal he revealed. "I got these made for us."

"How did you manage that?" Finley asked, accepting the crossbow Nord handed him with a look of reverence usually reserved for one of his cars.

Nord shot Finley an amused look. "I asked."

"And they just handed them over?"

"They couldn't very well send us on a hunt unarmed."

Finley let out a low whistle, returning his attention to the weapon cradled in his hands.

Lina watched Nord select a long spear out of the pile, wondering if he'd chosen it for her, when he stopped in front of Quinn.

Her eyes bounced from the weapon he held out to her and then back up to him. "You're shitting me, right?"

"I never joke about weapons."

Quinn blinked. "I don't think any of us are under the impression that I'm actually going to be useful out there. It's not exactly like I can convince it to sit there quietly while we murder it." She shot Nord a hopeful look. "Can I?"

"I doubt it."

She sighed. "Yeah, my gift has never worked on animals. So really, our best-case scenario is me staying out of your way."

"I'm not letting you go out there without a way to defend yourself. Here, like this," Nord said, placing the smooth wood in her palms and then moving to stand behind her. He gave her a critical once-over, positioning her body until she was holding it the way he wanted her to. "When in doubt, use the pointy end," he told her with a smile.

Quinn smirked at him. "Famous last words."

Nord shook his head, going back to retrieve a hand ax from the pile. Lina let out a soft gasp as he held it out to her. The wood was a gleaming ebony, the ax head a flinty silver with loving details etched into its surface. Lina carefully traced one of the symbols. "This is for me?"

"Your magic will always be your best weapon, but if you get in a situation where you don't have time to use it, I wanted you to have something versatile." Nord cleared his throat, seeming suddenly uncertain. "Do you like it? I asked Strega to include the markings I requested for mine."

"Be still my heart," Quinn said with a dramatic sweep of her hand up to her forehead. "The man got them his and hers axes. Isn't that like the Viking equivalent of wedding rings?"

Lina's heart raced at the thought, and she couldn't resist stealing a look at Nord, shocked to find him blushing. He cleared his throat again and then pointed to the symbol she'd been tracing.

"It means Tor, thunder. That was my father's name. He always carried the sigil into battle for luck, and I continued the tradition. It's probably silly," he said, running a hand along the back of his neck.

"No," Lina insisted, lifting it up and loving the weight of it in her hand. She curled her fingers around the throat of the haft, and it settled against her skin like it had been handmade for her. "It's perfect. I love it."

Nord grinned, looking relieved as he went and grabbed the two much larger axes he'd gotten for himself.

Lina's eyes narrowed playfully as he slid them haft first into the holster he'd strapped to his back. "Wait, how come I get the baby one?"

"Be thankful you got one at all," he replied blandly, but his eyes glinted with humor. Lina grinned, recalling all the times she'd begged him to give her a weapon and he'd refused.

"Well, we all have to start somewhere," she replied.

They shared a smile.

Nord looked away first, his eyes brushing over all of them before he dipped his chin in a decisive nod.

"Now we're ready."

CHAPTER 14
NORD

"The nest is just up ahead," Søren said, his eyes trained on the sky where his bird was little more than a speck amongst the clouds.

After spending the last few hours in Søren's company, there was very little doubt in Nord's mind that the man was a worg and the bird his familiar. He'd known a few in his time, and there was no mistaking that soul-deep bond between man and beast.

"So, what's the game plan?" Finley asked, eyes roaming over the winding mountain path ahead of them.

Björn turned back to look at Finley, the heavy chains he carried over his shoulder clinking together as he did. "You tell us. It's your hunt."

Thus far, the only similarity Nord could find between Björn and his mother was the silvery-blue hue of their eyes. He'd never have known they were related otherwise. The man's head was shaved down to the skin, and his full beard was a mess of bright orange curls, braids, and beads, which hung about mid-chest. And while built like the bear he was named for, Björn had more in common with the stuffed toy than its wild ancestors.

Finley twisted to face Nord. "What's the game plan?"

A smile tugged at Björn's lips while Strega openly snickered. She'd warmed to them considerably since their first meeting a few days ago. Søren, as usual, didn't react at all. Though Nord was starting to believe that had more to do with the fact he was focused on what he could see through his familiar's eyes rather than the conversation taking place around him.

"Wyvern are fierce predators. They're one of the rare creatures that kill because they can and not just as a means of survival."

"So we lure it out," Finley said, already following Nord's line of thought.

"If the beast senses easy prey, it shouldn't be able to resist the urge to finish the kill."

"That doesn't sound very sportsmanlike," Quinn said, leaning heavily on the spear he'd given her.

Nord's lips twitched. "It's not. But against a creature like this, we need every advantage."

"Fair enough," she said, gratefully accepting the flask of water Lina handed her.

"What are we going to use for bait?" Lina asked, her eyes sweeping over the mountain's barren landscape.

They'd seen little in the way of wildlife as they'd hiked up the mountain pass, which made sense, given most animals' natural instincts would have driven them as far away from the wyvern's nest as possible. And for those it didn't, well, they'd likely made an excellent meal.

"That's where you come in."

Her brows furrowed for a second, and then her nose wrinkled as she worked out his meaning. "You want me to conjure a wounded animal?" Lina bit her lip. "I'm not sure if I can. I've never tried to create a living thing before."

"Good thing it only needs to be half-living," Quinn said with a forced smile as she capped the flask and tossed it back to Lina.

"It doesn't need to be real," Nord assured her. "It just needs to look and smell like it."

"I can try," Lina said, still looking a little uncertain.

He could see the Novasgardians out of the corner of his eye, staring hard at her as she drew upon her power. He bit back a smile. The wyvern wasn't the only thing Nord was setting a trap for. It was not so much a trap to trick them, but rather to ensure he and Lina passed today's test.

It was the reason he'd come up with this plan. Since Lina was still mostly untested in actual combat, there was no guarantee how she'd perform under pressure. But when it came to her innate mastery of her magic, there was no way she could fail to impress. Ensuring she had an opportunity to showcase it was a surefire way to prove her worth as an ally.

Lina took a deep, centering breath, her eyes squeezed shut as she focused on whatever mental image she wanted to call into existence. When there was no immediate change, Björn and Strega shared a look, but Nord knew better than to underestimate Lina.

He focused intently on the clearing ahead of them on the path, evaluating it while he waited. The winding route they'd followed up here was fairly narrow where it curved in and around the mountain, but the path had leveled off and opened up to be about the size of an American football field. It almost looked like part of the mountainside had been sheared off to create the flat open space. But regardless of how it came into being, it was an ideal place to fight since they'd have room to maneuver and only a handful of trees and boulders to work around.

The only potential downside was the sheer drop off the edge that ran along the entire right side of the clearing. They'd have to be careful not to stray too far to that side.

One moment the area was empty, and the next, a ripple shimmered in the air, like heat wafting up from the ground, and then it was there. An injured mountain lion right in the center of the clearing, its fur smeared with blood and dust.

Strega sucked in a shocked breath, which was apparently the cue Lina had been waiting for, because she opened her eyes and released a shaky one of her own. But instead of looking relieved, her brows furrowed, and she moved to stand beside her apparition. Nord and the others followed, forming a loose circle around Lina's creation. From here, he could make out the coppery scent of blood in the air.

"It's too still," she murmured distractedly, her fingers twitching as if they were trying to mold whatever she pictured in her mind.

Even though he'd witnessed the extent of her power firsthand, Nord couldn't help his reaction when the animal's tail twitched, and its ribcage rose and fell. His body tensed, ready to deal with the threat before he remembered it wasn't real.

When the creature didn't move a second time, Lina sighed. "I'll have to keep focusing if we want it to seem like it's still alive," she said, sounding apologetic. "Keeping an object in motion isn't something I've had to do before, I—"

Nord cut her off by leaning over and pressing a swift kiss to her lips. "You're incredible. Do what only you can do. The rest of us will get into position."

She blinked up at him, her cheeks tinging pink at his words. "Okay."

He gestured with his head that the others should follow him, and they obeyed without a word. Now that Lina had baited the trap, there was no telling how soon the wyvern would arrive to investigate.

Nord's eyes fell on the chain coiled over Björn's shoulder. "Can we count on your help, or are we on our own?" he asked even though he already knew the answer.

"Our instructions were to only intervene if necessary."

Nord held out his hand. "Then I'm going to need to borrow those."

Björn handed the heavy length and its accompanying hooks over. Nord took a second to test the weight of them in his hand. It'd been a while since he'd had to throw something a vast distance, but he was fairly confident, given the size of the target, he wouldn't miss.

"We won't have much time to act once it arrives. It will be distracted by the scent of blood, but it will shift focus as soon as it catches our scents. We'll need to strike fast. Aim for its eyes, belly, or wings. And whatever you do, watch out for its tail."

Quinn blanched but tightened her grip on her spear and nodded along with Finley. "What's that for?" she asked, pointing at the chain.

"Our best bet is to keep the beast grounded. I'm going to try to attach the chain to one of its legs to prevent it from taking flight."

"And then what? Turn it into a kite?" Quinn asked, her eyes blown wide.

"Something like that."

"You're fucking crazy," she said, shaking her head.

"No," Björn corrected, seeming proud, "he's a berserker."

"Same thing," Quinn muttered.

Björn and Strega chuckled, and even Søren seemed to crack a smile. Nord shared their amusement. She wasn't wrong.

"All right, you two stand over there by those trees and wait for my signal."

"What's the signal?" Quinn asked.

Finley grabbed her hand and started walking in the direction Nord indicated, answering as he did, "You won't be able to miss it. Trust me."

Quinn tossed a final, wide-eyed look over her shoulder as she trailed after Finley.

Nord turned his attention back to the others.

"If you're not here to fight, then stay back," he ordered. "I won't be held responsible for your injuries if you're stupid enough to get in the way." Then he dismissed them from his mind entirely as he searched for his hiding place.

He'd already given Finley and Quinn the spot with the best cover. There weren't many options left on his side of the clearing, save a skeletal tree and a pile of rocks that only went up to his knees. Neither provided much in the way of coverage, but the tree at least would camouflage the bulk of his body. And even a poor hiding spot was better than standing out in the open.

After a quick scan of the sky, his eyes darted to Lina, who was just about halfway between him and Finley, crouched behind a boulder with the cliff's edge at her back. She didn't seem to notice him, focused as she was on the animal she was giving life to. With nothing left to do, Nord settled in to wait.

It couldn't have been more than a minute or two at most before Søren let out a whispered shout.

"Incoming!"

His warning was cut off by a high-pitched shriek that was so loud, the very mountain shook from the force of it.

Nord's ears were ringing as he watched the wyvern come into view. The edges of its midnight blue scales were a reddish-brown, while its leathery wings were a deep inky black. Two jet-black horns curved up and back on either side of its glowing amber eyes. Sharp ridges started along its spine and ran all the way down its deadly tail, which ended in a barbed point.

He let the sight wash over him, the thrill of imminent battle bubbling up as he recognized the approach of a worthy opponent. It wasn't his first time facing off with one of the winged creatures, but it had been a while, and this one was bigger than he remembered. It was easily four times his size, with its tail making up half that length. He'd forgotten how imposing the giant reptiles were with their wings fully extended, claws outstretched, and toothy maw open on a mighty roar.

The wyvern let out another blood-curdling scream as it prepared to land, its wings arched back to slow its descent. His bloodlust slipped over him then, sharpening his senses and narrowing the world down to this exact moment.

The time for battle was upon them.

As the wyvern landed, a slight tremor ran through the earth

upon impact. The creature pulled its wings in tight as it took a few lumbering steps closer to Lina's grisly offering, the ground continuing to tremble with each powerful stride.

When it dipped its long neck to claim its prize, Nord jumped out from behind the tree with a savage cry. He ran forward, swinging the chain over his head like a lasso, once, twice, three times before he let it fly. The coiled length slid through his fingers toward its target, but the wyvern was fast. Faster than a creature of its size had any right to be.

Its head swung in Nord's direction; its eyes narrowed into two angry, yellow slits as it sidestepped away from the chain with ease.

Nord began to draw the metal links back to him, preparing to try again when the creature took its first threatening step forward, and then a second. From the corner of his eye, he could just make out Lina's trembling form pressed up against her boulder.

His heart gave a panicked lurch. Even if he managed to catch the giant lizard, Lina was far too close to it for his liking. The beast would likely lash out at the nearest enemy, which was currently her. And with her proximity to the edge, she might accidentally topple over it in her attempt to back away.

He couldn't risk it.

Nord dropped the chain, pulling the first of his axes free as he started sprinting.

"What happened to the plan?" Finley shouted in his mind.

"Fuck the plan!" Nord yelled, the words turning into a battle cry as he closed the distance, using Lina's boulder as a launching pad as he ran up, and then propelled himself off of it. He was airborne for only half a second, his ax on a downward swing aimed at the wyvern's exposed neck when the creature's wing slammed into him and knocked him off course.

Nord flew back practically the entire distance he'd just run, dust flying up as he made contact with the rocky surface. The bloodlust blunted the pain, and he rolled, immediately pushing himself up into a crouch with a snarl.

The wyvern stalked closer, letting out its own bellow of indignant rage.

Nord could see Finley and Quinn creeping out from behind the trees in an attempt to flank the beast while Lina slowly backed away, her eyes darting around as if searching for inspiration. Wanting to keep the monster's attention on him to buy the others the time they needed, Nord hefted the ax in his hand, changing his grip so that he was holding it closer to the bottom of its haft before pulling back and chucking it straight at that massive face.

The creature reared back, his ax falling uselessly to the ground. Nord ground his teeth together, preparing to grab his second weapon, but then he heard the familiar thrum of a crossbow releasing its bolt. The metal tip tore through one of the monster's wings, causing it to shriek and spin in rage.

It turned and ran at Finley, its mouth snapping closed mere feet in front of him.

There was one second of wild-eyed panic, and then Quinn shifted her position so that she was holding her spear like a bat instead of a javelin. She swung, crashing the flat side of the wood against the beast's snout.

It swiveled its head, bellowing as the wood splintered and cracked. Quinn gaped at the two halves she was now holding before they clattered to the ground, and she scrambled backward.

Nord was already up and moving, his second ax in hand as he made use of the wyvern's distracted state. Lina apparently had the same idea, but there wasn't time for Nord to figure out what she was trying to do before the beast—likely realizing it was surrounded—pushed itself into the air.

The wyvern's flapping wings created huge buffets of wind, kicking up dirt that flew into his eyes, making them water. He squinted, trying to shield against it as he searched for the next opportunity to strike.

Lina, meanwhile, seemed to be keeping herself busy playing support. She'd repaired Quinn's spear and had also managed to conjure a ballista. Or what he assumed was supposed to be a ballista. It was essentially Finley's crossbow, but larger and mounted. Nord could only guess Lina had seen the wyvern barely react to the bolt and decided they needed something bigger to take it down.

"Brilliant woman," Nord muttered, impressed that she'd managed something so intricate in the midst of this fray.

The wyvern was less impressed. Its focus was still leveled on Quinn and Finley. It snarled and gnashed its teeth, making like it was going to bite them again. Nord saw the snaking tail too late.

"Look out!" he shouted.

But the barbed tip was already coming straight at Quinn. Finley dove, knocking them both to the ground, though he wasn't quick enough to miss the sharp edge of one of the barbs. Finley grunted in pain as blood spurted out of his arm.

"Hey! Douche bucket!" Lina shouted, letting her ax fly and pulling the creature's attention before it could make a second attempt.

Lina! No!

He couldn't manage to form the words as he watched her sprint —weaponless—in the opposite direction from where Quinn and Finley were sprawled on the ground as she tried to draw the wyvern away from them.

With her attention divided between where she was running and the creature chasing after her, she wasn't prepared when the strike came.

Luckily, her escape route led her straight toward him, so Nord— who felt like he was watching things unfold in slow motion—was right there when the wyvern made its next attack. Its thick tail snapped forward like a whip, but instead of piercing Lina, it hit Nord.

Lina cried out as she watched the razor-sharp tip sink into and then through him.

Nord grunted and clenched his teeth against the blinding flash of pain. His options were limited, impaled as he was. Already, he was being lifted up into the air. He wrapped his hands around the scaled flesh like he was preparing to pull it out.

"Lina, run."

"I'm not leaving you."

"Dammit, woman. Fucking run."

"No!"

Nord couldn't waste another second, not when the wyvern was preparing to make a meal out of the both of them. As the creature's head dipped and its fetid breath fanned over his face, all he could hope was that he was faster.

He wasn't.

The wyvern lifted Nord higher, as if he weighed nothing at all, and slammed him against the side of the mountain. The metallic taste of blood coated his mouth as his head cracked against stone, momentarily blinding him.

"Nord!" Lina screamed, but he was having trouble hearing her over the sudden rumbling of rocks breaking free from up above.

The wyvern's head dipped lower until Nord was looking straight into those reptilian eyes. Knowing all he could do now was buy the others time, Nord embraced the full fury of his berserker, tightening his grip on the beast's tail and pulling himself further onto it. He hissed out a breath as not even the bloodlust could fully protect him from the searing pain. With mere seconds left before boulders began to rain down upon him, he did it again until he was in range of those deadly jaws.

But the impact never came.

He risked a glance up, shock and then pride rippling through him as he realized Lina had managed to create a barrier between him and the rocks above. They smashed into her shield and then clattered down its sides.

That one small shift in the tide was all Nord needed.

With a bloodthirsty cry, he grasped the wyvern's jaws in each hand and pulled. The muscles in his neck and arms bulged as he grappled with the beast. It began to thrash its head in earnest, trying to get free of Nord's hold as he forced its mouth further open. It was no use. Infused with the divine strength of his fury, Nord managed to pry the creature's jaws apart, not stopping until he heard a sickening crack.

It wasn't enough to kill the wyvern outright, but it was something.

The wyvern wailed, flailing beneath Nord's vise-like grip and causing some of its teeth to cut into the skin of his hands. But what were a few more cuts when the frenzied movements caused the barbed spikes inside him to tear deeper into his skin, sending warm trickles of blood spilling down his back and chest?

That's when he heard it.

The sweet, familiar *thrum* as the ballista bolt tore through the air and went straight through the wyvern's skull, pinning it to the mountain and killing it instantly.

The giant body sagged, the tail taking Nord with it as it fell bonelessly to the ground.

For a second, all he could hear was the ragged thumping of his heart.

"I've got you," Finley said, eyes shining silver as he got to work removing and then repairing the damage caused by the wyvern's tail.

Nord couldn't care less about his injuries. His eyes slid to Lina, who'd dropped to her knees beside him.

"You did good," he said, his mouth feeling like sandpaper.

"So did you." Her voice didn't betray her nerves, but her eyes did. This was the second time she'd seen him nearly die, and she'd barely recovered from the first.

"I'm proud of you."

Lina bit her lip, looking like she was about to cry as her hand found and squeezed his.

"But next time, when I tell you to run, you fucking run."

Her mouth dropped open, and then she snapped it closed, the

ghost of a smile playing about her lips. "Never gonna happen. We're a team, remember? Where you go, I go."

He would have kissed her if he could move. Instead, he settled for staring into the crystalline depths of her eyes and imagined what he would do once they were alone.

"Well done," Björn boomed. "That was one of the most impressive displays of skill and magic I've ever seen." He turned to Quinn with a smirk. "Well, for the most part. You do know how a spear works, don't you?"

Her eyes narrowed, and their wine-colored depths began to swirl hypnotically. "Hey, buddy. How 'bout you do me a favor and kiss your own ass?"

Björn's expression went slack, and he started twisting this way and that. With a look of pure consternation, he bent over and shoved his head between his legs with a grunt.

Strega stood agape while Søren stared at Quinn with a piercing intensity. Finley paused what he was doing only long enough to see what was happening. Then he grinned and shook his head.

"Better him than me," he muttered.

"Quinn," Lina said with a quick shake of her head. "Stop."

"What are you doing to him?" Strega asked, looking equal parts horrified and impressed.

Quinn's expression was fierce, though she never looked away from the squirming Viking who was moments away from falling onto the ground with his failed attempts to turn himself into a pretzel.

"No one speaks to me that way and gets away with it," she ground out.

"I know, sweetie," Lina said soothingly. "And now, so do they."

Quinn allowed the compulsion to continue for a second longer before she released him.

Björn's jerking movements stopped, and he stood red-faced and panting with his hands on his knees. "Apologies. I meant no offense. Won't happen again."

Strega looked between Björn and Quinn, though her loyalty seemed divided. "My husband has a habit of putting his foot in his mouth. I assure you, his words were in jest. He will not make the same mistake twice. That was . . ." she trailed off, not seeming to have the words. "Well, it was fucking incredible, is what it was. Can you really make someone do whatever you want them to?" she asked, frank respect shining in her eyes.

"Want to find out?" Quinn asked with a wicked smirk.

Strega hesitated a second before answering. "I think I'll pass."

"Good choice," Quinn said before shifting subjects. "So I'm just curious. At what point were you guys going to step in? Was body maiming not enough? Did someone actually need to get eaten first, or . . ." She let the question hang.

Nord huffed out a laugh. The woman had balls of fucking steel.

"You seemed to have things well in hand," Strega said. She walked closer as she spoke, and Nord caught a glimpse of the axes she'd retrieved for them cradled in her arms.

Quinn let her eyes pointedly drop to where Finley was still intently repairing the gaping hole in Nord's chest.

"Riiiight. I'd hate to see what you consider out of hand. Also, for the record, your armor is bullshit. What's the point of even wearing it when that thing cut through it like it was a piece of wet paper?"

"Everyone knows not to get hit by a wyvern's tail," Søren said with a shrug.

Quinn stared, color flashing high on her cheeks, but all she said was a hollow, "I'll try to remember that."

"There," Finley said, his eyes hazel once more as he sat back on his heels. "All done."

Nord sat up, cracking his neck before inspecting the melon-sized hole in his chest plate. A couple inches to the left, and it would have gone straight through his heart. He could have died.

Not sure what to do with the revelation, Nord grasped Finley's forearm, holding it just below the elbow. "Thank you, brother."

Finley waved the thanks away, mirroring Nord's hold on his arm.

"Anytime." There was a beat of silence as they stayed that way. Then Finley grinned and dropped Nord's arm. "Besides, I made a promise to get us all through alive. I intend to collect my reward for a job well done."

Quinn's face was carefully blank as she inspected her nails. "Who said anything about a reward?"

Finley blinked at her. "You've got to be shitting me," he growled.

She smirked. "Don't get your panties in a twist, Batman. It's not like I have access to my stash right now, anyway. What did you think was going to happen?"

While they stared at each other, Lina slid up beside Nord.

"Are you okay?" she asked, wrapping her arm around his waist.

"Good as new."

She seemed to melt into him for a second, but her expression was set when she turned back to the Novasgardians.

"So, did we pass your test?" she asked.

"What do you think?" Strega asked.

"That if we didn't, you can take it and shove it up your ass," she replied with a tight smile.

Nord tightened his hold on her, loving how fearless she could be. And how fierce.

There was a moment of silence, and then all three of them started to laugh.

Lina's brows lifted. "Did I say something funny?"

"I don't think you'll ever have to worry about fitting in with us, häxa," Søren said. "You are a Viking at heart, if not by blood."

"What did he just call me?" she asked Nord under her breath.

"A witch."

Her eyes narrowed as if she wasn't sure whether or not she should be insulted. Eventually, she asked, "So now what?"

Søren grinned, his face transformed by the act. "Now we feast."

CHAPTER 15
LINA

Søren's fist slammed into the jaw of his opponent, sending blood and spit spraying over the cheering crowd.

"You know . . . when he said feast, this wasn't exactly what I pictured," Lina said, tilting her chin toward Quinn but leaving her eyes trained on the spectacle before her.

"Expecting something a little less bloody?" she asked with a teasing grin.

Lina winced as Søren landed another series of powerful blows, sending his opponent flying backward into the crowd. They jostled the man, pushing him until he stumbled back into the center of the makeshift fighting ring.

"I mean . . . I expected there to be more food and some drinking horns at the very least. Maybe some music . . ."

Quinn pointed to where Nord stood with Finley, a black and white horn in his hand. "There's one."

Lina grinned. "I should have known my berserker wouldn't let me down."

"The food was good while it lasted," Quinn said.

"True, I just hadn't anticipated having to dodge elbows while trying to get it."

Quinn laughed as Lina gingerly rubbed her arm. "We're lucky we managed to snatch up what we did," she said as the crowd let off another raucous cheer. "And there's music," she added, gesturing to a trio of musicians playing in the corner. "You just can't hear it over all the yelling."

Lina's eyes trailed over the room, skimming across the beautiful wooden walls and antler chandeliers, lingering for a moment on the massive hearth that took up almost a third of the wall and eventually landing on the man and women playing instruments. If not for the fighting pit that currently took up the entire center of the room, it had all the makings of a beautiful reception hall.

"At the end of the day, they're celebrating," Lina said with a shrug. "Who am I to say what that should look like?"

"Exactly," Quinn agreed. "But you have to admit, there's something pretty hot about watching Søren beat the shit out of that other guy."

"Is it the violence you like or the fact that they're both shirtless, sweaty, and built like a couple of—"

"Vikings?" Quinn supplied with a laugh.

"Exactly."

She grinned. "A little of column A, a lot of column B."

Lina snickered. "Welcome to the club."

"I think I'm going to like it here," Quinn said.

Søren circled his opponent, his face coming into clear view as he briefly paused to crack his knuckles. Dark strands of inky hair stuck to his face, and a savage grin twisted his full lips.

"It's the quiet ones you have to watch out for," Quinn added, her voice oddly yearning. "They're always the kinky bastards."

Lina raised an eyebrow. "Satori, *you're* a kinky bastard."

"Obviously."

"So what's the problem?"

"Who said there was one? I was just saying. The quiet ones are almost always beasts in the bedroom."

A delicious tingle rolled through Lina and settled low in her belly as the memory of Nord from the other night filled her mind. *You can say that again,* she thought with a smile.

Before Lina could reply out loud, Søren leaned forward and raced toward his opponent, sending him flying up and over his shoulder. The man landed with a pained groan. There was a moment of sudden silence as the crowd waited, and then an earsplitting cry when he didn't get back up. Søren lifted his arms up and dropped his head back, shaking his hair and beating his chest as he let out a victory cry that could have rivaled one of Nord's.

"Maybe you should go congratulate him," Lina said.

"Um . . . I don't think I'm his type," Quinn replied half a second later as Søren locked eyes with another man in the crowd, walked over, grasped him by the back of the neck, and then laid one on him.

"Now that's hot," Lina said, feeling her cheeks grow suddenly warm.

"Amen, sister," Quinn agreed, fanning her face.

"Guess you'll have to find someone else to play your bedroom games with."

"What makes you think that's what I'm after?"

"Um. Is that an actual question? Because you've all but tattooed your name on our friend Batman."

Quinn's gaze shifted from the two men kissing and landed on Finley. Her eyes burned with longing for a split second and then shuttered, blocking out her feelings completely. "A girl like me should always keep her options open."

"Quinn—"

"Things are complicated enough already."

"But you two clearly want each other—"

Quinn shook her head. "Drop it, Cuska."

"Fine." Lina blew out a breath. "But this conversation isn't over."

"Sure it is."

Lina rolled her eyes. "You can be a real asshole, you know that?"

"That's why you love me," Quinn said, blowing her a kiss.

"What are you two talking about?" Finley asked as he and Nord joined them.

"What an asshole Quinn is."

"So the usual then," Finley said with a smirk.

"Pretty much," Lina agreed with a nod.

"Cute," Quinn said. "You two done now?"

"Depends," Lina said. "You going to tell me what I want to know?"

"Nope."

Lina pressed her lips together to keep from laughing. She knew Quinn would talk to her when she was ready and not a second before. Pushing the issue would only annoy the both of them. Deciding a subject change was in order, Lina turned to Nord.

"How long do these feasts usually last?"

"Why? Tired already?" The question was teasing, but his eyes were serious as they scoured over her.

Actually, she was. Between the near heart attack she'd had watching that thing practically tear Nord in half and a full day spent hiking up and down a fucking mountain, all she wanted to do was crawl into bed and sleep for a week or so. The way she figured, she'd more than earned it.

A frown worked its way between Nord's brows as he read her answer from her expression. "I can take you back—"

"No," she insisted with a firm shake of her head. "You can't leave. They threw this thing in your honor."

"Our honor," he corrected as a couple moved into their view. Nord glanced at them with a confused lift of his brow.

The man spoke, squeezing the woman beneath his arm. "Apologies for interrupting, Gunnar. Saxa here just wanted to come over and welcome you home." The woman blushed fiercely as she gave Nord a little wave. "It's such an honor to meet one of the true heroes of our people."

"Oh, um, thank you," Nord said, looking uncomfortable.

There was an awkward beat of silence as the couple stared adoringly up at Nord.

"Anyway," the man said with a chuckle, "we'll see you around!"

Quinn and Finley exchanged an amused glance while Lina waved a hand at the couple's retreating backs.

"You were saying?"

"What?" he asked.

"I don't see anyone coming over here to speak with us, Gunnar," she replied.

Nord grasped her lightly by the chin, leaning down until his lips hovered just over hers. "That's not my name," he said, kissing her softly. "Not anymore. The man they think I am is dead."

Lina's heart gave a little twist in her chest because she understood exactly what he meant. He was Gunnar in the same way she was Evalina. The people those names belonged to were long gone, along with the lives they'd intended to lead. In their place were two strangers who'd been reborn in the ashes.

"We really were made for each other," she murmured.

"You sound surprised. I told you that the first night I met you."

"Yeah, well . . . I was a little distracted."

He grinned. "Fair enough."

There was a swell in the music before it cut off entirely, and the room fell to an expectant hush. Lina glanced around, seeking out the source of the sudden silence. She found her answer almost instantly.

Astrid was easy to spot as she moved through the crowd, offering smiles or quick handshakes as she made her way to the slightly raised area where the band had been playing. Once there, she held out her arms, her voice carrying without any noticeable means of amplification. Unless you counted the room's vaulted ceilings, which Lina supposed might just be the reason.

"Friends, we have so much to celebrate tonight. First, the continued peace between us and our neighbors to the west."

Cheers rang out at Astrid's words, but Lina struggled to pay attention as she continued with her speech. Especially once Nord slipped his arms around her waist and pulled her back against him. The heat of his body seeped into her tired muscles, and it wasn't long before she was fighting to keep her eyes open.

"Not to mention the return of one of our own!"

Lina jerked upright at the dull roar those words caused.

"It is not every day you get to see a berserker take down a wyvern with his bare hands, but from what I am told, the legends about Odin's warriors have not been exaggerated."

Finley coughed. "From the way she's carrying on, you'd think he single-handedly slayed the beast," he muttered under his breath.

Lina shot him a smile. "Don't worry, Fin. We all know who made the killing shot."

His dimples flashed as he smiled at her. "And who made it possible in the first place."

Nord's arms tightened around her waist, and his lips dropped to her ear. "Indeed. Your quick thinking is the reason all of us are standing here alive."

Warmth blossomed at their praise. She may not be a kickass fighter—yet—but it was nice to know they thought of her as an integral part of the team.

"It's cool, guys. No need to spare my feelings. We all know I'm the weak link," Quinn said.

"After the stunt you pulled, I doubt anyone here considers you weak," Nord said.

Quinn beamed. "Yeah, I'm kind of awesome, aren't I?"

"You're something all right," Finley said, laughing when Quinn shoved him. "What? I agreed with you."

Quinn narrowed her eyes, but Astrid's next words had all four of them turning their attention back to her.

"Gunnar, if you'd please join me."

Almost as one, all eyes turned to Nord. He stiffened, and Lina could feel the tension thrumming through him as he forced himself to let her go. The look he gave her as he walked away was unreadable.

"Has he always hated being the center of attention?" Quinn asked.

Finley considered the question for a second before answering. "It comes with the territory when you're a Guardian. We work best in the shadows without anyone ever realizing we were there. Public recognition of any kind is generally a bad thing."

"Even for a job well done?" Lina asked.

"Did the Director strike you as the type of guy who recognizes or rewards that kind of thing?" he asked with a raise of his brow.

"Well, when you put it that way . . ." Lina said softly, her attention never leaving Nord as he reached Astrid's side.

"In the longstanding tradition of our ancestors, I wanted to present you with proof of your victory. May it serve as a reminder of your fearlessness in the face of danger and act as a warning to your enemies."

With that, Astrid reached out a hand. Björn, as if waiting for the signal, moved forward and placed one of the wyvern's deadly fangs into her palm. With a look of pure pride, Astrid held out the macabre trophy to Nord.

Despite the crowd, the room was silent. As if everyone within was holding their breath while they waited to see Nord's reaction.

Lina was biting down hard on her lip, oddly moved as Nord accepted Astrid's gift. His fingers ran the length of it, and his throat bobbed before his eyes lifted to hers.

"Thank you," he said in a gravelly rasp. Then, he turned to face the crowd, his eyes pausing on Lina for a single moment before his eyes blazed with a familiar light, and the berserker lifted it high in the air and let out an earsplitting cry.

The crowd went nuts. Lina had never seen anything like it. The closest comparison she could even think of was the crowd at a sold-out rock concert, but even that didn't capture the feeling of awed reverence of the people welcoming Nord home. There were cheers, beatific smiles, and more than a few tears as they began chanting his name. Bodies surged forward, shoving their little group back as everyone else tried to get close to the small makeshift stage, hands reaching out to touch Nord.

"I would have worn different shoes if I knew there was going to be a mosh pit," Quinn said with a startled laugh as she stumbled into Finley, who wrapped a protective arm around her shoulders to help steady her.

All Lina could make out now was the top of Nord's head as people continued to swarm him. Then the crowd parted just enough that she caught a glimpse of his face. A smile lifted her lips at the sight of his elated grin. She couldn't recall a time she'd ever seen him quite so happy.

"Hey, guys," she said after his head disappeared from view, "I'm going to head back."

"I'll come with you," Quinn offered, already untangling herself from Finley's hold.

"No, no. You guys stay."

"You sure?" Quinn asked, her eyes searching.

"Totally. If we all go missing, Nord will worry, and he deserves to enjoy this. I'm just going to go lay down. I'm wiped."

Finley and Quinn shared an uncertain look.

"If you're sure . . ." she eventually said.

"I am. Night," she said, giving them each a quick hug before turning for the door.

The walk back to their suite was a short one. Lost to her thoughts as she was, Lina barely noticed the stars twinkling overhead or their reflection dancing on the water's surface. She even passed the entrance to their building and didn't realize it until she was about halfway down the next block.

Mentally chiding herself, she hurried back the way she'd come and sighed as she eyed the stairs. Leaning heavily on the rail, she slowly made her way up, her overworked muscles screaming in protest with each step.

By the time she'd made it to their door on the top floor, she was all but dead on her feet, having used the last of her energy to reach it. She was contemplating whether she needed a shower as she waved her hand in front of the door the same way she'd seen the others do. It opened without issue.

Kicking off her shoes, she decided the shower could wait, but as she turned to shuffle her way into the bedroom, a flash of white caught her eye.

Lina stopped, her heart thudding heavily in her chest as her eyes landed on the pair of familiar envelopes. Her emotions tangled, exhaustion giving way to a sharp stab of grief and curiosity.

Shoulders slumped, she changed course and padded over to the table where her uncle's will and the letter he'd written her had remained since dinner their first night here. She stared at them for a long moment before reaching out trembling fingers and running them along the top of the smaller envelope. She traced the lines of her name, emotion tightening her throat at the familiar slant of her uncle's handwriting.

Thinking of Nord and how he always managed to face the situations that made him most uncomfortable head-on, Lina decided it was time for her to do the same. All plans of bed and sleep gone, she sat down heavily in the chair and slid the envelopes closer.

"All right, Uncle Alistair. What did you want to tell me?"

CHAPTER 16
LINA

Lina pressed down so hard on either side of the packages that little impressions of her hands remained once she finally reached for the larger envelope.

She shook so badly that it was a struggle to open the flap, but finally, she managed. She pulled out the formal-looking document, a few words and phrases jumping out at her as she briefly scanned it. Things like 'bequeath' and 'Evalina' and 'all my earthly possessions.' She dropped the papers as if they burned and jumped a little at the unexpected clink of the envelope hitting the glass tabletop. With a frown, she lifted it, spilling the rest of the contents out on top of the will.

She stared at the two keys. One was clearly his apartment key; the other was less obvious. It was thick and weathered, the gold chipped and faded.

She studied it curiously before turning her attention back to the other envelope, assuming any answers would be waiting for her there.

Not giving herself time to think, she ripped the envelope open, squeezing her eyes shut for just a second before pulling out the letter. Sucking in a breath, she started to read.

My dearest Evalina,

If you're reading this . . . well, I guess you already know what's become of me. Please believe me when I say the last thing I ever wanted was to leave you, my sweet girl. Especially when I only just got you back.

I am so sorry for any pain my passing has caused you, but I hope that there is comfort in knowing that I do not do so willingly. Know that I fought until the last to get back to you and that if my death was the only way to keep you safe, I would gladly die a thousand times over again. It is every father's wish to protect his daughter, and if the cost for that is laying down my life, well, that is an easy price to pay.

No matter how much you are hurting, Sweetling, you cannot lose yourself to grief. Too much hangs in the balance. You are so much more important than you could ever know. Not just to me, but to our people. It is time for you to become who you were born to be.

To that end, I've put things in place so that I might continue to be of help to you even now. I cannot risk my words being found by someone other than you. So, turn to the last of my gifts for solace.

I may not be with you, but know that you are never alone, my girl. It was the greatest pleasure of my life, helping raise you into the magnificent woman you've become.

Until we meet again,

ALISTAIR

A TEAR ROLLED DOWN HER CHEEK AND SPLASHED ONTO THE PAPER. LINA shoved it away, not wanting her tears to ruin her uncle's last words to her. Her heart felt as though it had been carved from her chest. Her eyes were blurred with tears she was fighting hard not to shed, and it was almost impossible to breathe around the meteor-sized lump in her throat.

But she managed.

Alistair had asked her not to fall apart. The least she could do was try. For him.

Lina tried to distract herself by lifting the keys, wondering if they were the gift he was referring to. Before she could do more than consider the possibility, the door opened.

She spun in her chair, the keys clattering to the table as one hand flew to her chest. "Nord, Jesus, you scared me."

"You left—" he started, but he cut himself off when he saw her face.

His eyes dropped to the papers scattered in front of her, and his expression went from fierce to tender as he moved to her.

The tears she'd tried so hard to fight pushed past every defense as he held his arms open to her. Lina stood with a hiccup and blindly crashed into him as she lost the battle, silently hoping Alistair forgave her for this moment of weakness.

Nord cradled her against him, one hand wrapped around her back while the other cupped her head. He'd dropped his face so that he was kissing the top of her head, holding her while she sobbed.

Eventually, Lina pushed back, just far enough to look up at him. "I'm sorry," she croaked.

Nord shook his head, moving his hand to brush away the tears still rolling down her cheeks. "There's no need to apologize for what you're feeling, Lina."

"H-he told me not to lose myself to it," she told him.

"I do not think he meant that you're not allowed to grieve at all. But rather, to keep moving forward despite the sadness."

Lina nodded, knowing he was right. Then she let out an embarrassed laugh as she wiped at her dripping nose. "I'm a mess."

Nord kissed her forehead. "No, you're not."

She gave him a look, and he smiled.

"Okay, fine. But you're my mess."

Some of the tightness in her chest eased at that.

"Can I get you anything?" he asked, taking a step away like he was ready to grab whatever she might need.

"No, just—" She fell silent as Alistair's cane came into view. Her breath left her in a whoosh.

'Turn to the last of my gifts.' His cane. The one object Cora made a point to give her that never seemed to make much sense. As her eyes landed on the hissing serpent handle, she knew without a doubt that's what Alistair's letter referred to.

She pushed past Nord to where the cane was leaning against the wall, lifting it carefully.

"Lina?"

"Alistair left something for me to find," she said distractedly as she turned the cane over in her fingers, wondering how she was supposed to unlock its secrets.

On impulse, she tried to twist off the top. It moved easily beneath her hands, coming loose with only a few twists. After a quick check, Lina let the length of wood fall to the ground. She moved over to the couch, Nord trailing her as she sat down, cupping the Cuska family crest in her hands.

She ran her fingers along every dip and crevice, searching for a hidden latch or button of some kind. But after the third round, she was forced to admit there was nothing there. With a sigh, she let it drop to her lap.

"I'm missing something," she huffed.

"What does that say?"

"What does what say?"

Nord reached out and pointed to a tiny line of text that curled around the underside of the crest. Lina squinted, barely able to make out the words even after Nord pointed to them. It was so small it just looked like a scratch.

Lifting it back up, she held it close to her eye, and there was something about the script that felt familiar. Like it was something she'd seen, often. She just couldn't quite make out the letters outside of a 'sol.' That's when the second part of Alistair's message clicked into place. *'Turn to the last of my gifts for solace.'*

"It's the Cuska family motto," Lina whispered. "*Spes meum solatium.* Hope is my solace."

As soon as the words left her lips, there was a bright flash of light. Lina lifted a hand to protect her eyes, and when she lowered it, she let out a startled scream.

Standing in front of her, no more than six feet away, was the flickering lavender form of her uncle.

"I knew you'd figure it out," the apparition said with a smile.

Lina risked a glance at Nord. "You're seeing this too, right?"

His eyes were narrowed as he nodded. "And hearing."

"Thank fuck." She let out a relieved breath. "Uncle Alistair? Are you a . . . a ghost?" she asked, wondering if he'd managed to somehow bind his spirit to his cane.

The lavender form faded for a second before her uncle's voice sounded once more. "Not a ghost. Merely a recording."

"Oh," she whispered, oddly disappointed by the revelation. "So, um, how does this work?"

Another flicker, and then, "I recorded a message for you with instructions. I also anticipated a few questions you might have. If the spell recognizes a series of keywords, it will trigger what I hope is the appropriate response. I didn't have time to test it out, so apologies if it's a little buggy," he said with a familiar chuckle.

Lina's heart squeezed, and a couple tears trickled down her cheeks.

"I'm sure you have a lot of questions," the hologram said when she didn't immediately speak again. "But we do not have much time before the spell burns out."

Nord took her hand in his, giving it an encouraging squeeze.

"Oh, okay," she said, straightening and wondering what she was supposed to say to trigger his instructions. "Um, tell me what to do, I guess."

The image wavered, and her uncle's face turned serious as he came back into view. "The first thing you need to know is that the Codex is safe. When I suspected I'd been found, I hid it, along with the pages I'd managed to translate. No one but you will be able to unlock the entrance to my sanctuary. It will require a test only a Cuska can pass. You'll know what to do when the time comes. To get there, you will need the key I left you. The address is listed in my will along with the various other properties and holdings you've inherited. That is as much as I feel comfortable saying, even now. Trust that you already have the answers you need."

Lina swallowed, feeling a little lightheaded as she tried to make sense of everything he was telling her. "What am I supposed to do once I get the Codex?"

After the now familiar flicker, her uncle's expression turned even more earnest. "Use it. Study it. Discover all of its mysteries—especially the ones we've already discussed. The Codex is the key, not just to unlocking your full power, but to saving our people. I know you fear it, that you worry craving power will make you like your father. That could not be farther from the truth. You are your mother's daughter. Trust in her, if not yourself."

Lina's eyes darted to Nord. She could see the questions blazing in his eyes, but he was holding onto them for now, giving her room to voice her own.

"Do you . . ." she faltered and licked her lips before trying again, "Do you know who did this to you?"

This time his answer was not quite a perfect fit, but it still caused ice to run through her veins. "The Drakes have always been our greatest rivals. Do not trust Mikel, and do not underestimate his reach. You will find few friends amongst the Council. Be careful. It is not what it once was."

Aware that the clock was ticking but not sure what else to ask, she said, "Is there anything else I need to know?"

After a second, the hologram said, "The first thing you need to know—"

"Stop. Never mind," Lina interrupted, not wanting to waste what time she had on a repeat. "Is there anything else you want me to know? Something you recorded but haven't said yet?"

Once the flickering was done, her uncle was smiling, his eyes warm. "I'm so very proud of you, Lina. I have no doubt that you will go on to accomplish great things, many of which may feel impossible at first glance. Surround yourself with people that you trust, who are strong where you feel weak. That is the wisdom of a true leader. And when you claim what is rightfully yours, do not be afraid to let go of tradition and forge your own path. Oh," he added, as if it was an afterthought, "for what it's worth. I approve of the Viking. He's a good man—even if he is part of the Brotherhood. I could not have chosen better for you myself."

Lina and Nord shared a glance, her lips lifted in a small smile, his eyes uncharacteristically misty.

"My time comes to an end—"

"Wait!" she said, jumping up as the apparition started to fade. "Not yet. Please."

"This is not goodbye, Lina. Merely farewell. I'm always with you, Sweetling. Those we love never truly leave us."

With that, he winked out of existence. Lina was left staring hard at the place where her uncle once stood, her heart thundering in her chest.

"He was a good man," Nord said as he rose.

"A great man," Lina agreed.

His fingers skimmed her arm before weaving with hers. "Are you okay?"

One last tear rolled down her cheek, and Lina wiped it away. "Not yet, but I will be."

And this time, as she said the words, she truly believed them.

No matter the reason, or the limitations, she was just thankful her uncle had the foresight to leave her a gift that would allow her to see and hear him again, if only for a little while.

Getting to hear that he was proud of her, that he approved of her choices—those she'd already made and those that she might make in the future—it was the kind of closure few ever got when they lost a loved one. And knowing that he believed in her helped her believe in herself.

Intentionally or not, Alistair's final gift wasn't the Codex, or his advice, or even closure . . . it was hope. And as it had been for her ancestors, it was solace.

CHAPTER 17
NORD

Lina turned to him, her eyes blazing with determination despite her tear-spiked lashes. "I'm sure you have questions..."

"None that require answers right now."

There was a beat of silence as she tilted her head to the side and studied him. "You know, for a man that can be utterly demanding, you sure are patient."

"Benefit of living for as long as I have," he said, settling back in the sofa and throwing his arm along the top. "You learn that things have a way of happening in their own time."

"Perhaps," she said as she walked over to the table and lifted the small stack of papers and the keys before returning to join him on the couch. Tucking her legs beneath her, she rested her elbow on the back of the couch and propped her head on her fist. "But don't you think this would have been good to know before we came here? We could have saved ourselves the trip and be that much closer to dealing with the Drakes once and for all."

"But we wouldn't have secured allies."

"True."

"It's also likely that had you opened his letter immediately, you might not have been in the right frame of mind to make the connections you needed to make. Who's to say you would have put things together any faster?"

"I suppose," she said, her eyes dropping to the papers she'd set in her lap.

"Any idea where he was referring to?"

Lina shook her head slightly as she flipped through the pages. "I didn't even know Alistair owned property beside his condo." Her eyes widened as she turned the page over and then continued on to the next. "Let alone this many." Her eyes shifted to his. "Where do you think he got the money if my family really was indebted to the Drakes like he claimed?"

Nord shook his head. "No idea. Mind if I take a look?"

She handed him Alistair's will without comment.

"This is an impressive list," he said, counting fifteen properties that spanned the globe, in addition to several boats, cars, undeveloped plots of land, commercial holdings, and a sizeable investment portfolio. "Seems like your uncle had some secrets."

Lina snorted. "Just a few." She waved a hand at the papers he was holding. "How am I supposed to know where to start with a list that size?"

"He said you'd know it when you saw it. What jumps out at you?"

She tugged the list of properties out of his hand, mumbling the name of various locations as she read through the addresses. "New York, Key Largo, Quebec, Edinburgh, Tuscany, Berlin . . ." Lina straightened, her eyes darting back up. "Wait, I think this is it." She turned the page and tapped to the fourth one from the top. "See the street name?"

"Hope Street," he read aloud, looking up at her. "What about it?"

"What are the chances that one of the trigger words for my uncle's spell happens to be the name of the street where one of his homes is located? That can't be a coincidence, can it?" she asked, seeming excited.

"I don't believe in coincidence."

She grinned. "Looks like we're going to Scotland."

"Who's going to Scotland?" Finley asked as the door opened, and he and Quinn walked into the room.

"The four of us," Lina said, circling her finger in the air as if she was rounding them up.

"I thought you were going to bed?" Quinn asked, her eyes landing on the papers scattered between them. "What did we miss?"

"Alistair told me where he hid the Codex."

"Thus Scotland," Quinn said, sitting down on the arm of one of the chairs. "When do we leave?"

Lina looked to Nord. "Uh . . . now?"

"Is that really a good idea?" Finley asked, waving his hand to close the door. "People are still after us."

"That's why it can't wait," Lina said, leaning forward and clasping her hands together. "Whatever Alistair found in that Codex, he believes it will help us. We can't risk it getting into the wrong hands."

"Explain to me again what's so special about this history book," Finley said.

"What isn't special about it?" Lina returned with a shrug. "In addition to the history it contains, there are spells, secrets that have been lost over time . . . It might contain information on a way I can unlock the full potential of the Cuska line. For that possibility alone, it's too important to leave unprotected. We can't ignore anything that will give us a leg up on the Drakes—or them on us if they get to it first."

"Be that as it may, I doubt fleeing in the middle of the night is the best way to go about things. We came here for a reason. Are we really just going to up and leave after only a handful of days?"

"The suit has a point," Quinn agreed.

"Whose side are you on?" Lina accused, though there was little heat in it.

"Yours. Always."

Lina gave her a crooked smile. "You were there when Alistair told us about it. You saw how important he believed it was. Do you really think it can wait?"

"No," Quinn said bluntly. "But our problems don't just up and disappear because we get that book. It's not like we know what we'll find. Or how long it will take for you to even perform whatever ritual it might contain once we get our hands it. We need to be prepared for the possibility that leaving here will initiate a countdown, and we have no idea how much time is on the clock."

"What do you think?" Lina asked, turning to face Nord.

"I think a fight is coming whether we're ready for it or not. It's not a matter of if, but when. There's a lot we don't know about the Drakes, but the one thing we can assume is that they are far more prepared for a showdown than we are. And that's not even considering what the Director and the full might of the Brotherhood can do. The only way for us to even the playing field is to put ourselves in a position to overpower them. If this book's secrets could give us the advantage we need, it's foolish of us to ignore it. The longer we wait, the less likely it is we'll get the advantage we need."

"I'm not saying I disagree," Finley started, holding up his hands when Lina was about to cut him off. "Hear me out. What if our going there simply leads our enemies straight to it? Is that really a chance we can afford to take if this spellbook is as important as you claim?"

"What if they find it anyway while we're sitting here with our thumbs up our asses?" Lina countered.

"Is that really a possibility?" Quinn asked. "The only reason you even know where to look is because of Alistair's will."

"True, but you're forgetting that Alistair knew he was being followed. Who knows how long they tailed him or what they managed to learn while they did? The Drakes may know exactly where Alistair hid the Codex, even if they don't yet realize that's what he's hidden."

A heavy silence filled the room as they all considered the possibility.

Nord shifted so he was sitting with his elbows resting on his knees. "The whole reason we came here was to buy ourselves time to figure out our next move. Thanks to Alistair, we have it."

Lina shot him a grateful smile.

"Okay, so we go and get it. Can't we just bring it back here after?" Quinn asked.

Nord could see where she was going, and the suggestion held definite appeal, though he was disinclined to go that route. "Technically, yes. Assuming Astrid would allow us to come and go as we please. But we put the people of Novasgard at risk every time we do."

"How so?" she asked, her brows furrowing.

"Anyone can travel through a portal while it's open," Finley answered. "All it would take is one Guardian slipping through with us, and the secret of Novasgard and its people is lost."

"Wouldn't the Director know of them already, after what he did to Nord?" Quinn asked.

"In all likelihood, though he currently lacks a way to find us here," Finley said.

"Because the gateway can only be accessed by direct descendants, and Guardians can only create portals between places they've actually been," Lina said.

"Which wouldn't be an issue any longer once another Guardian was able to open a portal for him," Quinn added with a heavy sigh.

"Exactly," Nord said. "If it was just the Drakes we were dealing with, I'd be less worried. But we know Guardians hide in plain sight and that they are actively searching for us. We cannot overlook the possibility they'll be watching us the second we set foot back in their world."

"So it's a one-way trip," Quinn said.

"At least until we're certain we can travel back safely," Nord confirmed. "The Novasgardians may be our allies, but I rather not bring war to their sanctuary. Not if we can avoid it."

"Me either," Lina agreed. "I don't want to put their home at risk."

"Well, I guess it's decided then," Quinn said as she stood. "For better or worse, we're going home."

Lina nodded. "Looks that way."

"I still think we should at least get some sleep and leave in the morning," Finley said. "If things do go to shit straight away, at least we'll be well-rested. We're no good to anyone in our current state."

"Agreed," Nord said. "And that gives us a chance to say goodbye to Astrid."

"Then I guess it's time for bed," Lina said, pushing to her feet.

"At least we know packing will be a breeze," Quinn said, already moving to her bedroom.

Lina chuckled. "You coming?" she asked, turning to look back at him.

"Be right there," he said as he stood.

Once they were alone, Finley gave him a careful once-over. "You good with all of this?"

"I don't see another choice, do you?"

He blew out a breath. "No. But it doesn't mean I like it. There are too many unknowns. For all we think we know, we're still walking into this blind."

"We've won under worse odds before."

Finley smiled, but it didn't quite reach his eyes. "True. But we never faced off against our Brothers before."

It was then that Nord realized just how much this change in status had to be eating at him. Unlike Nord, who'd been practically blackmailed into joining, Finley had willingly signed up with the Brotherhood because he believed in their mission. The fact that Finley had been declared a traitor by association was entirely his fault.

"Fin, I—"

"No. This isn't on you."

"The only reason you're even on the run is because of me."

"I couldn't just stand aside after what the Director did to you. He's undermined everything the Brotherhood stands for—or what it used to stand for. If that means they'll strip me of my title, well," Finley said with a twist of his lips and the shadows of his past reflected in his eyes, "it wouldn't be the first time. The only difference between you and me is they already made it official."

"You don't deserve this."

Finley shrugged. "Neither do you, and yet here we are."

"Here we are," Nord agreed.

"Guess that means you're stuck with me."

Nord groaned, but his smile was genuine as he placed one of his hands on Finley's shoulder. "I couldn't ask for a better man to watch my back or one that I'd trust more with mine and Lina's lives."

Finley's eyes dropped, and he had to clear his throat before he replied. "Knowing the men you've fought beside, I take that as a mighty compliment."

"As you should. You're a good man, Finley—one of the best. No matter your title." With that, Nord clapped him on the shoulder and started for the hallway.

"And all this time, I thought you barely tolerated me," Finley called after him.

Nord glanced over his shoulder. "Because I do. You might be a good man, Fin, but you're still a fucking pain in my ass."

Finley's laughter followed him as he made his way to his bed and the woman lying in it.

"WHAT'S THIS I HEAR ABOUT YOU LEAVING SO SOON?" ASTRID ASKED, setting her glasses on top of whatever she'd been reading when he'd walked in.

It had only taken about twenty minutes from the time Nord told Søren their situation had changed and they needed to get back, to them receiving a summons from Astrid. He'd arrived on her doorstep less than fifteen minutes later, with the others and their bags in hand. Since the summons was for him specifically, they were waiting out in Astrid's living room.

"It's true, I'm afraid," Nord said, meaning it. It would have been nice to have more time getting to know her and the others. But he knew their paths would cross again.

"But we've only just gotten used to you."

"I know. When we arrived, we had no idea how long we might need to stay. I don't think any of us expected to find what we needed in a matter of days."

She turned thoughtful. "Does this have anything to do with those enemies you spoke of?"

"It does."

"So then the path ahead is a dangerous one," she surmised.

"When isn't it?" Nord asked, his berserker's thirst for violence seeping into his voice.

Astrid laughed. "Such is the life of one of Odin's chosen, I'd suspect."

"We can only run from who we are for so long," Nord agreed.

She smiled at that, something like respect shining in her eyes.

"Well," she said finally, clasping her hands in front of her, "I'm glad that your journey brought you back to us, even if only for a short while. Perhaps in the future, you will not let so much time pass before you come back to visit us."

"I'd like that," Nord said.

She must have heard something in his words, because she added, "You will always have a home here if you choose it. These are your people as much as they are mine. Perhaps more so, though you'd have to kill me if you want to take my place," she said. Although she was smiling, Nord knew she was absolutely serious.

"I have no intention of ever trying to make that claim. Novasgard is yours."

"Good, I'd have hated to destroy you for trying."

Nord laughed, a deep booming laugh that rolled through his stomach. The woman knew what he was capable of, and yet he had no doubt she absolutely would stand against him if required. He was also willing to bet she'd make him work hard to beat her. A part of him looked forward to testing the theory.

"I'd expect nothing less, cousin."

"I'm glad we understand one another."

"As am I."

The moment stretched as a comfortable silence fell between them.

"So, when do you leave?"

"Now, actually. I just wanted to make sure we had the chance to say goodbye."

"Well," she said as she stood, "I don't want to keep you. It seems like you're in a hurry for a good reason. Let me go say goodbye to the others and see you all off properly."

"Actually, would it be all right if we created a portal here instead of using the gateway?"

After their conversation last night, Nord hadn't been sure portaling out of Novasgard was a good idea, but Finley had pointed out that no one would know where to look for them until after they returned. As such, using the portal to get back wouldn't be an issue. So long as Astrid allowed it, of course.

She paused beside him, considering his request. "I don't see why not."

"Thank you, it saves us at least half a day's travel."

"Of course. It's nice to know that I can help in some way."

"You've helped more than you could know."

She smiled but kept her eyes trained forward as they reached the living room. "Well, that's what family does, isn't it?"

Nord hesitated for a second, his steps faltering as he watched her disappear into the other room.

Family.

His eyes closed against the weight of emotion that single word sent cascading through him. Then he opened them and joined the rest of his family in the other room.

Lina's gaze immediately found his, and a little furrow worked its way between her brows. Silently, she moved to his side, slipping her hand into his.

"We ready?" Finley asked, their bags in a stack at his feet.

Nord dipped his chin.

"For better or for worse, right?" Quinn asked, looking grim.

"Let's hope it's better for you and worse for your enemies," Astrid said.

"I like the way you think," Lina said.

Astrid winked. "Selfishly, I'm just hoping you'll come back to visit once things blow over."

Lina beamed. "We definitely will."

"Well, then. Hurry off so you can come back."

"You heard the lady," Lina said with a laugh.

Finley held out his hand, his eyes swirling silver with his power. "One portal to Edinburgh, coming up."

CHAPTER 18
LINA

As she stepped through the portal, the first thing that caught her attention was the smell of damp earth and clean air. Like a storm had recently blown through. As the city came to life around her, the second thing she noticed was the moon.

"Uh, wasn't it just morning?" she asked, taking a few steps forward and checking out the lamps that lined the cobblestone street.

"We were in a different realm," Finley said, totally nonplussed as he closed the portal. "You can't expect time to function the same."

Something about his phrasing made Lina suspect he wasn't just referring to them crossing an interdimensional time zone. "What are you saying?"

"For us, it's only been about six days since we were last here. But, for this world, we could have been gone hours or months."

Lina blinked at him. "Don't you think you should have mentioned that?"

Finley lifted a brow. "Would it have changed anything?"

"I guess not," Lina conceded. "But how are we supposed to know *when* we are?"

Finley glanced around; his gaze narrowed as he scanned the darkened street. Without a word, he turned and moved toward a pile of trash. Crouching down, he sifted through the top layer.

"I think he finally lost his mind," Quinn said, standing with her arms crossed beside Lina as they watched his rummaging.

"It was bound to happen."

Letting out a satisfied, "Ah-ha," Finley straightened and held up a crumpled newspaper. "Bingo." Shaking out the pages, he gave it a quick once-over. "There we go. Easy. According to this, it's January 14th."

Lina gaped at him. "Are you telling me we just lost six *weeks*?"

Finley folded the newspaper and tossed it back onto the trash pile. "So it appears."

"Damn. We missed Christmas *and* New Year's Eve. You owe me presents," Quinn said, poking Lina.

Lina rolled her eyes. "I think you're missing the point. We were gone for six days, but the assholes plotting against us have had six *weeks* to plan and scheme. Do you have any idea how much can change in a single week? Let alone six?"

Nord wrapped his hand around Lina's hip and pulled her back against him. "It's more likely they've been wondering how we remained hidden for so long. Plans are useless if the person you're plotting against is nowhere to be found."

Lina pressed her lips together. He was probably right, but she was still reeling.

"Think of it this way," he continued, "your argument for expediency was more valid than you knew."

"Are you trying to make me feel better by telling me I was right?" Lina asked with a smirk.

"Is it working?"

"Maybe."

His chest vibrated against her back as he chuckled.

Feeling marginally better, Lina looked around again. "This place is like something out of a history book," she said. "Hell, there's a castle right there."

"That's because Edinburgh was one of the few places that didn't get bombed during World War II," Finley said, hands deep in his pockets, his expression unreadable.

Lina sometimes forgot that Finley had been around almost as long as Nord. It was mind-boggling the things they'd seen and lived through. She sensed he had history here, and as tempted as she was to find out what it was, Nord had just finished reminding her they were short on time.

"Anyone know where Hope Street is?" Lina asked, searching for a road sign. She found one that said "High Street," but it didn't do much to help orientate her, seeing as this was her first time here.

Quinn pulled a cell phone out of her back pocket, her fingers tapping furiously on the screen.

"You remembered to bring your cell phone?" Lina asked.

"You didn't?"

Lina bit her lip. She couldn't remember the last time she'd seen the handheld device. Instead of answering the question, she asked, "How is it even still charged?"

"Rookie," Quinn said with a sad shake of her head. Pulling out a square object with a cord from her pocket, she explained, "Power bank. I never go anywhere without it. These suckers hold a charge for like ever. I plugged my phone in as soon as we decided we were coming back."

Lina stepped out of Nord's loose hold, grabbed Quinn's face, and gave her a loud, smacking kiss on her forehead. "You're my very own Mary Poppins. Saving the day with compacts hidden in your bra and fancy gadgets in your pockets. What would I do without you?"

Quinn slapped Lina's arms away, but she was smiling as she did. Holding out her phone, she said, "There. Looks like we're about a mile away. We just need to go," Quinn looked up, squinting as she searched for the correct direction. "That way," she said, pointing.

"Lead the way."

Phone in hand, Quinn guided them to the top of a street that appeared more like an alleyway as narrow and curved as it was. The shops lining the street were already closed for the night, but there were numerous pubs near overflowing with rowdy patrons. A couple of men, both clad in kilts, stumbled out from one such bar, loud music and laughter pouring out as the door swung closed behind them.

"I . . . didn't think people actually still wore those," Lina said, watching them try to prop each other up as they made their way to their next stop for the evening.

"Welcome to Scotland," Finley said with a laugh. He pointed to the pub the men had just vacated, and Lina could just make out a ceiling lined with assorted flags through the window. "Should we pop in for a pint first?"

"Tempting, but we're in a hurry, remember?" Lina said. Finley looked truly disappointed, so she couldn't help but offer, "Maybe once we get what we came for?"

He winked at her. "I'm going to hold you to that."

About twenty minutes later, the four of them were standing on the sidewalk looking at a black door with a gold sixteen above it, the building's blond brick blackened by years of soot and grime.

Lina stared at the three-story building, wondering what secrets she'd discover inside.

"You guys ready?"

They nodded, and since she had the key, Lina took the lead as they crossed a small concrete bridge that separated the building from the sidewalk. She slid the key into the door, her eyes falling closed as she mentally prepared herself for the potential emotional onslaught being surrounded by her uncle's things might cause. With a gusty sigh, she turned the key in the lock and crossed the threshold.

There was an expectant feel to the air. As if the house was holding its breath, waiting for whatever happened next. The back of her neck prickled, and the hairs along her arms stood on end.

With an involuntary shiver, she groped along the wall, searching for a light as the others filed in behind her. As Lina's hand finally found the switch and light flooded the entryway, Finley simultaneously closed the door. There was a lone moment of perfect quiet, and then the house seemed to shudder.

A low moan sounded behind her.

"Everything okay?" she asked, peering over her shoulder at Quinn.

"It wasn't me," she said, her black hair flying out behind her as she shook her head.

Lina's eyes met Nord's a second before a phantom appeared right behind him. "Watch out!"

Nord ducked as the apparition shot forward, its skeletal arms outstretched.

Finley dove for the wall, pulling Quinn with him out of the apparition's path.

"What the—"

That was all Lina managed to get out before a second figure popped up on the stairs beside her. Lina swallowed back a scream of fright as the phantom dove straight at her, it's eyes glowing white-hot.

Nord crashed into her, causing them both to collide with a small side table and send its lone picture frame clattering to the floor.

Lina instinctively pressed her body closer to Nord's, her fingers biting into his arms as the single moan turned into a deafening chorus. It was nearly impossible to hear anything over the ghostly wails, which sounded as if they were coming from the walls of the house itself.

"These guys don't seem to like us being here very much," Quinn said.

"Maybe if we ask them nicely, they'll just go away?" Lina suggested.

But then a third shadowy figure joined the others, quickly followed by a fourth.

One for each of us, Lina realized.

"We need to get out of the hallway," Nord said. "We don't have enough room to maneuver."

The stairs were ahead of them on the right, but there was a wide opening into another room off to the left, as well as a door that led to the back of the house at the other end of the hallway.

Lina swallowed, her eyes lingering on the closest phantom. "After you."

Nord only made it two steps to what Lina assumed was the living room before one of the figures came flying at him, blocking his path.

A deep growl sounded low in his throat as Nord started to rage.

"I don't think you can really beat the shit out of a ghost," Lina pointed out.

"Watch me," he said, taking a running leap at the form, only for it to vanish and appear behind him, effectively cutting him off from the rest of them.

"Lina, do something," Quinn shouted as one of the figures opened its mouth and shrieked.

Lina's mind raced as she tried to figure out what was happening. Clearly, her uncle had set up some sort of magical security system. She just wished he would have left her a hint about how she was supposed to turn it off.

She had a growing suspicion that the longer it took her to figure it out, the more violent these creatures would become. Considering they were made of shadows and air—as best she could tell anyway —there wasn't a whole lot any of them could do to fight back. Which meant getting them out of this mess was up to her.

Think, Lina. Think.

There was another piercing wail, this one so shrill it seemed to shoot straight through her brain. Her unease compounded as something warm and wet began to trickle down the side of her neck. Lina wiped at it with the back of her hand, feeling nauseous when it came away smeared in blood.

"They're getting restless," Quinn said, her voice tense with warning as one of the figures swiped at her. She jumped back into Finley, who quickly pushed her behind him.

Recalling how Nord had to use his blood to prove he had the right to open the gateway, Lina ran her bloody hand along the wall, thinking maybe the house would recognize her as Alistair's niece.

Nothing happened.

Feeling stupid, Lina shoved her fingers into her hair and gripped the sides of her skull, trying to alleviate the building pressure as the specters took turns letting out their unearthly cries. Her head felt like a balloon that was a few shots of helium away from exploding. "This can't be right. Why would Alistair ambush us?"

"Think, Kærasta. The key to ending this is something only you could know," Nord called to her as two screeching phantoms flew at him. He ducked in the nick of time, popping back up and throwing a powerful uppercut into the nearer of the two's faces.

It scattered into glittering black dust, and Lina was just about to let out a huge breath of relief when the particles seemed to freeze and then coalesce back into a single floating form mere inches between Nord and Quinn.

The figure wasted no time before it lunged.

Once again, Finley threw himself in front of her best friend to try to protect her from the attack. This time, however, the phantom's strike landed. It didn't move through Finley, as Lina expected. Instead, its claws raked across his face, the blow containing enough force to send the Guardian to the floor. His head hit the ground with a resonating *thud*.

Lina's heart twisted, and her breath caught in her chest when Finley didn't move.

"Fin!" Quinn shouted, dropping down and curling her body over his.

"Fuck," Lina growled, her mind scrambling.

She needed to act. Now.

The longer it took, the more empowered the creatures became.

The answer to disarming this trap was something only she could know. Something obvious. At least to her and Alistair. It had to be unique to them."

As she thought through it, fragments of their conversations and time together drifted through her mind. His letter. When he revealed that he named her. When he confessed to loving her mother and then offered insights into who she'd been and how alike they were. His endless patience when she was first learning how to use her magic. Their not entirely sanctioned conversations in the Archives, and that time she summoned them two glasses of whisky.

When the answer came to her, she wasn't quite sure it could be that simple.

And yet . . .

Calling on her power, Lina pulled the image into her mind, focusing on the specific details she needed. When she opened them, the Brotherhood's Archive surrounded her, and the phantoms were nowhere to be seen.

Lina's legs gave out as the adrenaline wore off, and she sat down hard on a nearby desk.

"You fucking idiot," Quinn said, punching Finley in the shoulder.

He sat up with a groan, clutching his head. "Ow. In case you missed it, I just saved your bloody neck. Again. A thank-you wouldn't go amiss."

"I never asked you to protect me," she snapped, her eyes flashing like purple fire.

"You might as well get the fuck over it, because I'm going to protect you whether you like it or not."

Quinn stared at him for a second before leaning over and pressing a kiss to his stubbled cheek. "Thank you," she whispered.

Finley stared at her, looking stunned. "I think I might have hit my head harder than I thought."

Quinn sat back with a shrug. "Contrary to popular belief, I don't enjoy watching you get hurt."

His hazel eyes searched hers, and he gave her a slow smile. "I'll keep that in mind."

Lina released a shaky breath, glad that they were both okay.

Nord reached her then, a small tear in his shirt the only remaining sign of the scuffle.

"You okay?" she asked.

He nodded in a distracted manner as he took in their new surroundings. "Alistair hid the Codex here?"

"To be fair, this isn't the actual Archive. It just looks like it. And, I don't think it really mattered what I created. I just needed to use my magic to create the reality I wanted."

Nord gave her a searching look. "What do you mean?"

"It's something he used to say to me a lot when I was first learning," she explained. "*'Reality is yours to control, Evalina. It's your world. Color outside the lines. Make it unapologetically yours,'*" she quoted. Then she shrugged. "Anyway, the Archive is where we first found each other again, so it has sentimental value. We spent a lot of time together there. Plus," she added, pushing herself up and moving around the desk she'd been sitting on to pop open the secret cubby beneath, "it gave me a chance to give Alistair his hidden compartment."

"A hidden compartment?" Quinn asked, coming to stand beside her.

"Inside joke," Lina said as she reached in and moved her hand around. When she was just about elbow-deep, she smacked a cool leather surface, and tingles shot up her arm. Excitement bubbled in her chest, and she grabbed the book and the rolled-up stack of papers that laid on top of it. She carefully pulled them both out and then set them on top of the desk with a little flourish.

"Ta-da!"

Quinn snickered. "Ta-da?"

Lina was too excited to take offense. "I mean, it's not a rabbit, and the cubby wasn't exactly a hat, but you've gotta admit, that was one hell of a magic trick."

CHAPTER 19
LINA

Lina scooted the chair closer to the desk, her anticipation building as she eyed the Codex. A part of her still didn't believe she'd pulled it off.

From her perch on top of the desk, Quinn turned to face Lina, sitting with one leg bent on the polished surface and the other planted on the floor. "I still don't understand how the actual Codex is here if we're not really here—at the Archive, I mean."

"Honestly," Lina said with a little laugh, "I'm not entirely sure I understand it myself. The only way I can think to explain what happened is like this. I *knew* the real Codex was already hidden somewhere in the house. So if you think of what I did like remodeling, I updated the interior but kept some of the original structure."

"So you gave the kitchen a facelift but kept the pipes. The pipes in this case being the Codex?"

"Pretty much," Lina said.

Quinn pursed her lips. "Neat."

"Well, are you going to open it?" Finley asked, propping one hand on the back of Lina's chair and the other on the desk as he leaned over her shoulder.

"Don't you think the girl might want a little space?" Quinn asked as she played with the ends of her hair.

Finley jumped up. "Oh, sorry."

"No. No, it's okay. You're fine." Lina took a deep breath. "I just can't believe we found it."

"We have what we came for. You don't have to rush this part if you're not ready," Nord said from her side.

She glanced up at him. He was leaning against the desk beside her, his arms folded across his chest and his legs crossed at the ankles. Stretched out as they were, his legs completely blocked the walkway between their two desks. For someone who didn't look like they'd enjoy scholarly pursuits, he sure seemed at home here.

"It's not that," she said, finally giving in to temptation and allowing herself to run her palm over the Codex's forest-green cover. "It's just a little overwhelming. Alistair kept it hidden for decades, you know? And I can't help but feel like everything is going to change as soon as I open it."

"That's totally understandable—and probably not far off, to be honest. But he's also the one who told you to find it and study it," Quinn pointed out.

"True," Lina said with another heavy sigh. "Very true."

Not giving herself a chance to chicken out, Lina lifted the cover by the bottom right corner and gently opened it. The first page was blank, snowy white parchment, which was odd given the book's age. Chalking it up to some sort of preservation magic, she flipped the page and found the Cuska family crest intricately detailed in gold ink.

For a second, she just stared, allowing her eyes to drink in the gilded lines. How many generations of her ancestors had come before her, seeking the Codex and its secrets? In a way, it was humbling to know that she was following in their footsteps. She only hoped she proved herself worthy.

The next page was a pen and ink illustration of a woman standing in a jungle. Her dress was slit up to her thigh, revealing a snake curled around her calf. Her hair blew in the breeze and completely obscured her face, which was angled down toward the serpent at her feet. As Lina watched, the picture seemed to shift and move, the woman's hair and dress blowing in the invisible breeze. Lina could actually feel the warmth of the sun and the cool air against her face. Could hear the flutter of leaves and the snake's sibilant hiss echoing in her ears.

Nord's concerned voice reached her then.

"Lina?"

She blinked, coming out of her trance with an embarrassed chuckle. "Sorry. I'm here," she said, quickly turning the page.

This one was filled from top to bottom with words and symbols she couldn't read. Reaching for the rolled bundle of papers, Lina untied the black ribbon and carefully flattened them out beside the Codex. There was a soft pang in her chest as she recognized Alistair's writing, but she was too focused on her task to do more than acknowledge it.

"What's it say?" Quinn asked, leaning forward.

"Looks like some sort of creation story," Lina murmured, her eyes skimming Alistair's notes. As far as she could tell, they were more of a play-by-play than literal line-by-line translation.

"As fascinating as I'm sure that is, you should probably skip ahead to the good stuff," Quinn said.

"You're one of those people that reads the end of the book first, aren't you?" Finley asked with mock accusation.

Quinn shrugged. "So what if I am?"

"The list of things wrong with that are too numerous to name."

"Guys," Lina said, looking up, "Shut up or go somewhere else."

"Sorry," Quinn said. "I'll behave. No promises about him, though," she added, jerking her thumb at a scowling Finley.

With a slight shake of her head and a 'can you believe those two' look she cast at Nord, Lina returned her attention to her uncle's summary.

The creation story was interesting in that it seemed to be a variation on what happened between Eve and the snake in the garden of Eden. It was less about original sin and temptation and more about protection in exchange for knowledge. Apparently, Adam wasn't a fan of the serpent, but Eve convinced him to spare its life. In thanks, the serpent gifted Eve and her descendants with its considerable gifts.

Intrigued, Lina flipped through the pages, noting the repeated mention of the name Sofia. What her uncle hadn't been able to discern was whether this was an actual person or a persona selected because of its connection to the word wisdom. It didn't seem to matter either way, except insofar as Sofia seemed to have included personal messages at the start of each chapter.

The chapters, as best she could tell, were really just categories with Sofia's intros providing a bit more insight as to what the reader could expect to find in that section. Her uncle had created a table of contents that listed out the three major sections. There was one on history, another on lineage with references to the emergence of various powers throughout the years, but the majority of the book appeared to be a collection of spells and rituals. This is where her uncle's notes became more detailed.

Lina also noticed that the ink on these pages was fresher, meaning Alistair must have been working on them recently. That alone was enough to garner her interest. If he'd spent the bulk of his efforts there, it must be what he'd wanted her to see.

She read through his notes quickly, her attention sharpening when she came to a page with one heavily underlined sentence.

The heart of our power comes from the Transference.

She scanned the rest of her uncle's translation, her palms starting to sweat and her heart speeding up with each new word. When she reached the end of the passage, she straightened, her eyes shooting first to Nord and then to Quinn.

"What is it?" Quinn asked.

Lina licked her lips, nervous energy buzzing through her. "I think I found what Alistair thought was so important."

"About accessing your power's full potential?"

"I . . . think so."

Quinn raised a brow. "Well, either you did, or you didn't. Which is it?"

Laughing nervously, Lina rubbed at her forehead. "Remember how he mentioned the Transference?"

"Technically, I was the one who explained it to you guys, but yes," Quinn said, her eyes narrowing with interest. "Why? What's it got to do with *your* power?"

"Apparently . . . everything," Lina said, her gaze shifting nervously to Nord for a second time.

He watched her intently. While he couldn't possibly understand the meaning of her words, he clearly picked up on her reaction to them. She could tell that he was waiting for her to explain, but he was giving her room to come to terms with what she'd found before pressing.

If what her uncle wrote was true, then Nord was the key to everything. But, if they were wrong . . .

Well, it was a hell of a risk to take. And, ultimately, not a choice she could make alone.

"What's the Transference?" Finley asked, still reading over her shoulder.

"That's the million-dollar question, isn't it?" Lina replied, still reeling from her discovery.

She opened her mouth to try to explain and then shut it again. How did she even start? Where did she start? She looked at Quinn, begging her to come to her rescue.

Quinn, who knew what the Transference involved, even if she didn't have the full details, immediately jumped in.

"Simply put, the Transference is something that occurs between true mates. It ensures that they are true equals, their powers shared between them."

Lina could feel her cheeks heating as Quinn explained. She could also feel the weight of Nord's stare on her, even though Quinn was the one talking.

"If," Lina chimed in. "The power is shared between them *if* the mates are deemed worthy."

"What do you mean?" Quinn asked.

"According to this, if an animagus believes they have found their true mate, they can choose to undergo the Transference. The process is . . . intense. In addition to binding their souls to each other, it also binds their power. It was a way of ensuring that one partner isn't vastly more powerful than the other, creating an imbalance among two who should see each other only as equal. It's also a way for animagi to mate outside of our species without power dynamics— such as one species feeling inferior to the other. Whatever power one mate has, the other gains. So long as the mates are found deserving, that is."

"And if they aren't?" Nord asked.

She forced herself to meet his gaze. "Then they die."

Before Nord could respond, Quinn asked, "Finding a mate is great and all, but I still don't see what it has to do with you accessing all of your family's animagi abilities. That is what Alistair said he'd found, isn't it?"

Lina tore her eyes away from Nord and stared at her clasped hands. "It is."

"You're going to need to give me more than that," Quinn said.

"The Transference is old magic. The oldest magic, actually. It is believed to be the process undertaken by Eve and the serpent to create the first animagi."

"You're saying that Eve, the actual, honest to God Eve, is your great-grandma a billion times removed?" Quinn asked.

Lina smiled slightly. "If the story is to be believed."

"Well, that explains how the Cuskas came to be, but what about the others?"

"According to Alistair's notes, there were similar acts of selfless-ness between the first humans and the creatures they shared the

Earth with—the Codex refers to them as the Ancient Ones—where power was gifted as a reward for a selfless act. But that gift also set the animagi apart from the other humans. There was jealousy, fear, and of course, in the rare instance an animagi found love, they'd be forced to watch their mortal partner age and die. So, they found a way to create true equals—by replicating the spell that the Ancient Ones used on them."

"So what happened?" Finley asked.

"What always happens when power is craved above all else," Lina said sadly. "It was abused."

"How?" Quinn asked, her voice hushed.

"Well, initially, no one realized that undergoing the Transference actually tapped into the line's full power because the first of us always had access to it. But as time went on, and our magic diluted, it became apparent that the only way to regain what had been lost was through the Transference."

From the corner of her eye, Lina saw Quinn press a hand to her mouth, as if she could already tell where Lina's story was going.

"In their quest for power, animagi began to use the spell en masse. They would kidnap those whose abilities they wanted for themselves so that in addition to their own animagi abilities, they'd also gain access to their mate's. But in this blind pursuit, they forgot something important. The Transference always hinged on the vessels being found worthy—it was the Ancient Ones' power being granted, after all. And it probably goes without saying that they were not pleased with how their gift was being misused.

"People were slaughtered because of our obsession with power. There's a reason animagi were feared and mistrusted above all others. Why our kind was hunted to the point of near extinction. So, to remove temptation and keep those of us left safe, the secret was locked away. Shared only with those who proved themselves. Because the price of being deemed unworthy was too high. Especially as our numbers dwindled."

Silence settled around them as she finished speaking, and Lina clasped her hands tighter together, waiting for someone to confirm what she'd already decided.

It was over. The Codex was a dead end. She may as well offer herself up to the Director because attempting the Transference was a death wish.

"Does that book tell you what you need to do to perform the spell?" Nord asked.

"Yes, but—"

"What do we need?"

"Nord," she said, her heart pounding as she shook her head, "I can't ask you to do this."

"You aren't asking. I'm offering."

She blinked back tears as she looked up at him, stunned by his offer. "Did you just hear anything I said? We could die."

"We won't."

"How can you be sure?"

"I don't need a spell to prove what I already know in my bones to be true. No one is more worthy than you."

She gave him a disbelieving laugh. "I highly doubt that."

"You're selling yourself short."

"How can you say that? The entire reason we're even considering this is to help give us an advantage against the Drakes and Brotherhood. Given my people's history, that doesn't seem like the kind of thing that goes over well in this process. In fact, that's the sort of thinking that made the survivors hide the information in the first place."

"You aren't taking into consideration the fact that you're not seeking this power for yourself. Think about it. You have nothing to gain from choosing me. I have no gifts to offer you. My magic was taken from me. So, realistically, while you would gain a few new abilities if we are successful, I am the one who truly benefits. Second, this is not a selfish grasp at power. You're only considering it as a last resort to protect the people you love. And perhaps most importantly, the person you're willing to share your power with is someone who truly loves you. Who wholeheartedly trusts and respects you. In the instances of misuse you mentioned, not one of those attributes was present."

"You're biased," she managed once she could speak around the ball of emotion in her throat.

"Doesn't make me wrong," he said with a one-shoulder shrug.

Finley rested his hand on her shoulder. "For what it's worth, I think he's right. And I have no reason to be biased."

"You're my friend," Lina pointed out.

Finley pointed to Nord. "I've been his longer. You really think I'd let you risk his life if I had any doubts?"

"You guys, this is crazy. What if we're wrong?"

"Then we die anyway. It's not like the Drakes or the Brotherhood are planning on letting us waltz off into the sunset and live happily ever after, so what does it really matter?" Quinn asked. "I don't think any of us are sitting here under the assumption that this is going to end with everyone alive and singing Kum Ba Yah when all is said and done. People are going to die. We need to do everything we can to ensure those people aren't us. But, if it is, at least this way, it's your choice and not at the hands of your enemies."

Lina stared at her best friend. "That might be the most dismal thing you've ever said to me."

"I think it's time for us to face a couple hard truths, don't you?"

"I'm pretty sure that's all I've done since I've come back, thank you very much."

Quinn reached over and rested her hand on top of Lina's. "You've got to do this, Li. Alistair wouldn't have pointed you in this direction if he didn't believe in you. My mother wouldn't have gotten involved if she didn't believe it too. All of us are sitting here right now because we believe in you. It's time for you to start believing in yourself."

"If it was just my life on the line, this wouldn't even be a question. You know I'd risk it in a heartbeat. But you're asking me to put Nord's in jeopardy, and I just *can't*."

"Kærasta," Nord said tenderly, pushing off the desk and squatting down beside her to take her hand in his, "what sort of life do you think would be left for me if you weren't in it?"

Lina opened her mouth to answer, but he stopped her with the brush of his thumb over her lower lip.

"I've already lived a dozen lifetimes without you. Now that I've experienced one spent by your side, there's no going back. We're a package deal, remember?" he asked, borrowing her words from the day of the hunt. "Where you go, I go. And if that happens to be the afterlife, then so be it. So long as we're together."

Lina's heart felt like it contracted in on itself, the intensity of her emotions sitting heavy inside her chest.

"I hate you," she said, her lip quivering beneath his soft touch.

The side of his mouth twitched up. "Ah, Kærasta. That's not hate you're feeling."

"No," she agreed. "It's love."

CHAPTER 20
NORD

A deep crease formed between Finley's brows as he read over the list Lina had handed him.

"You're sure it calls for all of this?" he asked, cocking his head up to look at her.

"You're welcome to look over Alistair's notes yourself if you'd like to double-check," Lina said.

"No, it's not that I don't trust you, it's just . . ." He scrubbed a hand down the back of his neck as he trailed off.

"What's bothering you?" Nord asked, not needing to rely on their years of friendship to read the troubled look on Finley's face.

"The majority of these ingredients are known psychedelics. They're used to induce powerful trances."

"Isn't that essentially what we're trying to do?" Lina asked.

"Since none of us have ever seen the ritual performed, we can only guess what's going to happen," Finley said. "But I do find it concerning that you have seven different variants on this list alone when only one is necessary to get the job done. On top of that, when you include the other items on here—like the crushed bloodstone, which is a magical amplifier, or the infused crystal, which acts as a focus—it's entirely possible that you're going to be trapped inside the spell until it runs its course. There's a very good chance that we won't be able to reach you if things go sideways."

"So what you're saying is it's dangerous," Quinn said, grasping the list out of his hand and looking it over. "We already knew that."

Nord was inclined to agree. "Do you know where we can get what we need?" he asked.

Finley's voice sounded in his mind. *"I know you love her, but are you sure you want to do this?"* It was the first time in a while he'd defaulted back to their old method of communication. He'd been actively working on breaking the habit in deference to Nord's new station, and falling back now only underscored how unsettled he must be.

Nord kept his unwavering gaze trained on his friend's face, letting it speak for him. While he could appreciate Finley's caution, especially since it was his and Lina's lives on the line, they'd already decided on their course. Which meant that the time to second guess themselves had passed.

Now all they could do was see it through. Come what may.

Finley exhaled loudly, likely letting go of whatever other words of warning he'd been planning to say. "I have most of these items at the Bunker. They're common enough, but this last ingredient, the Tears of Destiny, I've never even heard of it before. It could be anything as far as I know."

"Actually, it couldn't," Quinn said. "It's quite specific, seeing as how there's only one known vial in existence."

"So you're the expert on obscure magical items now, are you?" Finley shot back.

"When it's something I've already had to acquire before, yeah, actually, I am."

Finley pressed his lips together, a muscle in his jaw flexing. "Then you know where we can get our hands on some."

"I do," Quinn agreed. "But you're not going to like it."

Prickling along the back of his neck told Nord he knew what she was about to say, but Lina beat her to answering.

"Crombie," she said, her voice flat.

Quinn set the list down with a sigh. "It was one of the first jobs I did for him."

Nord's hands balled into fists at his sides, a familiar red haze sliding over his eyes as fury swelled within. He hadn't forgotten what the bottom feeder had done to Lina. Part of him looked forward to repaying that kindness with some of his own. The other part knew that they couldn't afford the distraction.

It was only a matter of time before their enemies found them. The best thing right now would be to get what they needed without anyone being the wiser. The more time they wasted dealing with the sorry excuse of a fae, the more likely their whereabouts would be reported back to both the Brotherhood and the Drakes.

He blew out a deep breath, forcing the rage down as he did. If they were going to accomplish their mission, he needed to keep a cool head. A berserker in the midst of a rage was hardly something that went unnoticed for long.

"And you're certain he didn't auction it off?" Nord asked.

"No. He said he wanted it for his personal collection."

"So if we want to get our hands on it, we'll either need to ask him nicely—" Lina started.

"Which we know always goes over oh so well, generous, selfless soul that he is," Quinn interjected.

"—or we steal it," Lina finished.

"Why go through all that trouble? Can't you make him give it to us?" Finley asked Quinn.

"I'm not sure," she replied, not meeting their eyes.

"Wait, you never used your gift on him?" Lina asked.

"I never wanted to find out what happened if I failed," Quinn said, looking like the admission cost her. "He's fae, and they have a natural resistance to any sort of mental tampering. Likely because so many of them have compulsion abilities of their own. With him being of royal blood, I just didn't want to risk it."

"All right," Lina said after a beat, running her hands up and down her thighs, "so break in it is. I'm assuming we need to go to The District?"

"He keeps his private collection at his home," Finley answered. "He has a library of sorts, where his prize pieces are showcased."

"And you know this how?" Quinn asked, her eyes narrowed with suspicion.

"I've been there."

Quinn raised a brow. "I find it hard to believe that he just let a Guardian stroll right into his house."

"He didn't get much of a choice. It was official Brotherhood business."

"But that's good news for us, right?" Lina asked. "It means you'll be able to portal us there?"

"Definitely."

"What about wards or a security detail?" Nord asked. It seemed unlikely someone as powerful as Davis Crombie would leave his house unguarded, especially if he kept priceless treasures inside.

"If we run into anyone, I can make sure they forget we were ever there," Quinn said.

"Unless they're fae," Finley said.

Quinn shot daggers at him with her eyes. "Have you ever seen him near any of his kin? Crombie despises the fae. It won't be an issue."

"That takes care of one problem, but what are we supposed to do about the wards?" Lina asked.

Finley's eyes blazed silver. "I paid attention when Crombie broke through the Brotherhood's wards. I'm pretty confident I can replicate the magic he used to breach his own."

"What if you can't?" Nord asked.

"Then we break in the old-fashioned way and get the fuck out of there as soon as possible," Finley said.

"The real question is when do we want to do it?" Quinn asked.

"Sooner would be better," Nord said.

"Well, what time is it in Bell Falls now?" Lina asked.

Nord did some swift calculations in his head. "It's about nine p.m."

"That's good for us," Quinn said, "it means Crombie will likely be at the club. We'll have at least a small window to get in, grab the vial, and get out before he realizes anyone's there."

"So we go now," Lina said, pushing up to her feet, her expression steeled with determination. "While he's distracted." She glanced around, her eyes briefly landing on each of them. "Unless there's anything you guys need to do first."

Quinn gestured to Lina's replica of the Archive. "I'm sitting in a secret hideout in Scotland, on the run from not one, but two supernatural secret orders—one of which I technically belong to. What else, exactly, do you think I have on my to-do list right now, besides getting out of this fucked-up situation we're in as quickly as possible?"

Lina laughed, and the sight of her smile punched through him. Not for the first time, it reminded him of the first ray of sunshine breaking through the clouds after a storm. He wasn't sure when exactly her happiness had come to mean more to him than his own, but he'd hazard a guess it was right around the first time she aimed one of those sunbeam smiles at him.

"I don't know. I was just asking. The Tears aren't the only item on the list. Maybe Finley would rather stop by his Berserker Bunker first to grab the rest of the supplies so we can come straight back here after our little B&E. Or maybe you guys might want to restock our go-bags properly at the penthouse. There's been a lot of running from point A to B without time for much else recently. Does the fact that I'm the reason we're stuck in this endless parade of shit mean I have to keep making decisions without any input from you guys? Aren't I allowed to just check in with the group sometimes?"

Quinn gave Lina a long, considering look. "I'll allow it."

Nord hid a grin behind his hand. Their bickering was almost as entertaining as Quinn and Finley's.

"So we going or what?" Quinn asked, blowing Lina a kiss as she picked her jacket up from the back of a chair and pulled it on.

Lina gave Quinn an exasperated eye roll and then turned to face Nord. "I know how you feel about Crombie. You can stay here if—"

"Not a chance."

She dropped her voice, her eyes earnestly searching his. "I know you're pissed at him. Trust me, I am too. But there's no shame in staying back if you're not sure you can control yourself—"

"Now you're just being offensive," Nord said, but he couldn't keep his lips from twitching up since she so clearly saw through him. "I have perfect control."

The slight rattle in his chest belied his words. But she didn't need to know that.

"You might as well save your breath, love. You know he'd never let you do something this stupid without being nearby to swoop in and save you," Finley said as he buttoned up his coat.

That was also true.

Lina raised up on her tiptoes, her hands resting lightly on his shoulders as she pressed a kiss to his cheek. "As long as you're sure."

"That my place is at your side?" he asked, capturing her hand with his as she stepped away. "There was never any doubt."

Her expression went soft, her gaze tender as it met his.

Quinn started gagging obnoxiously. "I think I just got diabetes. You guys are disgusting."

Lina opened her mouth to reply, but Nord tugged her back, slanting his lips down and over hers in a kiss that was pure possession. After a stunned second, Lina arched into him with a low moan.

"Annnd now I'm pregnant."

Smirking, Nord pulled away, holding Lina steady as she rocked back on her heels.

"You and me both," she said, her cheeks flushed.

"Point taken, big guy," Quinn said.

Nord winked at her.

"There was a point to that?" Lina asked, still slightly dazed as she glanced between them.

Quinn laughed. "Only that your man is pro-PDA, and anyone who isn't can fuck right off."

Finley let out a grunt of frustration, drawing their attention to him right as the expanding portal fizzled and died.

"What's wrong?" Lina asked.

"The wards around Crombie's estate extend farther than I thought," Finley answered with a frown. "It's going to be a bit of a hike to get to his place."

"What else is new?" Quinn muttered. "If it's not murder stairs or ancient bell towers, it's a Swedish forest or Scottish alleyways. Why would this be any different? Fucking Crombie."

Nord pressed his lips together to keep from laughing. She reminded him of a disgruntled cat airing its grievances, all fluffed up fur and yowling meows.

"Just think how great your ass is going to look after all the cardio we've been doing recently," Lina offered, her shoulders shaking slightly as she fought off her own amusement.

Quinn turned to the side and checked herself out. "Fuck cardio. My ass is already perfect."

Since the two women were focused on each other, Nord was the only one that caught Finley's muttered, "Bloody right, it is." Then his eyes flashed silver once more, and a second portal formed, this one without issue. "Best we get moving," he said. "We're going to be out in the open longer than originally intended, so don't stop running until you reach the barrier."

Lina's nose scrunched as she glanced over at him. "How will we know when we reach it? I've always just gone through wards."

"With the amount of magic this thing is pumping out, I'll be able to spot it a mile away. Keep up with me and you'll be fine." With that,

Finley stepped through the shimmering surface of the portal, and the others filed through behind him.

Finley was already sprinting up a grassy hill by the time Nord stepped through. There was a brief moment of pride as he spotted Lina just behind him, easily keeping pace.

"Home sweet home," Quinn said, casting her gaze out over the twinkling lights of Bell Falls seated at the bottom of the hill before glancing up at the moon hanging heavy in the starry sky. Then she looked at the others and groaned. "The asshole just had to live in the middle of buttfuck and nowhere, didn't he?" she grumbled before half-heartedly starting to jog after Lina and Finley.

Nord took off, passing her with only a few steps. He turned and jogged backward. "Need me to carry you?"

"Don't tempt me, gorgeous. Now turn around before I make you trip over your own feet."

Nord flashed her a grin before he raced away. As he crested the hill beside Lina, Crombie's estate came into view. Even from this distance, he could tell that the bastard's house was as pretentious as he was.

It appeared more castle than modern home with its stone façade, multiple wings, and soaring turrets. Nord could just make out a hedge maze near the back of the property, and a sparkling fountain lit up and bubbling in the front courtyard. There was no telling what other secrets the twenty-acre property held as he sped down the other side of the hill, but at least he could be sure there wasn't a moat.

Finley held a hand out as he started to slow. Nord assumed he'd spotted the ward until Finley cocked his head and held a finger up to his lips.

Tension coiled in Nord's muscles as a preternatural stillness took hold of him. It was the berserker readying itself to strike.

Not even a second later, Nord heard it too. A low growl that was far too deep to be something as mundane as a guard dog. Then a shadow broke free from his periphery.

Not waiting to see what the shadow was, Nord plunged into the rage, welcoming his ever-present fury as it took control of him. Teeth clenched, he spun in the direction of the shadow, cataloging details as they emerged.

It was not a beast he'd seen before, but it didn't matter. The four-legged, fur-covered creature was similar enough to a canine that it was all he needed to know.

"Keep going," Nord ordered, never taking his eyes off the prowling fiend. "I've got this covered."

Finley knew better than to second guess him. His eyes flashed silver as he scanned the horizon and then silently motioned for the women to follow him. Lina hesitated only a second before she obeyed.

Saliva dripped from the midnight-colored beast as it let off another warning growl.

Baring his teeth, Nord did the same.

The beast's ears twitched, as if insulted Nord would dare to threaten it, and then it lunged. It leapt through the air like it had wings, arcing forward with a speed that should have been impossible.

But Nord had fought far deadlier things and won. The thrill of impending battle rushed through him, setting his blood on fire with the promise of violence.

A moment before the snarling creature would have collided with him, Nord plucked it out of the air by the head—like it was some kind of ball instead of a couple hundred pounds of killing machine—and twisted. There was a yelp of pain and then silence as Nord dropped the now dead beast on the ground.

It was over so quickly there was almost a ripple of disappointment.

He was just about to turn and rejoin the others when another shadow peeled away. And then a second, and a third.

The berserker's eyes narrowed as he tracked the movements of the rest of the pack. Then he grinned.

This was more like it.

Sliding himself into a defensive stance, Nord braced himself for the next attack.

"Here, kitty kitty."

CHAPTER 21
LINA

Lina bit down on her lip, her eyes swinging back the way they came for the dozenth time in the last few minutes. She knew Nord could take care of himself, but she was seriously contemplating running back and seeing what was going on when Finley's hushed voice greeted her.

"All right, we should be good to go," he said. His eyes flashed a blinding silver and then returned to his warm hazel as he faced her and Quinn. "Ready?"

Lina glanced back, about to say 'no' when she caught sight of Nord running toward them. Tension she hadn't noticed melted away as he came into view. Then her eyes snagged on the bloody claw mark running down the length of his face, and she raced toward him.

"What the hell happened?"

Nord, looking like the somewhat demented warrior he was, gave her a smug grin. "Merely a flesh wound."

Exasperation warred with amusement as she crossed her arms and narrowed her eyes. "Only you could look quite so giddy while saying something like that. You're having fun, aren't you?"

"Is that a crime?"

Lina shook her head. Frankly, it would be more concerning for a berserker not to find enjoyment in a little bloodshed.

He curled an arm over her shoulders, and they quickly made their way back to where Finley and Quinn were waiting for them.

"Want me to take care of that?" Finley asked, reaching up to grab Nord's jaw.

Nord ducked out of his hold. "We'll deal with it later."

Fin nodded. "Right. In that case, Lina, you're up." He pointed to the left side of the towering house. "See that window? First floor, third from the left?"

"The one with the light on?"

"That's the one. His library is toward the back of the house, but if you can use your magic to get us through that window undetected, it should be a straight shot down the hallway to the library. It's the most direct route, unless you rather creep around the side of the house and come from the back garden. But we run the risk of running into other defensive measures if we go that way."

"Window it is," Lina said.

"Whatever gets us out of here faster," Quinn agreed.

For just a second, Lina imagined shattered panes of glass and the heavy blue curtain flapping the breeze. But she dismissed the image just as quickly—if Finley had intended for her to simply break a window, he would have taken care of it himself. And as enticing as it was to leave behind proof that they'd bested Crombie . . . it was safer all around not to. So, instead, Lina settled for converting the glass panes to an open set of French doors they could easily pass through.

It took all of thirty seconds for the image in her mind to become reality.

"Nice work," Nord said with a slight smile.

Lina shrugged. "It's just a door, not a big deal."

"Your conjuring is almost instantaneous and your manifestations more detailed. That speaks to control, which is a big deal."

She dipped her face to hide the grin his words of praise caused. "Thanks."

Finley carefully made his way across the lawn, taking lead like last time. He paused by the open doors and then gestured for them to follow.

Lina's heart thumped erratically in her chest as she crept toward the house. They were actually doing this. They were going to steal from Crombie.

If she hadn't known how dire their situation was, she would have thought they were all suicidal. The truth was, this act of pure stupidity might be the only way to save them all. It was an absurd situation, but that pretty much summed up the entirety of her life. A series of absurd, impossible situations.

Finley ducked his head into the house, looked both ways, and then disappeared inside. Nord and Quinn went in next, and Lina ducked across the threshold last, taking a second to return the window to its original state before tiptoeing down the hallway behind the others.

Lina was so focused on the space between Finley's shoulder blades that she barely noticed the details of the interior, except that it was decorated in shades of silvery blue and accented with white and navy. There were a few paintings on the walls, but if asked, she couldn't have said what the subject matter was.

She was just thinking about how lucky they were Crombie chose such a plush carpet since it helped muffle the sound of their footsteps when Quinn's shocked inhale stopped her dead in her tracks.

Ice rolled down Lina's spine as two men rounded the corner, their mottled gray skin, burly build, and black eyes identifying them as two of Crombie's gargoyle guards.

"What the fuck are you doing here?"

She heard Nord growl low in his throat and braced herself for a fight, but it was Quinn, not her berserker, that stepped forward. She pushed around Finley and into the center of the hall, her steps sure and unhurried.

"You're confused."

Lina held her breath as the two guards' expressions shifted from enraged to dazed.

Quinn continued to speak in a calm, measured tone as she approached them, hypnotizing them with her voice every bit as much as her eyes. "You heard a sound, but when you came to investigate, there was nothing out of place." Reaching behind her back, Quinn gestured for the others to move past her. Then she placed a hand on either of the gargoyle's shoulders and said, "There is no one here. Everything is as it should be. On the count of three, you're going to go to the kitchen and make yourself a sandwich and stay there until your shift is over."

Quinn made sure that they were well away from the bodyguards before she started counting. By the time she whispered, "Three," she was standing behind them, whispering the word in their ears before turning and racing back to join Lina and the others.

Lina risked a glance back at the gargoyles in time to see them blink and shake their heads.

"I told you there's nothing here. No one would dare fuck with Crombie. Let's go see about something to eat."

Lina shook her head, the adrenaline surging through her body calming only slightly. "You're scary, you know that?" she whispered as the two men walked in the opposite direction.

Quinn's lips quirked up in the barest hint of a smile.

"Library's just ahead," Finley said in a hushed voice as he gestured to a set of wooden doors. "Let's go before anyone else finds us."

Lina wiped her sweaty palms on her pants, her head filled with the sound of blood rushing through her veins. They were almost done, but she was suddenly more nervous now than before they started.

Nord tested the knob, but the door swung open with ease. Using his back, he pushed it all the way open so the others could rush past him. Once they were all inside, he carefully shut it once more.

Heart in her throat, Lina glanced around the sprawling library. It was two stories with curving staircases on either side of the room, and a number of comfortable-looking chairs and lounges spread throughout. The shelves were filled with books of every size and color. Between every few stacks, there were shadow boxes with spotlights on their various contents. But the central focus of the room was a massive fireplace. The four of them could easily stand shoulder to shoulder within its black stone walls with room to dance if they should wish to.

"Searching might be faster if we split up," Lina said, turning in a small circle as she tried to take everything in.

"Agreed," Finley said. "What are we looking for?"

"The Tears are in an amethyst-colored vial about the size and shape of a pepper," Quinn answered, holding her fingers apart to show what she meant. "The topper is gold filigree, and the bottom is also tipped in gold."

"Probably best we don't touch anything unless we're sure," Nord said.

"If you think you've found it, I can confirm before we grab it," Quinn offered.

The plan seemed straightforward enough, but Lina still couldn't quite shake her nerves. "As soon as we get it, we portal back to Hope Street. No dawdling, got it?" she asked.

Finley and the others nodded their agreement.

"I'll be ready with the portal as soon as Quinn confirms we have the right vial."

Lina licked her lips. "Okay then. You two take upstairs. Nord and I will search down here."

There was a single moment of tense silence as the four of them exchanged determined looks. Then Finley and Quinn split off, each soundlessly walking up one of the white and black marbled staircases.

"I'll be right over there if you need me," Nord said, reaching out and giving her hand a tight squeeze.

"Let's hope I don't," she said with a wry twist of her lips.

Nord returned her smile with one of his own and then headed for the left side of the library.

Lina spotted the closest shadow box and got to work. The knowledge seeker in her struggled to ignore the rows upon rows of books with their gilded and unusual titles. It was only due to sheer force of will that she kept moving, dismissing the illuminated contents on display as quickly as possible.

Crombie's collection, at least the small part she'd seen, was impressive. There were runed blades, enchanted orbs, even a book that was chained shut and bound in what she could only assume was flesh. She didn't need Finley's Guardian abilities to tell that these objects were magical to the nth degree. A fact that only emphasized how powerful the contents of the vial they sought must be.

Five minutes later, she'd just about finished searching the back wall when she found it. The tiny purple bottle perfectly matched Quinn's description. Her heart gave an excited jolt, and she instinctively reached out to rest her fingers against the glass. It seemed silly to wait for Quinn's confirmation when this was so clearly what they'd been searching for.

"Guys!" she hissed as loudly as she dared.

When she didn't immediately hear an answering shout or the rush of footsteps, she started checking the glass box for some sort of hinge.

"I found it," she called out again, tapping her foot in nervous agitation when there was still no answer.

Maybe she was too far away?

Lina bit her lip, debating whether she should go back to the center of the room and call for them or if she should just grab it. If it was already in hand when they regrouped, that was a few minutes less they had to spend in here before they could leave . . .

Mind made up and mouth drier than a desert, Lina willed the front of the glass display case out of existence. Since the glass had been pristinely clean, there was no discernable difference between it being there or not. It wasn't until Lina tentatively reached out and her fingers met no resistance that she let out a gusty exhale. The slight twitch of her hand was the only outward sign of her nerves as she moved it deeper into the box before she finally came into contact with the warm, textured surface of the bottle.

Closing her fingers around the vial, Lina quickly jerked her fist back out, and then on instinct, created a duplicate of the delicate bottle where the original had sat. Once she was certain the details were perfect, she replaced the glass and shoved the real vial in her pocket.

Heart thundering wildly, Lina gave up all pretense of stealth and cried out, "I've got it!" as she booked it back to the center of the room.

Nord was there to greet her, his intense gaze moving over her as if ensuring that she was all right.

A frazzled-looking Finley peered down at her from over the baluster. "What the hell happened to waiting before touching anything?"

"Yell at me later," she said to both of them. "It's time to go."

Shaking his head, Finley started for the stairs, muttering to himself, "Why doesn't anyone ever stick to the bloody plan?"

Quinn came into view seconds later, wasting no time as she ran down the stairs. "You found it?"

Lina pulled the vial out and held it up for her to inspect.

"That's the one."

She shoved it back in her pocket, idly noting that it felt warmer now than it did when she first touched it. Chalking it up to body heat, she dismissed the thought and quashed the urge to tell Finley to hurry up with the portal.

They'd been on borrowed time since they first set foot in Bell Falls, and it was well past time to get the hell out of here.

Nord moved behind her, dipping his head so his mouth was beside her ear. "We're going to have a talk later about you taking unnecessary risks."

She craned around to give his marred cheek a purposeful look. "Only if I'm allowed to talk to you about the same."

His lips flattened, but his eyes seemed to shine with laughter.

"Okay, everyone through," Finley said, the visage of the Hope Street house undulating beside him.

Quinn dove through the portal first, and Lina was right behind her. She didn't start breathing again until all four of them were standing on the sidewalk, looking at the door to Alistair's hideout.

The overdose of adrenaline left her shaky, and Lina sat down hard on the neighboring stoop, dropping her head between her knees as she let out a disbelieving laugh.

"I can't believe we just did that."

There was no answer.

In fact, she couldn't hear anything. Not the distant sound of pub patrons or late-night traffic. Not the rustle of leaves in the wind or animals scurrying past. The silence was absolute.

Lina's blood turned to ice as she lifted her head and spotted a very familiar, very unwelcome face above her.

"You have some explaining to do."

This can't be happening. Lina squeezed her eyes shut as dread pooled in her stomach. *He wasn't there. You were alone. He can't possibly know you took it . . . unless there was some sort of spell on the bottle itself.*

"Closing your eyes won't make me disappear, sweetheart," Crombie said in his darkly seductive voice.

Lina forced herself to open her eyes and stand, leaning heavily on the wrought iron railing as she took in the time-frozen forms of her friends. "How did you find me?"

"You and I are connected now, remember?"

"Unfortunately," she said through gritted teeth, some of her anxiety being replaced by anger.

Crombie's eyes narrowed at her hint of temper. "You've been hiding from me," he said, tilting his head as he studied her. "I've felt no trace of you for weeks, until tonight. Where have you been?"

The smallest flicker of relief ignited within her. He didn't know. He must have sensed some sort of disturbance when she'd returned to Bell Falls, if he even realized she'd been there at all, but he had no idea what she'd been up to.

"I really don't think that's any of your business," she replied, crossing her arms and fighting the urge to wrap her hand protectively around the vial that sat heavy in her pocket. She didn't dare tempt fate and draw attention to it.

"Ah, you see, sweetheart. Until you make good on our little deal, everything you do is my business," he said.

Lina decided it was time to go on the offensive. "How did you get here, anyway? Last time I checked, portals weren't part of your skill set."

Crombie's full lips lifted in a dangerous smile. "Don't presume to know anything about my skills, Lina. You know only what I want you to."

It was Lina's turn for her eyes to narrow. "What do you want, Crombie?"

"I want what you owe me."

"I'm a little busy right now, so you're going to have to wait. Believe it or not, you're not the biggest bully on the playground."

Until now, Crombie had stood with his hands casually placed in his pockets, his demeanor somewhat cold, but nonthreatening. At her words, that all changed. His expression twisted, his smile turning cruel.

"Think again, Lina. There is *nothing* scarier in this world or any other than me, I promise you."

Lina's eyes shot to Nord's furious but frozen expression. Crombie had managed to trap the berserker in the midst of taking over, and Nord's towering frame screamed of coiled violence. "Somehow, I doubt that," she mused, then added in a more conversational tone, "He'll kill you if he hears you talking to me like that."

Crombie snorted. "As if I'm afraid of one of Odin's dogs."

"Then why freeze him?" Lina taunted. "If you're Big Bad Untouchable Crombie, then why worry about him at all?"

"I'm tired of our conversations always getting interrupted by the riffraff."

"That riffraff happens to be my family and friends. I don't appreciate you insulting them."

"They started it," Crombie hissed.

"Then be the bigger man," Lina shot back. "What are you, a child?"

Crombie glowered, a muscle fluttering in his set jaw. "I don't make a habit of playing nice with my enemies."

Lina pressed a hand to her temples, feeling suddenly exhausted by the loss of adrenaline and rapid shift of her emotions. "We aren't your enemies, Crombie. I wanted to be your friend, remember? But then you used my time of need to trick me into becoming bloodsworn."

"No," Crombie said, his voice ice cold, "*you* changed the rules first. When you allowed your little weaver to extort me and then had the audacity to come back and demand more. As if making a mockery of me once wasn't enough. All I did was ensure that you'd have to keep your promise in exchange for my assistance."

"And I *will*," Lina insisted. "Once we deal with the Brotherhood and the Drakes, I swear to you, Crombie, I will get whatever shiny artifact you want from the Vault so badly. But I'm not exactly able to waltz into the middle of the Mobius Council right now."

"You're an heir. You can do exactly that."

"The Drakes declared war, Crombie. I can't step foot near Mobius right now. Not until Mikel is dealt with."

Instead of anger, Crombie seemed to grow calm at the mention of her feud with the Drakes. "I've heard whispers about that. Pity about your uncle. He seemed like a tolerable man."

The words stabbed through her. It wasn't exactly a warm hug, but coming from Crombie, it was probably as close as she'd ever get.

"Thanks," she gritted out, hugging herself. "So are we good?

You'll give me some space to take care of these guys. And then, once I've dealt with the rest of this nonsense, I'll help you?"

Crombie studied her, his expression unreadable.

"Please, Crombie," she said, placing one of her hands on his forearm, hoping her touch might reinforce her words.

He felt like a statue beneath her hand, his arm hard and unyielding. His eyes dropped to where she touched him, and they flickered with something she couldn't name as he stepped out of her range.

"You can have your time for now. But I expect you to hold up your end of the bargain when I come to collect. I will not wait forever for you to deal with your problems. My patience only extends so far."

"Thank you," she breathed, sincerity coloring her words. She knew he didn't have to give in to her demands. Frankly, he had no reason to do anything for her, but she hoped that his goodwill would last long enough for them to do what they needed to. "Will you let them go now?" she asked.

Crombie glanced at the others. "I prefer them this way."

"But I don't."

He shook his head. "Your taste in companions is questionable, sweetheart."

"I like you," she pointed out. *Sometimes.*

"Like I said. Questionable." Then he seemed to take in their surroundings. "Why Edinburgh, by the by?"

"Alistair sent me here."

"Interesting."

He started to saunter away, pausing briefly beside Nord. He gave the gash along his cheek an interested once-over. "Run into some trouble?" he asked, glancing back at Lina.

"Something like that," she said, her head feeling light.

"Hmm," Crombie murmured before placing two fingers on Nord's shoulder and giving a little shove. It shouldn't have been possible, given Nord's size and the insignificance of the push, but Nord went flying backward, landing about halfway down the block with a heavy thud.

"Hey!" Lina shouted in protest, watching as Nord pushed himself to his feet, his expression murderous.

Crombie smirked. "He had it coming."

Then the sounds of the evening returned, and the next thing Lina saw was Finley shooting forward and grasping Crombie by the neck of his expensive shirt.

"Listen, you cockwomble. I've had just about enough of your bullshit—"

Crombie rolled his eyes. "Until next time," he called over his shoulder, then lifted a hand, snapped his fingers, and disappeared.

"Where'd he go?" Finley asked, his hand now clutching air.

"I have no idea," Lina said, just as shocked as he was.

"I hate it when he does that," Quinn said, far more calm than the rest of them.

"You knew he could just vanish like that?" Lina asked.

Quinn shrugged. "Crombie's fae. They have a lot of tricks up their sleeves."

"The next time I see that faerie prick," Nord snarled, "I'm going to make him wear his ass as a crown."

"Is that even physically possible?" Quinn asked, her brow furrowed.

"It will be once I harvest his spine for my ring collection."

"I thought you only made rings to mark the special battles?" Lina asked, only half joking.

"Trust me," he muttered darkly. "The day I rid the world of that ass, it will be a very special day indeed."

CHAPTER 22
LINA

"Are you sure he didn't know about the vial?" Lina asked Quinn. "He loves fucking with us. Maybe he just wanted to watch me squirm?"

"Trust me, Li," Quinn said, curling her legs up beside her on the oversized armchair. "He couldn't have known. The time between us snatching it and returning here, and then him showing up, is just too tight."

"But that could be the exact same argument as to why he must have known. Maybe he had some sort of spell attached to the vial that brought him to its current location," Lina mused as she paced back and forth in front of Alistair's new fireplace. Her first order of business once they'd stepped inside had been reverting the home back into a cozy living space instead of the Brotherhood's Archive. Unfortunately, the warmth of the roaring fire did little to soothe her frazzled nerves.

"And he just happened to let us keep it, no questions asked? Yeah right. That's not the King of the Underground I know and despise."

Lina's pacing paused, and she bit the side of her nail as she considered Quinn's explanation. "Yeah, I guess so."

"Come and take a seat," Quinn said, patting the cushion next to her. "You're going to wear a path in the lovely carpet you just created, not to mention stress me out if you keep up that pacing much longer."

Lina's eyes dropped to her sock-clad feet. "The carpet's fine."

A pillow hit her square in the face. "Sit. Down. You are driving yourself crazy."

She stared at the cheerful yellow square and sighed. Picking it up, she stomped over to the couch and flopped down with a huff. "Better?" she asked as she tossed the pillow down and pulled her knees to her chest.

Quinn studied her intently. "Not really. You're wound up tighter than a virgin on her wedding night."

Lina propped her chin on her knees. "I'm just worried. So many things could go wrong."

"The hardest part is behind us."

"Ha," Lina said with a snort. "You're just saying that because you're not the one who has to perform the death spell."

"It's not a death spell."

"It may as well be when it kills as many people as it works for."

"Lina . . ."

Her eyes lifted from her toes back to her best friend.

"You're spiraling."

Lina's shoulders slumped. "I know."

"Everything is going to be fine."

"Then why isn't Finley back from the Bunker yet?"

"Because he's only been gone twenty minutes, and it takes time to collect all the things we asked him to?"

"I hate it when you're reasonable."

"Nord should be almost done with his perimeter check or whatever weird alpha commando thing he's off doing, and when he gets back and sees you like this, he's just going to say the same thing I am."

"Yeah, but I'll believe him when he says it."

"Bitch," Quinn snapped, chucking another pillow at her.

Lina laughed and knocked it away before it could hit her. "You know, just because they're named throw pillows doesn't mean you *have* to throw them at me."

"Stop staying stupid shit, and I won't have to."

Quinn's sisterly banter had managed to do what her words of wisdom had not. Lina took her first full breath since they'd made it out of Crombie's. "Thanks," she said softly.

"Don't mention it," Quinn said, resting her elbow on the padded arm of the chair and leaning her head against her fist. "So what's really bothering you?"

"What if it doesn't work?"

"It will."

"Okay, but what if it doesn't?"

"Then I guess you'll both die," Quinn said pragmatically.

"Gee, thanks."

"Is that really so terrible?" Quinn asked.

Lina gave her a look.

"No, seriously, I mean it. You both go out together. You don't have to deal with the Director's or Mikel's hard-on for revenge. Is dying really the worst thing that could happen to you?"

Lina lifted her arm and pointed at the Prism inked into her skin. "I can't die, remember? Not really. And turning back into a ghost, existing alone in a world without him is pretty much one of the worst outcomes I could imagine."

"You've got me there," Quinn admitted.

"You are supremely terrible at this."

Quinn shrugged. "I'll say a lot of things, Li. But I won't lie to you just so you can feel better. Our situation's fucked, but you know that. It has been for a long time now. My lying about it isn't going to change that. But I will say, for the first time in a really long time, I truly believe we're going to get through this."

"You do?" Lina asked, her heart lifting at the sheer conviction she heard in her friend's voice.

"I do. The Codex changed the game. If this goes the way I believe in the very marrow of my bones that it will, then you and Nord are going to become the most powerful pieces on the board."

"Perhaps, but we'll still be just two people. The Director and Mikel have entire armies behind them."

"Maybe. But I'd bet on you and your power over their numbers every single time."

Lina smiled and shook her head, finding it hard to understand Quinn's unwavering belief in her, when a thump from the other room had both women turning their heads to the doorway.

"He's back," Lina said, her heart speeding up as little tingles of electricity ran up her arms and back.

"It's showtime," Quinn said.

Finley walked into the room and dumped a duffle bag onto the coffee table before stepping back and running a hand over the back of his head.

"It went okay?" Lina asked, tossing him a glance as she started to unzip the heavy black bag. "You were able to get everything on the list?"

Finley nodded. "And a few extras I thought might come in handy."

"Thanks, Fin. You're a saint."

He smirked. "I've been called a lot of things, most justified, but I'm pretty sure that's not one of them."

"So," Quinn said, rubbing her hands together as Lina started setting out ingredients onto the table, "where do you want to do this?"

"Alistair said it needs to be performed under the stars. Something about heavenly light bearing witness to the offering."

"Does this place have a backyard?" Quinn asked, craning around in search of a window that might provide her with an answer.

"No, but there's a little park just across the street," Finley answered.

"I'm not sure we really want to start performing anything that might constitute witchcraft out in the open. Didn't they burn people at the stake for that?" Lina asked.

"Yeah, in the 17th century," Quinn answered with a laugh.

"Still, best not to risk it," Lina said. "People tend to freak out about that kind of thing."

"What's your other option? The roof?" Quinn returned. "We don't have the best track record with rooftops."

Lina pressed her lips together, fighting against a shudder as the vision of Nord being struck by lightning flashed through her mind. No, they definitely didn't. Then she shoved the memory aside with a sigh. But they also didn't have another choice.

"I mean, it's not the worst idea," Lina said slowly. "Unless you think an open window with moonlight streaming in might count."

"Do you really want to take a shortcut with all that's at stake?" Finley asked.

"Definitely not," Lina said, her legs bouncing with nervous energy. "Roof it is."

The sound of footsteps on stairs heralded Nord's return just as Finley said, "You only have an hour at most left before dawn. Are you sure you want to attempt this right now?"

Lina carefully set the purple bottle down in the center of the rest of the ingredients and then sat back and wrung her hands together. "Honestly, no. But I really don't see another choice. Crombie proved easily enough that we can be found at any moment. The longer we wait, the greater the chance someone else finds us too. An hour could be the difference between pulling this off or not. So ready or not, this has to happen now."

Her eyes met Nord's as she finished speaking. His arms were crossed, and he was leaning against the wall.

"I agree."

Finley's hands were on his hips, his head bowed as he blew out a breath. "All right. What do we need to do?"

Lina had read and reread her uncle's notes enough times that she knew the steps of the ritual by heart, but even so, she pulled the copy of it she'd transcribed from her pocket and smoothed it out over the table.

"It's pretty straightforward, as far as instructions go. We set a few things around the silver chalice and then add the rest of the ingredients into it, adding the Tears last. Once that's done, Nord and I speak some words in unison, and each take a drink of our magic potion."

"There's no chanting? No painting your bodies with magic symbols?" Quinn asked, leaning forward and trying to read Lina's notes upside down.

"A spell doesn't need to be a spectacle to be effective," Finley said, taking a seat on the arm of the sofa.

"No, of course not," Quinn agreed with a frown. "I just expected something this life-changing to have a bit more to it. Seems a little too easy to get off with just having to say the magic phrase and drink a potion."

Finley pointed at the items lined up on the table. "There is nothing easy about what the combination of those is going to put these two through."

"The potion is a catalyst," Nord added. "The magic is what happens after it's consumed."

Quinn blanched. "Maybe I spoke too soon."

"Do you two need to be the ones to mix everything together?" Finley suddenly asked.

Lina checked her notes. "No. Why?"

He looked at Nord, then back at her. "You guys could probably use a minute alone before we get started. Quinn and I will take this upstairs and get everything ready. May I?" he asked, holding his hand out for the instructions.

"Of course," Lina murmured, handing it over while Quinn gathered up everything Lina had so carefully set out.

That done, she stood and headed out of the room, pausing just outside to give Lina a parting look, which she interpreted as "Good luck."

"Come up and join us on the roof when you're ready," Finley said.

"Thanks, brother," Nord said, placing a hand on the other man's shoulder as he walked past.

Then they were alone.

Other than venting his frustration about Crombie, Nord had been pretty quiet since they agreed to go through with the Transference. Lina didn't believe for a second that he was doubting his choice, but she couldn't help but wonder what was going on in that head of his.

"You ready for this?" she asked, slowly pushing to her feet.

One side of his mouth quirked up. "To be bound to you irrevocably for all eternity? Why wouldn't I be? I made you a similar vow once. Was it not enough to prove myself?"

Lina laughed and rolled her eyes. "Our circumstances have changed a bit since then. Eternity is a pretty big commitment when both of us could potentially live forever. Though, if you got fed up with me, you could always ask Finley to send you to another world for a decade or so. Just because our souls are going to merge—or whatever is about to happen—doesn't mean that we have to spend every second with each other."

"Come here," he demanded.

Lina obeyed, not because it was an order, but because being beside him was where she always wanted to be. "Animagi aren't necessarily immortal, you know," she warned him as she wrapped her arms around his waist and rested her head against his chest. "Alistair suggested it, but I haven't seen mention of it in the Codex. To be fair, I haven't finished reading through everything, and a few parts are still untranslated, but it seems more like a possibility than a guarantee."

"Immortality is not all it's cracked up to be. Life holds more meaning when it's temporary," he replied, his chest rumbling beneath her ear as he spoke. "Or when you have someone to spend it with."

"Well, however long we have. Minutes," her voice caught on the word since it was a very real possibility, "or millennia, I'd be lucky to spend them with you."

Nord pressed a kiss to the top of her head, his hand moving soothingly against her spine. "Speaking of souls, did you know my people didn't believe in them? At least, not by your modern definition."

"No?" Lina asked, tilting her head back to look at him. "What did they believe?"

Nord played with the ends of her hair. "What you refer to as the soul—a singular entity—we believed to be composed of many parts, some which could leave us while we still lived. Each part was responsible for something different, but all were equally vital to our understanding of ourselves and our place in the world. So for me, it makes sense that my soul would be faceted, and you one of its pieces."

The beauty of the sentiment robbed her of words. Lina had always loved the idea of soul mates—that there was someone out there made just for her. But she never believed in them. Not until Nord.

She actually preferred his explanation of it to her own under-standing. That she was a vital, fundamental part of himself that affected the way he saw and viewed his own place in the world. Because that's what he was for her. They didn't need a spell for that. It simply was.

"I feel the same way about you," she said, pressing a kiss to his chest over the steady thump of his heart.

He gave her hair a little tug to bring her eyes back up to his. "Then whatever happens next is merely a formality."

All of her lingering doubt evaporated then and there. Because he was right. They were already connected in the deepest, most funda-mental way. Acquiring additional power, while nice, couldn't touch that truth.

Whether that made them more or less worthy of the Ancient

Ones' gift, Lina couldn't say. But she no longer feared their judgment.

Lifting up on her toes, she wrapped her arms around his neck and pressed her lips to his. "Should we get up there and get it over with then?"

Nord shifted, easily supporting her weight as he lifted her up. Lina instinctively wrapped her legs around his waist and tightened her hold.

"Let them wait a little longer," Nord murmured, a second before his lips landed hungrily on hers.

***

"Do you want to do the honors?" Finley asked, holding the purple vial out to her.

Lina was about to say no but hesitated and reconsidered. It felt right, somehow, that she would be the one to add the last ingredient. "Sure," she said.

Finley handed her the small bottle, and Lina was no less surprised by its innate warmth even though she was coming to expect it.

"Just one drop," he warned her.

"I know, Fin. I've got the spell memorized."

He offered her an apologetic smile. "Of course. We'll be right over there," he said.

They both knew there wasn't much he could do once the spell took hold, but she appreciated the sentiment regardless.

"Thanks, Fin," she said, giving him a quick hug, her eyes meeting Quinn's over his shoulder.

They'd said everything they needed to say downstairs, so they just exchanged small smiles as Finley pulled away to turn to Nord. After a long look and a quick nod, he joined Quinn and leaned against the rooftop's half-wall.

"Here goes," Lina said, mostly to herself, as she uncapped the gilded topper.

A tiny bead of molten silver flashed in the moonlight. She'd expected the liquid to be clear, perhaps because of its name, so the opaque and metallic nature of it caught her off guard. Her hand shook slightly, and only Nord's lightning-fast reflexes ensured that the drop splashed into the chalice and not onto the ground.

"Close one," she said with a nervous chuckle.

"Just breathe," Nord said, his deep voice reassuring.

Lina forced herself to take a deep breath in and out while she recapped the vial and placed it back in her pocket.

"Okay, now we each hold the chalice and lift it up to the stars," Lina said, cupping her hand around the stem of the ornate goblet, her palm pressed against the intricate design. At the same time, her fingers curled over the back of Nord's hand.

Once she had a firm grasp, they raised their offering up between them.

"And now we look into each other's eyes—"

A sharp thrill ran through her as his icy gaze caught hers, though there was nothing cold about it. The pure trust and love she found reflected in his gaze anchored Lina and reinforced her own.

"—and make our plea."

Lina breathed in and began to speak, Nord's deep voice wrapping around her own as he joined in.

The words were ancient and lyrical. Beautiful in a way that could not be replicated, only experienced, though their meaning had been completely lost to time. She'd worried it would be awkward attempting to form the foreign combination of vowels and conso-nants, but once she started, they flowed from her lips as if part of her native tongue. And perhaps, since it was the language of the first animagi, in a way it was.

With the final word of the invocation echoing around them, Lina realized that their breathing was perfectly in sync. Before she could wonder whether that was a coincidence, Nord lowered the chalice and held it up to her lips.

Still holding his gaze over the rim of the cup, she swallowed deep. The flavors were a confusing tangle, heady like wine but herbal like tea. It wasn't until she lifted the cup for Nord to drain the rest of the liquid that the heat ignited within her chest. And then, like an inferno, the heat exploded up and out until her breath caught and burned away.

Her world narrowed to a single pinprick of color as the rooftop faded. The icy blue reminded her of frost and glaciers, and then . . . home.

Lina's awareness shifted then. It wasn't color she was seeing; it was a vibrant wash of emotion. All of them, all at once. Joy, heartache, pain—so much pain. None of it hers, all of it consuming her.

Faces swam through her consciousness, their lips moving but their words silent. Silent, and yet she somehow knew exactly what they were saying. As if these people she had never met spoke their words of love, support, and condemnation to her.

One face crystalized, and her heart felt like it might shatter. *Móðir. Mother.* Not hers. Nord's.

She was laughing. Her white-blonde hair braided, her eyes crinkled and shining, hands ushering two teenage boys away from her workspace. The younger of the two scampered off. The older was slower, his mother's arm banding around him to pull him back as she pressed a warm kiss to his cheek. She smelled of sea and fire, and the brief moment of affection filled the boy on the brink of manhood with happiness. Though he feigned annoyance as he shoved her away.

Happiness cut through Lina like glass, its shards catching and snagging, making her bleed as the truth resonated deep within her.

It was the last time he ever saw her alive.

The world tilted again, the scene shifting as easily as a wave being pulled back into the ocean. As the next image—the next memory—crashed over her, this one filled her not with bittersweet joy but an anger that burned so hot she couldn't breathe around it.

War raged around her, and the sounds of battle assaulted her. Weapons crashing together. Men and women screaming. In this place, chaos reigned.

The need for blood surged through her veins, pushing her forward, giving her strength. A hand reached out, grasping her leg—no, not her leg. Nord's. This time instead of seeing him, she *was* him.

"Please," the blood-smeared face begged. "Mercy."

An answering growl rattled in her chest. She could feel the strength of her muscles as she heaved her weapon up and brought it down.

"The only mercy you deserve is death," she said, her voice coming out in Nord's deep snarl as she removed her weapon from the now still body, the hand clamped around her ankle falling limp.

Instead of finding relief, or even revulsion, from the utter brutality of the act, her fury only grew. Spurred her on. She wouldn't—couldn't—stop until the last of her enemies fell beneath her blade.

There was another shift. Another flash of Nord's past taking hold and forcing her to experience it as he once had. She was strapped to a chair. She bit the inside of her cheek until she tasted blood, the pain of the act helping her hold on to consciousness as a man demanded that she answer his questions. *The Director.* Lina knew what was about to happen, and the part of her that was still her rebelled against this memory. She didn't want it. Didn't think she could survive what she knew was coming.

But there was no stopping it.

When the Guardian tore through her mind with his power, shredding her will and tearing apart her very essence, she couldn't even scream past it. There was no escape. Only pain.

So much pain.

The agony of it seared through her. Cutting her open and pouring out of her until she existed only in a sea of blinding white.

That's when Lina knew. She'd just been unmade.

CHAPTER 23
NORD

Nord was no stranger to powerful magic. He'd been reborn from it more times than he cared to count. Not just when joining—and unceremoniously leaving—the Brotherhood. But when his physical body had been pushed beyond its natural limits, and only magic could stitch it back together.

As the spell took hold, he knew better than to fight its seductive pull. It wasn't easy to give in. To allow himself to be vulnerable to a force so far outside his control. But that lowering of his will, that small act of submission, he knew better than most how it could make all the difference when power such as this was at play. And he couldn't risk anything that might adversely affect the outcome of this particular spell. Not when her life was on the line.

So he gave in.

The warrior who learned to never back down, never show weakness, did just that.

For her.

Heat preceded the sweeping away of his ability to control his own body. It started as a soothing warmth that blossomed out from his chest and morphed into a sharp, inescapable sting. The sensation wasn't painful exactly, but it was far from comfortable. In a way, it reminded him of having the tip of a blade pressed against his throat. While the hold wasn't intense enough to draw blood, it was absolutely a warning. One wrong move could change everything in a heartbeat.

As the heat built, Nord lost all awareness of his physical self, the roof he was standing on, the chalice clattering to the ground, and even the woman standing in front of him. There was only this sense of rapidly expanding outward and then hanging there. Suspended. Looming. Observing.

That's when the kaleidoscope of images began to swirl and take shape. Having delved through others' minds countless times, he knew immediately what he was experiencing: memories.

None of which were his.

Given their clarity, these weren't just random snapshots selected without thought either. These were the turning points. The defining moments. The kind that shaped a life—for better or for worse.

A part of him rebelled and longed to turn away. To stop. Not because he might not like what he saw—it had nothing to do with his feelings at all—but because a person should have a choice whether or not they revealed these jagged, often broken pieces of themselves to another.

And yet, even knowing that, some inner voice warned him not to —though the voice he heard was not his. It was familiar, however, calling to mind a world of mist and a warning that to be worthy, he could not give in to his fear.

Stay, it whispered, beckoning him deeper. *Watch.*

Become.

Remembering the razor's edge on which he currently danced, Nord obeyed.

As always, the initial moments when he became someone else were jarring. His psyche still superimposed over theirs, making him feel like a voyeur rather than an active participant. But it faded as he sank deeper until he ultimately lost the ability to distinguish who he was from what was taking place around him.

Lina's emotions came first, cementing him in the scene and becoming his own. Shame, embarrassment, and the need for approval.

For love.

They tore at him, making him wish to be anywhere but here. Knowing he'd failed again. That he would never be anything more than a disappointment to the man on the other side of the desk.

His shoulders were curved inward, chin nearly touching his chest, as if he could disappear if only he made his body small enough.

"It should have been you."

Nord—as a young Lina—jerked, the pain of the words hurting more than if the blow had been a physical one. He gasped, hearing Lina's heartbroken voice as he said, "Papa, you don't mean that—"

"That I wish you had died instead of her? I've never meant anything more. Go. Get out of my sight. You disgust me."

The image rippled and wavered, like someone had run their fingers across the surface of water. He was ripped out of the memory, but the lingering emotions were slower to fade as the next scene took shape.

A sense of dread built deep within him as it came into view. This memory he recognized, if only because of Lina's vivid recounting. As each second ticked by, he knew exactly what would come next.

The dark basement with its flickering candles. The sound of footsteps approaching from behind and the wet scrape of a tongue sliding up his cheek. The sharp press of a dagger into his chest. The sound of Lina's screams ringing in his ears until everything fell silent.

There was a fleeting moment of lucidity, where Nord consciously reached for his berserker in response to Lina's fear and pain, even though they'd already dealt with that particular threat.

But his inner monster lay dormant, inaccessible to him here.

As the world swirled and distorted a third time, Nord braced himself, anticipating the worst as the next memory began to crystalize. So far, the spell had only seen fit to shove him into the worst, most brutal memories. Why should this one be any different?

And yet somehow, it was.

For one thing, he had no body. For another, it wasn't a single, static moment, but a series of them strung together. The only constant as the world changed around him was the overwhelming sense of loneliness. Time went on, but he remained the same. Separate and apart from everything and everyone.

While these memories were nothing like the others, they were no less brutal. The desire to be seen, to be heard, was so acute he ached with it.

He'd tasted despair enough times in his own life. But never like this. For all her jokes of roommates and reality TV with no off button, Lina's time as a ghost was the cruelest joke of all. A prison sentence with no escape.

Nord had thought he'd understood what Lina had gone through, but there was no comprehending the reality. Not until he'd lived it himself.

With that thought came a fundamental shift within him. Like someone had turned a light on, and he could finally see something that had been right in front of him, but always just out of view, hidden by the shadows.

He saw it clearly now. He saw *her* clearly now.

And what he saw was beauty in its purest, rawest form. Every perfectly imperfect piece.

Electricity crackled through his veins, the sensation lighting him up from the inside out. The feeling built, the intensity ratcheting up beyond what should have been an endurable level. If he would have been in control of his physical form, he'd have dropped to his knees and cried out. Assuming he had any breath left to make such a sound. As it was, all he could do was exist through the molten heat surging through him.

The sparking energy reached its pinnacle, and Nord felt the way a star must feel at the end, in those last few milliseconds before implosion. First, there was a drawing in and rapid collision of every discernable part of himself. Then a frozen intake of breath when time went absolutely still. And finally, the thundering boom when it cranked back up and all of those ping-ponging molecules burst outward in a supernova of earth-shattering proportions. It was the death of everything that had once been and the creation of something completely new but no less powerful.

As the feeling of being scattered throughout the universe started to fade, Nord slowly returned to himself. His heart felt sluggish, as if someone had turned it off and it was trying to restart but had to pump peanut butter instead of blood. His breath scratched at his throat and his lungs seized as they struggled to function. But despite the ongoing trials of his internal organs, the rest of his body stood motionless.

Lina's stunned eyes peered into his, and he knew without her saying a word she was experiencing the exact same thing.

"Uh, guys?" Quinn asked in a stage whisper. "Everything okay over there?"

"Did it work?" Finley asked, taking a hesitant step forward.

Nord ignored them.

Still not feeling entirely in control of his own body, Nord lifted the hand that had been holding the now-forgotten chalice. Across from him, Lina did the same, her movements smooth and sure. Never once looking away from each other, they reached forward, like they were performing a choreographed dance and their muscles knew the steps even if their brains did not.

"Guys? What's going on?" Quinn asked, her voice pitched high with her mounting concern.

When there was less than a millimeter separating their hands, that electric energy that tore through him crackled between their palms.

Then they were touching.

At first, there was only the feel of her skin sliding against his, but as their fingers locked, the lightning crashed into him once more, and the only thing keeping him upright was Lina's grasp on his hand.

His head flew back, and power pulsed outward with the force of an atomic bomb. He expected the shockwave to be accompanied by the sight of smoke and flames, or even that intangible lightning, but there was nothing overhead except the last glimmer of the night's stars.

Then, with a soft hitch of breath—both his and Lina's—it was done.

As his head tipped forward, his eyes found hers once more.

"Are you all right?" he asked.

Her tongue darted out to wet her lips, and her chest rose and fell with rapid breaths. After a few seconds, she nodded. "And you?"

"Fine."

There was a low grunt beside them. "Why is it that I always seem to be picking myself up off of the floor thanks to you?" Quinn asked with a groan.

Nord finally turned to glance at the place Quinn and Finley had been standing, only to find them on opposite sides of the roof, both knocked flat on their backs, though they were in the process of pushing themselves up into sitting positions.

Finley lifted his hand from the back of his head with a curse, the dark smear of blood across his fingers visible even in the dim light. "Bloody hell." He let out a wheezing laugh as he gave Nord and Lina a quick once-over before turning his attention to Quinn. "I think we might have spoken too soon, love."

"Next time we decide to experiment with magic, I'm keeping watch from behind closed doors. Or a military barricade," Quinn said as she started to stand.

"Here, let me help you," Lina said, finally dropping Nord's hand as she rushed over to Quinn's side.

Even though he wasn't ready to let her go, Nord didn't resist and used the freedom to go to Finley.

Quinn lifted her hand, waving Lina off. "I'm not sure I want you touching me right now. No offense." She brushed her dark hair off her face as she looked at Nord with a quirked brow. "I saw what happened last time."

Nord was already grasping Finley by the forearm and deftly helped him stand.

Lina scrunched her nose up and gestured toward the two men. "See, there's nothing to worry about—"

"All the same. I've got this," Quinn said, proving her words true as she stood up and then immediately leaned on the roof's half-wall. "Jesus, you really knocked the wind out of me that time." She peered intently at Lina. "How are you feeling, by the way?"

Lina shrugged. "Fine."

Quinn squinted. "Fine?"

"Well . . . yeah."

"How is that possible?"

"What do you mean?"

Quinn sighed loudly. "Do you want to help me out here?" she called to Finley, though her eyes never left her friend.

"I think what she's trying to ask is, how is it you two were at the epicenter of that power surge and are completely unharmed, while we were just the bystanders and both feel like we just had our asses handed to us?" Finley asked, his eyes moving curiously over Nord.

Nord would have thought the check merely cursory if not for the glint of familiar silver light shining in his friend's eyes.

"What do you see?" he asked, his voice pitched low.

Finley's brow was furrowed as they returned to Nord's. "You look the same."

Nord performed a quick internal inspection, realizing now that the aftershocks of the spell had subsided, he felt completely normal. Just as he had before they kicked things off. But since both he and Lina were still standing here, very much alive, the spell must have worked, so how was that possible? To be touched and changed by that kind of power *must* have left a trace.

"You can't see the remnants of the spell's magic at all?" he asked, his brows dipping low.

"I didn't say that, mate. I said you look the same. This place, however, is dripping in residual magic. That burst you two just set off might as well have been a damn beacon. You know as well as I do that there's no hiding our whereabouts now. They may not be looking this way yet, but the Mobius Council, just like the Brotherhood, has eyes everywhere. They'll find out about this soon enough. And when they do . . ." Finley didn't need to voice the rest.

The unspoken words rang loud and clear in Nord's mind regardless. *They'll be coming for us.*

He growled low in his throat, the looming threat more real than ever. They'd had a target on their back from the moment Lina set foot back in this world and Nord chose to defy everything to help her. It had always been a matter of time before others came gunning for them. So while tonight's events hadn't really changed their situation, it may very well have just upped the timeline.

And unfortunately for the four of them, they were out of places to hide.

CHAPTER 24
LINA

Lina had never been ignorant about the power of physical contact. Having existed for so long without it, she knew just how essential it could be.

In some ways, it felt like the entire course of her life had changed with just one touch. That first exquisite slide of Nord's calloused finger down her spine as he wiped away the beer he'd spilled. Not even when he'd pulled her body against his for their first dance had he anchored her to him more thoroughly.

Without a doubt, other forces were at play that night. The culmination of Quinn and Alistair's spell, the magic that brought them to the ball itself, fate, destiny, whatever you want to call it, it was undeniably there.

But the truth was, for Lina, her life started with that touch.

Tonight, it seemed that would be the case again.

Lina had always had an innate awareness of Nord. She could feel when he was looking at her or sense when he'd entered a room. But that was nothing compared to what she was feeling now. Ever since their hands connected on that rooftop, her awareness of him turned into a tangible thing. Like a rubber band stretched taut between them, and the further apart they were, the greater the ache in her chest.

Now, it wasn't just his presence that she could sense, but his emotions as well. Not like when they were under the effects of the spell and his mind had been fully open to hers. She couldn't hear his thoughts or see his memories, but she could feel the echo of what he was feeling.

And right now, Nord was worried—which meant that Lina was worried.

She wouldn't have known it by looking at him. Which she did, frequently. Her eyes kept finding reasons to return to him. The slight zing of awareness that shot through her every now and then told her it was the same for him.

Right now, though, his expression was untroubled, his body language relaxed as he sprawled in the room's oversized armchair, his attention focused on whatever Quinn and Finley were saying.

The lack of outward admission regarding his unease was what really concerned her. Because if Nord wasn't willing to give voice to it, it meant that whatever ate at him was big, and he didn't know what to do about it.

What Lina couldn't figure out, though, was whether the concern was new or if it had always been there, and she simply hadn't known it until now.

"Li? You coming?"

Lina blinked and realized the others were all standing. "Coming where?"

Quinn laughed. "To bed. Did you hear anything we said in the last half hour?"

Lina flushed, embarrassed to have to admit that she hadn't really been paying attention. She'd been too focused on trying to figure out what was bothering Nord and waiting for some indication that the Transference had actually worked.

Since neither of them appeared to be dead, she could only infer that it had. But until she or Nord showed signs of their newfound animagi abilities, neither of them could be truly sure. The first thing they'd each done when they'd gotten back inside was tried to summon some magic. Nord hadn't been successful, and though Lina had managed to play around with the room's furnishings some more, it wasn't anything she hadn't been able to manage prior to attempting the spell.

Having just gone through her Awakening and knowing that there was an adjustment period between acquiring power and being able to harness it, Lina wasn't overly surprised by the revelation. None of them were.

That didn't mean they weren't all a little disappointed, though.

It was also why she'd been so inwardly focused. She was on the lookout for the first sign that either of their new powers was about to emerge. No matter how subtle the sign might be.

"I'm not even sure I could fall asleep right now," Lina said. The yawn that immediately followed her declaration made the others laugh.

"Come on," Nord said, with a soft smile playing about his lips. Holding out a hand, he helped her back to her feet, murmuring as he did, "Bedtime for you."

He might be eager to get her in bed, but Lina didn't believe for a second that sleep was what he had in mind. Apparently, neither did Quinn.

"Can you guys at least try to keep it down tonight?"

"Since when are you a prude?" Lina teased, curling herself around Nord.

"Since I can't remember the last time I had eight hours of uninterrupted sleep."

"Who says nights are for sleeping?" Nord asked, his hand roaming possessively down Lina's back.

She could feel color creeping into her face and was suddenly much more eager to get to bed.

"Well, if I spent my nights the way you two do, maybe I'd care less," Quinn said with a laugh. "But since my bed is cold and lonely, the most I can hope for are sweet dreams."

Lina looked to Finley, waiting for him to deliver one of his usual flirty lines. But he surprised her.

"She makes a good point," he said. His eyes gleamed with amusement, but his expression was serious as he added, "We should probably make the most of the quiet while we can. There's no telling how long it will last."

Lina could only assume Finley had no idea just how prophetic his words would turn out to be.

As they started turning off lights and making their way to the various bedrooms, the first strains of Billie Eilish's "bad guy" cut through the silence. The unexpected music made Lina jump, her heart taking off like a shot.

Quinn started laughing. "Chill you guys, it's just my phone."

Lina pressed a hand to her chest and let out a little laugh, feeling stupid for overreacting. She laughed again when she turned back to Nord and spotted him with a piece of what had once been the stairs' banister in his hand.

"Didn't like my redecorating choices?"

"I needed a weapon."

"And that was your first choice?" she asked with a lift of her brow.

"The item rarely matters. Anything's a weapon when you're a berserker."

"At least this time, it wasn't inflatable."

He smiled slightly at her teasing, but his focus shifted back to Quinn, who now held her cellphone in her hand. Her expression went from confused to worried as she read the screen.

"Who is it?" Lina asked, her own amusement fleeing.

"It's my mom," she said, her eyes shooting up. "Should I answer it?"

"Why wouldn't you?" Lina asked, but even as the question left her lips, the answer came to her.

Cora was part of the Mobius Council. She'd been working with Alistair—with them—behind their back. Keeping secrets. Actively hiding their whereabouts from Mikel, and by extension, the Council as a whole. As one of the group's leaders, there was no bigger betrayal. It wasn't a far leap to think that Mikel might have caught wind of it. That he could be the one on the other end of the line. Especially since Cora made it a point to limit all communication with her daughter.

"Answer it," Nord demanded.

Finley moved to stand beside Quinn, ready to offer his support if she required it. "Put it on speaker," he said, his voice gentler than Nord's by a mile.

There was no hiding the slight tremor in her hand as Quinn pressed the icon and held the phone out between them. Her face took on an eerie cast, lit from below by the phone's glowing screen.

"Mom?"

Lina knew she was trying to keep her voice casual, but she could still detect a quaver in the greeting.

"Quinn," came Cora's frantic cry. "Get out. Now!"

"Mom? What—"

"Run. All of you. There isn't much time. They're already there."

Lina's blood turned to ice. There wasn't time to think, let alone ask anything further, like who was there or how she knew about it. When Cora told you something, you accepted it as fact and went from there.

The phone fell from Quinn's hand as Finley grasped her by the wrist and started pulling her toward the front door.

"Wait," Nord hissed. "Not through the front. They'll be expecting us."

"If they're already here, we're likely surrounded," Finley whispered back. "That's our quickest way out."

"The roof?" Quinn asked, her already pale skin completely leeched of color.

Nord shook his head. "They could already be up there."

A soft thump, followed quickly by a dozen others, seemed to prove him right.

"Well, if we can't use any of the exits, how are we supposed to get out?" Lina asked.

Nord stared hard at the wall. She recognized that considering look in his eye and could feel his sudden surge of fury as if it were her own.

"Nord . . ." Lina said, having only half a second to brace herself before his foot crashed through the wall. Plaster and drywall rained down as he pulled his leg back through the hole he'd created.

"Pretty sure they heard that," Finley said dryly.

Nord grasped pieces of wall in either hand and ripped them free as he created a hole big enough for them to get through. "Probably."

Then he was diving through. Lina was right behind him, Quinn on her heels and Finley bringing up the rear. Thankfully, the building next door seemed to be empty. The furniture was draped with sheets, and all the lights were off. At least they wouldn't have to worry about disgruntled neighbors on top of everything else.

"Are we allowed to use this door?" Quinn asked as she looked around.

Nord considered Quinn's request but shook his head. "Best not. I noticed a basement that opens up to an alleyway when I was doing my rounds earlier. If we can get through there, we might get away before they realize which way we've gone."

One glance at Finley's face told Lina he didn't think the odds of that were very likely.

But their options were to run or sit and wait. And after all they'd already gone through, not one of them had it in them to give up now.

The sound of wood breaking and a rush of footsteps coming down the stairs decided things.

Without a word, Nord shot off toward the back of the house. The others followed, Quinn and Lina exchanging wide-eyed looks as they raced after him.

The stairs leading down to the basement were pitch black, but none of them dared risk a light. They moved as quickly as they dared in the dark, and more than once, Lina's frantic steps had her stumbling over herself or into the person in front of her.

When her feet found flat ground, she let out a small sigh of relief. She blinked a few times, trying to get her eyes to adjust to the darkness when she turned and spotted a soft trickle of early-morning light from the far corner of the room.

There. That was their escape route.

Lina waved her arms, trying to get the others' attention, but it proved unnecessary. Nord was already angling that direction. Reaching out, she grasped the back of his shirt as he moved past her, using him to guide her way. Though her heart was in her throat and her pulse raced in her ears, Lina's mind was calm.

They could do this. They hadn't been caught yet. It wasn't too late.

As Nord eyed the small rectangular window, Lina placed her arm on his bicep.

She started to shake her head. There was no way they could all fit through there. "I can—"

Nord lifted a finger to his lips to silence her. Then he pointed at the window and shook his head.

Lina squinted. If not through the window . . . but then he stepped back, and she saw what she'd missed. Nord had been blocking a cherry-red door.

Checking to make sure they were all ready, he reached for the handle.

She couldn't help but hold her breath as she waited. When he jiggled it and it didn't open, her breath whooshed out in a wave of disappointment.

Locked.

Not that Nord ever let anything as mundane as a door stop him. Without waiting, he dipped down and threw his shoulder into the wood with no little force, knocking the entire frame out of place.

Lina winced at the resulting crack, but there was nothing they could do about it now. Her solution might have been quiet, but she couldn't argue with his speed.

Nord poked his head out, checking the alley before gesturing for the rest of them to step outside. As they all filed out, the sound of slow, mocking applause bounced down the alleyway.

Lina's heart stopped. She squeezed her eyes closed and then turned to face the source of the sound. As she opened her eyes, her mouth fell open in utter shock.

There, standing at the mouth of the alley, was not Mikel Drake and his goons as she'd expected. In fact, it wasn't a group of people at all, as the footsteps chasing them through the house had led her to believe. But the sight of the lone man with his glowing jade eyes didn't diminish the threat.

If anything, it raised it. Because without witnesses, there was no telling what depths the fanatical asshole would sink to.

As if he could read the thought as it formed in her mind—which Lina remembered with dismay he absolutely could—the Director's lips twisted up in a mocking smile.

CHAPTER 25
NORD

"How considerate of you all to come to me."

Nord ground his teeth together as the Director's voice boomed in his mind. For a man who could wield his gift with the careful finesse of a surgeon using a scalpel, he chose instead to toss it like a grenade and inflict the most damage possible.

"Those wards were an inconvenience I didn't want to have to waste energy on. So thank you for making this so easy."

Rather than acknowledge the man, Nord surveyed his surroundings, making mental notes of where the others stood and what objects, if any, he might be able to use to his benefit. But other than a couple of rubbish bins and the odd plastic bag or gum wrapper, there wasn't much.

That was all right, though. As he'd told Lina, anything could be a weapon when you were a berserker.

Moving so his body shielded Lina's, he welcomed his building rage and stared the Director down. "I told you what would happen if you came after me."

"Yes, yes. You'll kill me." The Director waved a hand as if the threat was no more worrisome than a fly buzzing about his head. *"You'll have to forgive me if I'm not overly worried. I mean—"* The flood of words broke off as a low chuckle replaced them. *"—well, we've danced before, you and I. And I bested you then. So why would a Guardian ever fear his inferior? For that's what you are, Gunnar, inferior in every possible way."*

Nord growled as the rage swelled. He could feel Lina move closer to him and then the gentle brush of her fingertips against his back—her silent warning not to let the man's goading get to him.

"Only a weak man or one who feared what I could do in a fair fight would need to strip me of my power and tether me to a chair in order to beat me."

The Director tipped his head to the side, that damned smile still playing about his lips. *"What fight could ever be fair between two such as us? Stripped or not, your power was never any match for mine, and your brawn is insignificant when I can defeat you with little more than a thought."*

"Prove it."

"Nord," Finley hissed. He alone knew just how true the Director's taunt was.

But it didn't matter. He'd made the man a promise. And he intended to keep it.

As Nord called on his fury to fuel him, Quinn darted forward, her voice low and hypnotic.

"You don't want to—"

The Director barely spared her a glance as his laugh rolled through their minds. *"Cute."*

His green eyes flashed, and Quinn dropped to her knees, her scream shrill and endless as she lifted her hands to cover her ears.

"Stop it, you coward," Finley shouted as he ran to her. "A true Guardian would never use his power against an innocent."

"Innocent? Her? Do you even know who you owe your allegiance to anymore?"

Finley crouched beside a still screaming Quinn. Wrapping an arm around her, he pulled her body into his. "It's okay. I'm here. It's not real." He continued his soft murmuring, his eyes glowing silver as he tried to access his power to chip away at whatever the Director was doing to Quinn's mind.

"Stop it. You're hurting her," Lina cried.

"That was quite the point."

Lina tried to push past Nord, her expression murderous as she lunged toward the Director. "You dickless piece of shit! You like to fight women? Let's go."

The Director's bushy red brows lifted. *"Now that's an interesting proposition."*

The time for trading insults was long over. Nord would never allow Lina to fight this battle for him, nor could he give this pathetic excuse for a man the chance to harm her. There was little Nord could offer in the way of protection from an attack on her mind, save stopping it before it started.

"This one's mine," Nord gritted out, pushing her back as gently as he could manage.

He could see the need for blood shining in her eyes, but she gave him a jerky nod and staggered over to Quinn and Finley.

"Touching."

Knowing the others were—mostly—safe for the time being, Nord set his berserker free. He surged forward with a bestial roar, his arm cocked back and ready to deliver the first blow only to come up short as pain exploded behind his eyes.

The Director hadn't so much as blinked, and yet he'd unleashed a psychic attack so powerful Nord could already feel warm blood dripping from his nose and ears. Thankfully, his rage blunted enough of the pain that he could remain upright.

Spitting out a mouthful of blood, Nord fought hard to focus on the man a few feet away. Even though there were several other versions of him now weaving in and out of view.

"Too scared to fight me like a real man?"

"Big words coming from a man who can barely stand."

Nord wiped the back of his hand across his mouth, knowing the move only smeared more of the bright red blood across his face and beard. "Your little tricks may slow me, but nothing save death will stop me."

"I can make that happen."

"Are you sure about that? Because from here, it looks like you're too afraid to take me on equal footing."

There was the slightest flinch, a narrowing just about the eyes, that told Nord he'd struck a nerve. *"You and I will never be equals."*

Nord shrugged, hoping the move looked nonchalant as spots swam before his eyes. "Maybe not. But that should only make things easier for you, no?"

There was a sharp exhale, and Nord knew he had him. His words were meant to appeal to the man he used to be. The brawler who once built a living on violence and bloodshed. A man like that could hardly resist the temptation of taking on, and besting, a berserker.

At least that's what Nord was betting on. And as the Director removed his suit jacket and began to roll up the sleeves of his pristine white shirt, it looked like his bet was about to pay off.

"Fine. Have it your way. I don't care how I execute you, Gunnar Bloodaxe. Only that you cease to exist by the time I'm through. Just remember when you plead for mercy that you asked for this." Finished with his sleeves, the Director cocked his head to the side and gave Nord a smile as bloodthirsty as his own. *"You aren't the only one who enjoys bloodying your hands."*

The pain in his head disappeared so quickly, Nord staggered from the sudden shift, leaving him completely open to the Director's next attack. His fist collided with Nord's jaw, sending his face swinging to the side as more blood arced through the air.

A red haze clouded his vision as Nord slowly craned his neck back to the other man, noting both the blood and the silver glint of knuckle-dusters on the Director's fist. He had to give it to him; he was fast. Both with his attack and his use of magic. Nord hadn't even noticed he'd created the weapons.

"The first one was free," Nord snarled, slamming his fist into the Director's nose with every bit of his anger behind the punch. "The rest won't come as easy," he promised as the other man's head snapped back.

Nord didn't give him a chance to recover before raining a series of blows on him, including a powerful palm-strike to his solar plexus. By the time the Director managed to push Nord off, he wasn't smiling any longer. But Nord was.

The metallic flash in his periphery was Nord's only warning. He jumped back just as the Director swiped at his face with a knife.

Once again, he'd missed the other man's use of magic. Since he was currently without the ability to create any weapons of his own, he'd have to keep the man on the defensive to prevent him from gaining any sort of upper hand with his power.

Challenge accepted.

Nord bent low, rushing forward and aiming for the Director's knees, hoping to tackle him and take their fight to the ground. But the Director was fast—whether from years of experience or his enhanced abilities—and he dove over Nord, landing behind him.

Nord spun around, knowing better than to give the man his back. This time he didn't quite dodge the blade as it sliced through his arm.

He heard Lina's muffled cry, his eyes seeking her out even though he could hardly afford the distraction. Finley was holding her back, whispering fiercely in her ear as she struggled to break his hold. Quinn was unconscious on the ground beside them.

"Kill him," Lina mouthed, her eyes frantic, her fingers digging into the arm Finley had banded about her as she continued to fight his hold.

Gladly.

Cracking his neck, Nord took two running steps and kicked out, his foot coming down on the side of the Director's knee. His limb bent inward, his bones breaking with a sickening crack. The sound was a familiar and welcome one, but nothing was sweeter than when the Director audibly cried out.

The sound of his physical voice versus his mental one was like a shot of pure adrenaline to Nord's system. He grasped the man's shoulder and shoved him forward. Unable to support his weight because of his busted knee, the Director fell to the ground. He managed to shoot his arms out to catch himself, but Nord was on him immediately, pressing him into the wet ground with a hand on his neck.

With his free hand, he reached for the discarded plastic bag he'd spied earlier.

Anything can be a weapon.

Taking one side of the bag in his mouth, he used his hand to twist it, creating a makeshift garrote. Then in a lightning-fast series of moves, he released the Director's neck, slid his hand around to grasp him by the forehead, and pulled him back while bringing his other arm in front of the man's face. That done, he let go of the Director and grabbed the free end of his new weapon, wrapping it once around his fist before pulling it taut.

The Director gasped for breath, his hands coming up to claw at the bag wrapped around his neck. Just a bit longer, and he'd be disabled enough for Nord to finish him for good.

But he'd made a critical error. He'd underestimated his opponent.

The Director went slack, and Nord relaxed his grip. Not by much, but just enough that the other man could rear his head back and slam it into Nord's already injured nose. The momentum of the blow sent him back, and it wasn't until he felt the metal sliding into either side of his stomach that he realized the Director had used his distracted state to gift himself with another set of blades.

And he didn't stop there.

Nord should have known the man would never play fair once it was clear he couldn't win.

Pain lanced his head, robbing him of his vision and his breath. As more wet warmth dripped down his neck, Nord was half-convinced his brain was actually melting.

He fell back, the psychic attack rendering him momentarily paralyzed as he tried to work through the all-encompassing pain. His rage worked hard to boil it away, but the Director was relentless, sending wave after agonizing wave at him, leaving him with no relief.

That small window was all the Director needed. Nord knew how quickly the tides could turn when you were facing a skilled opponent. And no matter how much he hated the man, he had to admit, the Director was definitely skilled.

Twisting beneath him, the Director shoved Nord off and pushed himself up. Nord's muscles locked up, like whatever was tearing through his brain had also taken control of the rest of his body. He was helpless to do anything but lie there as the Director awkwardly made his way to his feet.

The Director pulled one of the daggers free from Nord's stomach, but Nord wouldn't have registered the action at all if he hadn't seen it happening. It was hard to focus on anything outside of the pain in his head.

Tossing the knife up, the Director's voice sounded in his mind. *"I expected more, to be honest. Pity that was the best you could do."*

Then he caught the weapon, though it was a dagger no longer. He'd changed it in the air, his Guardian magic turning it into something new and strangely familiar.

Nord couldn't place it. Not at first.

It wasn't until the hammer came careening down straight at his face that he recognized the Norse symbol. *Tor*. His father's rune. His father's *weapon*. It had been one of his favorites.

The bastard was about to kill him using his father's war hammer.

A roar built in his chest, pushing past everything and giving Nord a small burst of energy that staved off the worst of the ongoing psychic attack.

But it was too late.

The Director's strike landed true, the head of the hammer crashing into Nord's face before he could move out of the way.

The last thing Nord registered as the world went black was the sound of Lina's scream.

CHAPTER 26
LINA

"No," Lina shouted as Nord's body went limp. "Get up. Get up!"

Nord didn't twitch so much as a finger.

Even as she stared in mounting horror at Nord's unmoving body, she couldn't make herself believe it. Everything had happened so fast. One second, the Director's eyes were bulging and his face turning purple from lack of oxygen. The next, he's standing over Nord's supine form, swinging a giant hammer at his face.

It had been hard enough to walk away after the asshole's spineless attack on Quinn. Harder still after watching him draw first blood with Nord. But Nord had asked her to stand down, and when she'd tried to go to him against his wishes anyway, Finley had pulled her back, telling her she'd only be a liability.

All of that aside, even if she'd been allowed to help him, Lina wasn't sure she'd have been able to act quickly enough. It felt like the fight had started and ended in all of a minute.

She'd never seen anything like it.

Fury unlike anything she'd ever felt took hold of her then, and Lina turned her attention to the smirking man standing over Nord.

Lina forced herself to blink, to breathe. All it served to do was enrage her further. She embraced the anger, much preferring it to the alternative.

"You," she snarled, barely recognizing the voice that came out of her mouth as hers.

"Lina," Finley pleaded, trying to restrain her as she pushed to her feet.

She knocked him back as easily as if she'd swatted a fly.

The Director turned to face her, openly amused by her display of temper. *"Foolish child. Are you really so eager to meet your end?"*

Lina's hands clenched in tight fists. "I'm not the one who should be worried."

The Director may as well have yawned for all the reaction he showed. *"Come then. Let's get this over with."*

Had she been thinking clearly, she would have reached for her magic, used it to help arm or defend herself, but the need to destroy eclipsed all other rational thought. With each beat of her heart, her anger swelled and infused her body with foreign strength.

Violence had never been Lina's first choice, but she welcomed it now with an eager sort of glee. The thought of coating her hands in the other man's blood, in watching his eyes as the life faded from them, and hearing his final breath rattle past his lips filled her with unholy energy.

She would not stop until that image became reality.

Lina knew she was nowhere as skilled as Nord, but he'd trained her. And she was confident that the need driving her would more than make up for whatever expertise she lacked.

"Lina," Finley called urgently. "You can't kill him—"

"Watch me," she growled.

"Lina," he tried again. "He—"

This time it was the Director who cut him off. *"I don't recall anyone inviting you to this party."*

Finley let out a sharp grunt of pain, his hands flying up on either side of his head as if he could drown out whatever was happening.

Lina knew he was trying to fight off the mental attack. His jaw was clenched tight, his muscles straining as they tensed around the waves of pain.

Lina also knew it was a lost cause. Quinn and Nord had proven that. Neither one of them had been able to do anything but succumb. The trickle of blood dripping from his nose told her it would be a matter of seconds at most before Finley joined her best friend in an unconscious heap on the ground.

The Director's low chuckle rolled through her mind.

She slowly turned back to him. Her lip pulled back in disgust as she took in his amusement. He saw her as a joke and her friends as nuisances. He wasn't taking any of this seriously. It was a game to him, hurting people this way. He enjoyed it.

This man—this leader who prided himself on following rules—got off on harming those he was sworn to protect. He wasn't a man at all.

He was a monster.

The realization set off something inside of her. She no longer felt like she was alone in her body. There was something new there. Something wild and fierce and so fucking angry. The wild thing seethed as the Director's taunting smile stretched. It writhed in her chest, begging to be unleashed.

Letting out a bellow of rage, Lina took one step forward. Then another. By the third, she was launching herself into the air. Her feet continued to pedal, and it almost felt like she was running *on* the air as she cocked back her fist and aimed it at the Director's face.

He didn't bother to move at first, waiting until she was a millimeter away before dodging to the side and whacking her in the back of her head. The blow was powerful enough to set off little sparks at her periphery, but she shook it off as she landed and spun around, the slight pain only cranking up her fury.

She didn't hesitate before striking again, unleashing a flurry of blows at his ribs and face that he dodged with little effort.

Lina knew he was playing with her, that he didn't remotely see her as an actual threat. But while he had years of experience on her, there was a lot to be said for her pure, unadulterated hatred. So when one of her hits connected, the satisfying snap of his rib breaking was more than enough encouragement for her not to back down.

She pulled her arm back, ready to break a second one, when the Director's knuckles cracked across her cheekbone. He moved so fast she hadn't seen the backhand coming. There was just a moment of blinding pain, being airborne, and then having the wind knocked out of her as she crashed into the ground.

Distantly, Lina knew that after taking a hit like that, she should probably stay still. Take a second to catch her breath at the very least before sitting up. But instead, she blinked away the few stars in her vision and pushed herself up.

"You have heart; I'll give you that."

"In a few minutes, I'll have yours as well." Her voice came out rough and guttural. It hardly sounded like her at all.

The coppery tang of blood coated her mouth, and the feeling of something warm and wet dripping down the side of her face told her he'd split her cheek. Gingerly, she rubbed the back of her head. Her fingers came away coated in crimson.

That wild creature inside of her snapped at the sight of her own blood. Her vision changed, the world coming into sharper focus. Her chest vibrated with a growl that didn't sound remotely human.

It might have worried her, that sound, had she not been lost to her fury. But as it was, Lina wasn't exactly the one in control of her body any longer. The wild thing had taken over.

And it was going berserk.

She leaped up, charging full speed at the Director.

Maim.

Destroy.

Kill.

That was the extent of her plan as she jumped on him.

The Director's eyes went wide, and for the first time, they flashed with genuine surprise. He hadn't understood what he was dealing with. Now he did.

He grasped her by her hair, trying to pull her back that way, but Lina snapped her head forward, not even flinching when a fistful of her hair was ripped out. She fought with every weapon in her arsenal. She scraped at his face with her nails. Bit into the fleshy part of his neck. Kicked at his legs. Even tried to knee him in the groin.

He fended her off as best he could, but her attacks were so unpredictable, so feral, that he could do little more than block and dodge.

It wasn't until she'd managed to catch his ear with her teeth, blood that wasn't all hers dripping down her chin, that he let out a roar of his own.

"Enough!"

He'd managed to get his arm between them, his hand clenched around her throat as he tore her away from him.

Lina kicked and writhed in his grasp, her fingers tearing at the hand that held her aloft. She couldn't draw in a proper breath, but she wouldn't stop fighting until one of them was dead.

In that moment, she didn't exactly care which of them it was.

"I said enough," he snarled in her mind, throwing her with such force she went flying through the air and into the alleyway's two trashcans, knocking them over as she landed on the ground like a rag doll with a series of telltale cracks.

Lina tried to sit up but couldn't seem to make her body move. She heard her lungs rattle as she sucked in a breath and tried again.

Still nothing.

She gritted her teeth as the sound of footsteps coming closer preceded the Director's face coming into view above her. She couldn't help but feel a thrill of victory as she took in the number of bloodied scratches and welts that peppered his face.

He may have broken her body, but he'd never crush her will. And he wasn't walking away entirely unscathed.

He must have seen her celebration in her eyes because his

already thunderous expression darkened further. He grasped her by the throat again and lifted her back up as easily as a sack of potatoes.

She couldn't feel anything. Not even his hand against her skin.

"Are you ready for me to end your suffering?"

Lina was about to tell him to go fuck himself, but a slight movement behind him stayed the words. When her breath caught, this time it had nothing to do with the fact that a rib was likely puncturing her lung.

It was Nord.

As he silently rose to his feet, his eyes met hers over the Director's shoulder. His face was covered in blood, but his wounds were gone.

Her heart soared.

Not wanting to give Nord's position away, Lina forced herself to meet the Director's gaze.

"Finish it."

The Guardian's conceit worked against him. If he'd only thought to search her mind, he would have realized her words weren't for him.

Maybe then he might have stood a chance.

CHAPTER 27
NORD

Nord wasn't sure what he was aware of first. His complete lack of pain or Lina's white-hot fury. Regardless of when he became aware of it, once he was, it tugged at him, luring him out of the darkness.

He recognized that rage. It was a mirror of his own. But what could have possibly happened to send Lina into a bloodlust?

That's when the night started coming back to him. The rooftop. Lina's memories. The Transference. The alleyway.

Nord's eyes flew open.

Him.

He pushed himself upright, immediately spotting the Director's blood-splattered shirt and a battered Lina dangling limply from his one-handed hold.

His rage kindled instantly, but it wasn't the only power swelling up within him. The unexpected energy kept him from tumbling instantly into his berserker's lust. He inwardly poked at it, much like an animal might sniff another to get a feel for it. It was both familiar and new. Tasting of Lina, but also, surprisingly, of him—and more. So much more.

It wasn't like his Guardian power, which he'd always pictured like a reservoir in his chest. Something that he needed to consciously tap into before he could access it. This was different—as much a part of him as the blood pumping through his veins. It wasn't power he borrowed. It was his. And it came to his aid without conscious thought.

He instinctively knew it was the reason he was standing now.

Well, his new animagi power and the woman whose anger called to him like a siren's song.

Nord's eyes found Lina's. He could feel the threads of her relief weave themselves through her fury. Her expression never changed, but when she spoke, he knew her words were meant for him.

"Finish it."

With pleasure.

Nord couldn't resist the cruel smile that tilted up his lips. He knew exactly how he wanted to repay the Director for his kindness.

He merely had to think of what he wanted, and it was done. The weight of the hammer settling into his hand like an old friend. He didn't need to look to know that his father's symbol was proudly emblazoned on its side.

Nord swung the weapon at his side. It cut through the air without a sound, its balance perfect.

The Director started to squeeze Lina's throat harder. She didn't fight back. She couldn't. At least that's what the Guardian assumed. He thought he'd already won.

He didn't realize his mistake until Nord was a mere foot behind him, the hammer arcing toward the side of his head.

His eyes were all he had a chance to move. They swiveled to the side and widened in horror a second before the metal kissed his face.

Nord let go of the hammer in the same instant, moving to catch Lina as the Director's lifeless body lost its hold on her and dropped to the floor.

Once again, his power acted on instinct, pumping into her and repairing the damage the Director had caused. With each bone he repaired in Lina's spine, he had to consciously fight off the urge to break the same ones in the Director.

Thankfully, her own magic had already been at work, so it didn't take long at all for their joint power to heal her completely. He shifted his hold on her so he was cradling her back with one arm and her thighs with the other.

Lina wrapped her arms around his neck. "So that didn't quite go according to plan."

"There was a plan?"

One side of her mouth hitched up, and then her expression turned somber. Her eyes roamed over his face, as if she didn't quite believe he was real. "I thought he killed you."

"So did I."

"I . . . sort of freaked out."

"I could feel it."

Lina bit her lip, looking uncertain. "Is it always like that? The rage?"

"No. Sometimes it's worse. But I'll teach you how to rein it in, use it as a tool instead of letting it consume you."

She tilted her head to the side. "I wasn't prepared for it. Isn't that silly? We knew the Transference worked both ways, but I never even considered that I might become a berserker."

"To be honest, neither had I. We always discussed the transfer in terms of magic. I never think about my being a berserker as magical. It's just part of my DNA."

"And now mine," she said.

"And now yours," he agreed, taking great comfort in the thought of no longer being the last of his kind. There was also something intrinsically right about sharing that part of himself with her. It shouldn't have been possible—there'd never been a female berserker as far as he knew—but there was no denying it.

They truly were equals. Lina was his match in every possible way.

"You can put me down now," she said with a husky laugh.

"Not yet," Nord said, cuddling her closer. A small tremor worked through him as he recalled the state she'd been in when he'd come to.

Lina rested a palm against his cheek, her eyes softening with understanding. "We need to help the others," she reminded him.

Nord sighed, his eyes dropping to Finley and Quinn. He should have felt guilty it had taken him so long to remember them, but he didn't. The woman in his arms would always be his first priority.

He gently set her down, keeping his hand at the small of her back as they walked the few steps over to their friends.

"You take him; I take her?" Lina asked.

Nord nodded, already setting to work on undoing the damage caused to his friend's brain. Beside him, Lina did the same for Quinn.

Finley came to first, sucking in air like a drowning man. His eyes were wild as he surged up, grasping Nord's shirt like he was about to deck him. Then his brain must have registered what he was seeing because he checked the move and glanced between the two of them.

"You're alive," he said. "I thought . . ." He shook his head and turned his attention to a still-unconscious Quinn. "May I?" he asked Lina.

She stepped back, giving Finley room to take over the last of Quinn's healing.

He pressed a hand to her forehead, his eyes burning with silver light as he finished what Lina had started. Then he moved his hand and replaced it with his lips.

Quinn's eyelids fluttered, then slowly blinked open just as Finley lifted his head.

"Hey," she rasped, her voice rough from screaming. "What do you think you're doing?"

Finley's lips twitched. "Kissing you. Deal with it."

Quinn blinked at him, her expression open and unguarded just long enough for her to say, "Okay." Then she shoved him off and pushed herself up. "Is it over?"

"You don't have to worry about him anymore if that's what you're asking," Nord replied.

"What are we going to do about him?" Lina asked, moving to stand over the Director.

"Isn't he dead?" Quinn asked, her eyes darting between them.

"Not permanently," Finley answered. "The only way to kill a Guardian is to strip him of his power first."

Lina gave him a curious look. "Can you do that?"

"Not yet."

"Yet?" she repeated, her brows creasing.

"The secret of gifting and removing our power is limited to only those in the highest circles. So I don't know how to do it . . ." Finley's dimples flashed as he gave her one of his signature cocky grins. "But he does." His eyes shone silver as he dropped his gaze back to the man at his feet. "I have to admit, I've never been much of a fan of sifting through the minds of others. But I'm really going to enjoy this."

Nord knew exactly what he meant. After experiencing firsthand the various ways the Director abused his gifts, there was a definite sense of poetic justice in using those same tricks against him. It wouldn't even be possible for them to do so now if not for the fact that he couldn't maintain any sort of mental shields while unconscious.

It didn't take long for Finley to find what he was looking for.

"There you are," he murmured. Finley moved his hand so that it was resting just above the Director's heart. "I'm not one to take the law into my own hands—"

"Liar," Quinn said softly.

Finley grinned. "All right, I am. But in this case, I feel justified. If ever there was a man undeserving of his power, it's Colin Duffy."

It was strange how a title could give a man so much power. Colin Duffy was far less intimidating than the Director, and it had nothing to do with the fact that he was currently out cold. The Director had a reputation; Colin Duffy was nobody. Completely unremarkable.

Fitting punishment indeed for a man who'd built his life around the power granted to him by that title. Now he'd have neither.

"Go ahead," Nord said.

Finley nodded eagerly, his eyes glowing brightly as he used his power to take away Colin's.

Remembering the searing agony of being robbed of his own, Nord was surprised to see how quickly the matter was over. What had felt like hours when he'd gone through it had taken a couple minutes at most.

"There," Finley said. "All done. Would you like to do the honors?" he asked Nord.

"Wait," Quinn said, pressing her hand to Finley's chest. "Killing him now would be a kindness. I have a better idea. The only thing this man has ever cared about, besides himself, is his damned Brotherhood. What does he have left if he can't even remember it?"

Lina grinned. "Quinn, you're brilliant."

Nord had to agree. Death was easy. Having to live without anything to give your life meaning was the true punishment.

"Do it," he said.

Quinn beamed as she crouched down beside Finley, her eyes seeming to ripple as she started to speak. "As I was trying to say earlier before you so rudely interrupted me . . ."

Lina disguised her laugh as a cough.

Quinn continued to speak in her low hypnotic tone as she left Colin with the information she wanted him to have. Then she fell silent and placed her fingers on either side of his head. He'd seen her work before, modifying people's memories through suggestion, but never outright removing them. Seeing it now, he finally understood why they called her a weaver.

Her fingers were nimble, moving delicately as they moved around his head. When she would find a memory she wanted to reclaim, she'd pinch them together as if holding a needle and pull it away as if plucking the invisible strands from his mind. It didn't take as long as Nord expected, given the sheer amount of history she'd had to remove.

"Are you sure that's everything?" Nord asked.

Quinn nodded, the small smudges beneath her eyes a testament to how much of her power she'd just drawn on. "Not only does he not remember us or the Brotherhood, I also stripped him of all knowledge of the supernatural world. Colin Duffy is officially a mere mortal."

"Now what? Do we just leave him here?" Lina asked.

"No," Finley said. "I think it might be best if we call the Brotherhood to come pick him up."

Quinn balked at that. "Are you serious? They're the ones that unleashed this megalomaniac in the first place."

"Even though we've effectively neutered him, he's still their problem. Besides, it might buy us a little goodwill if they see that although we could have killed him, we didn't."

The thought of asking the Brotherhood for anything right now grated, but Finley was technically still among their ranks. Nord couldn't fault him for wanting to preserve his standing and perhaps repair his reputation.

Plus, he had a point.

Maybe in addition to clearing their names and getting the Brotherhood off their backs, it would also garner them another ally against the Drakes.

For that possibility alone, they had to risk it. They may have just dealt with one enemy, but there were still others out there more than ready to take his place.

With that thought at the forefront of his mind, Nord met Finley's gaze.

"Call them."

NATHANIEL COHEN WAS A MAN NORD KNEW BY REPUTATION ALONE. HE HAD a pristine service record and was known above all else to be fair and even-tempered. The fact that Nate was the one to pick up the phone when Finley called was a real stroke of luck.

Nate stood with his hands on his hips, watching as a couple other Guardians escorted a very dazed Colin to a waiting car.

"Thank you for calling us," he said in his calm, easy manner. "We both know you didn't have to."

Finley nodded. "Of course."

Nate turned and looked first at Finley, then at Nord. "I suppose you're both wondering what happens now."

"C'mon, Nate," Finley said with a roll of his eyes. "We all know what happens now."

Nate laughed. "The Brotherhood is nothing if not predictable. Well," he said, scraping a hand through his auburn hair, "pending the results of the investigation. You'll either both be reinstated—"

"I'm not interested," Nord said. "No matter what the investigation finds, I have no interest in rejoining the Brotherhood."

If Nate was surprised by the announcement, he didn't show it. "I can't say that I blame you, all things considered. But aside from that, your name would be cleared. That would make you a free man, Nord."

"And if not?" Lina asked as she returned from escorting Quinn back to her uncle's place. Quinn had been exhausted after dealing with Colin, so Lina had offered to walk her back so she could get some rest. She must have returned just in time to hear the end of what Nate said.

The Guardian had the decency to look apologetic as he answered her question. "If it's deemed that treasonous acts were committed, since both Nord and Finley were members in full standing at the time, they'll be sentenced accordingly."

The fiery spike of Lina's temper told Nord that not even she had any illusions about what the result of that would be. If found guilty,

Finley would be stripped of his power, and they'd both be imprisoned, if not killed outright.

"But, off the record," Nate added, scratching his jaw, "I don't see that happening. Given the Director going off the rails and deciding to play vigilante, it's unlikely that any tribunal will place the blame solely at your feet."

"So we're off the hook?" Lina asked hopefully.

"Not just yet. Think of this more like a cease-fire. You're not out of the woods, but you don't have to worry about the Brotherhood coming after you while the terms of the treaty are being negotiated."

Nord and Finley exchanged meaningful looks. It was something.

"Fin," Nate continued, "consider yourself on administrative leave. You'll still receive full pay and benefits, but you don't have to report in for the time being. We'll be in touch, okay?"

"Paid vacation? Couldn't ask for a better result, all things considered," Finley said, clasping the other man's hand.

Nate gave them all a nod and made as if he was about to leave.

"Wait, that's it?" Lina asked, grasping his arm to stop him. "What about the rest of it? Alistair was under your protection. Mikel Drake murdered him on your watch. Are you really just going to let that go?"

"Look, Ms. Cuska—"

"Lina," she corrected.

"Lina," he said with a soft smile. "I'm sorry to hear about your uncle. I genuinely liked the man. But the Brotherhood's stance is clear. We only get involved when our inaction would result in a cataclysmic event. I'm afraid that a single death doesn't quite meet the standard."

Nord had expected the answer. It's the same line he'd been fed not all that long ago. It didn't make it go down any easier the second time.

He could read the betrayal in Lina's eyes and feel the pulse of her surging anger like a second heartbeat. As far as she was concerned, these men may as well be complicit in her uncle's murder, given the fact that they'd failed to protect him and now refused to seek justice on his behalf.

For her, the denial of assistance was akin to a red flag being waved in front of a bull. Her rage spiked to dangerous levels, tugging on his own. Nord knew she was a mere heartbeat away from pummeling the man as her nostrils flared and color stained her cheeks.

He remembered just how volatile the rage could be in the early days. Hell, it was a struggle to contain even now. If he didn't act fast, Lina would attempt to tear Nate's head from his body before the Guardian ever realized what kind of danger he was in.

Nord knew he'd have to help teach Lina how to control that new part of her nature. He just hadn't expected to need to start her lessons quite so soon. Luckily for both of them, he knew all the best ways to sate a berserker's bloodlust.

"We understand," Nord said to Nate.

Lina turned furious eyes upon him. "The hell we do."

"If you'll excuse us," Nord said, shooting Finley a pointed look.

Finley took one look at Lina and nodded. "I'll finish up here and then go check on Quinn."

Nord gave him a grateful nod as he grabbed Lina by the arm and pulled her with him. "You're coming with me."

She fought his hold. "Hey. Let me go!"

"If I do that, you're liable to kill someone."

"If you don't, that someone might be you."

Nord grinned.

"I'm not joking."

"I know you're not, little berserker. And I look forward to the day we test our skills against each other as equals, but fighting you is not what I have in mind."

"Well, too bad for you, because a fight is exactly what I want," Lina hissed, finally ripping her arm from his grasp.

Nord grasped the hair at the base of her neck and gave it a sharp tug, using more force than was strictly necessary. Lina's eyes shone at the slight pain, her lips parting as threads of arousal shot through her anger.

He dropped his lips to her ear, not loosening his hold on her hair. "Remember what I told you in the shower? About how I deal with the bloodlust when there's no one left to kill?"

She licked her lips, her breath hitching. "I do."

"What did I tell you?" he demanded, noting the rapid flutter of her pulse as he dragged his teeth over the taut cord of muscle at the base of her neck.

Lina's answering smile was tinged with dark promise. "You fuck."

CHAPTER 28
LINA

One thing Lina knew with absolute certainty was that she was not remotely in control. Not of herself or what she was feeling.

Right now, her emotions had two settings: somewhat contained and off the charts. She was ping-ponging between the two extremes so fast she was giving herself whiplash. One second she was celebrating their victory over the Director; the next, she was ready to rip a man's heart from his chest because he refused to get his hands dirty on their behalf.

That wasn't the scary part.

The scary part was how easily she'd accepted that new, violent part of herself. Not just accepted—reveled in it.

She'd discovered a power there she'd never known before. A strength she welcomed. If staying furious meant that she was untouchable, then she was here for it. Because the second thing she knew was that she was done being someone else's plaything.

Unless that someone was a six-foot-six blond god named Nord. And even then . . . her new inner badass was demanding that he be the one to bend to her command.

As if he shared her thoughts, Nord's eyes caught and held hers. She knew he could feel what she was feeling. That he'd sensed her newfound rage had been seconds away from erupting back in the alley.

Just like he must know that the idea of unleashing all that pent-up frustration on his willing body was the only reason she was following him instead of remaining behind to 'help' the Guardian reconsider his edict.

The crackling energy running just beneath her skin was calm for the moment, like a storm on the brink of breaking free. But only because it was waiting for whatever came next.

Lina kept her eyes locked on Nord. Likely wanting privacy for what he had planned, he'd led them back to the abandoned building next to her uncle's. The basement door and its broken frame were hanging at a slant. He released her only long enough to summon the magic to repair it and hold it open for her to step inside.

A part of her noted his effortless use of magic. The Transference was clearly a success on all fronts, her going berserk and Nord's self-healing back in the alley were proof enough of that. But they'd have to explore just what that meant another time. Right now, the only thing she was interested in was how long it was going to take to get him inside her.

She could feel his breath on her neck as he followed her. There was a soft click as he locked the door behind him.

Then he was on her.

Wood cracked and shuddered as he slammed her against a sheet-clad piece of furniture. His hands fisted in her hair as his lips crashed down on hers.

The wild beast who'd taken up residence inside of her let out a fierce whoop, and distantly, Lina wondered why it felt like she was preparing for battle.

Nord's kiss was relentless, his lips firm and demanding as they took everything they wanted and demanded more. Usually, that alone turned her into a puddle of need. Not this time. The raging creature wouldn't allow it.

Ready to flip the tables, she bit his bottom lip and pulled until she tasted blood.

Nord's low growl as she cupped his rock-hard length told her he more than approved of her savage treatment. Though, to be fair, the flood of arousal she'd felt the second she bit down had given him away long before her hand ever found its target.

She'd thought it might get overwhelming, feeling everything another person was feeling on top of her own whirling emotions. But so far, all it served to do was crank up her own arousal up to a twenty.

As much as Lina wanted to free him and impale herself on his cock, what her berserker craved was his submission. It wanted him on his knees. Literally and metaphorically.

Lina shoved at his chest. Prior to tonight, such a move would have barely nudged him. Infused as she was with the bloodlust's strength, though, she sent him skidding halfway across the room before coming to a stop.

His lips curled up, one of his brows lifting in challenge. "Do you want to play, little berserker?"

Lina grinned, the husky pitch of her voice an echo of his. "I want to win."

She was running before she finished speaking, jumping up and wrapping her legs around him as she crashed into him.

Nord was ready for her, only taking a single step back as he caught her weight, his hands cupping and squeezing her ass as he pulled her into his body.

This time it was Lina who fisted his hair and tugged until his throat was bared to her. Still pulling his head back, she ran her teeth along the side of his neck in a similar fashion to what he'd done earlier. That similarity ended once she bit down into the corded muscle. Hard. Not unclamping her jaw until she felt the sting of Nord's teeth piercing her flesh, and he bit down into her shoulder.

It was like a bomb went off inside of her.

There was no pain, only pleasure.

She raked her hands through his scalp and down his back, letting the waves of pleasure ripple through her. Then she dropped free of his hold, kicking her leg out in an attempt to knock Nord to the ground.

He laughed as he sidestepped her clumsy move.

"You'll have to do better than that."

Lina rose to the bait, a small snarl escaping as she tried a second time to knock him to the ground.

When she got within range, Nord easily grabbed her before she could try anything. In one seamless move, he lifted her, spun, and dropped her so her back was somehow on the ground and her arms pinned above her head. It happened so fast that Lina wasn't even sure how she'd gone from standing to posed beneath him.

But she wasn't about to give in.

Not when his mouth met her skin and her eyes fluttered closed. Not when his hand ran down the front of her body, sending little bolts of electricity racing through her. Not even when he ground his erection into the vee of her body.

As good as it felt, she needed something else.

Allowing her body to relax infinitesimally, she tricked him into believing that he'd won. Once he pressed his weight deeper into hers, she rocked her hips up, using her body's newly discovered strength to push him up and over.

Now she was the one straddling him, her pelvis grinding into his.

"If you wanted to be on top, you only had to ask, Kærasta."

Lina leaned down until her lips were a breath above his. She stole a rough kiss and then leaned back to meet his gaze from beneath the sweep of her lashes. "I'm not asking for anything."

Nord's pupils flared wide until there was only a thin ring of icy blue around the black. "I don't mind topping from the bottom," he informed her, his smile slow and lazy.

It was like he knew what the words would do to her. Of course he did. They were a blatant challenge. Because he felt it too. The berserker's need for dominance thundering in his veins. The need to prove that he, and he alone, was the biggest, baddest alpha in the room.

Unfortunately for him, there was a new alpha in town. And she wasn't about to submit.

Not unless he earned it.

Lina kissed him hard and deep, sitting back with a tsk when he palmed her breasts. "Did I say you could touch?"

Nord let out a frustrated growl, reaching for her. Lina tried to duck out of his reach, but she was a hint too slow. Either that or he was simply more determined.

He caught her by the shirt, his hand fisting in the cotton and pulling her down to reclaim her mouth. While she was distracted by what his lips and tongue were doing, Nord ripped her shirt until it hung down on either side of her torso. By the time she pulled back to protest, he'd already tugged down both cups of her bra and bared her to him.

Before she could register what happened, he took one of her breasts in his mouth and sucked hard. Then he bit down on one nipple while pinching and rolling the other one until a breathless cry was torn from her throat.

"What were you saying?" he asked with an utterly unrepentant smile.

Lina let out a little growl and somehow managed to capture both his wrists and slam his hands down until they were on either side of his head.

Surprisingly, Nord didn't fight her hold. He must have felt her confusion because his lips twisted. "I like the view," he said, answering the question she never voiced.

Realizing her breasts were dangling in his face, Lina scowled and sat back.

"Still a great view," he teased, resting his hands beneath his head.

Seeing him stretched out beneath her, she couldn't help but silently agree.

Nord used her moment of distraction to his advantage, rearing up and flipping her over. Lina squirmed beneath him, managing to roll and get her knees and hands beneath her as he concentrated on slipping his hands beneath the waistband of her leggings and peeling them down.

During her frantic squirming, she'd managed to twist the fabric around her legs, turning them into lycra shackles. The slight restraint of her movement sent a hot pulse of arousal straight through her core. The crack of Nord's hand on her naked ass sent a second, much stronger pulse right on its heels.

It was harder to fight her way through the fog of lust clouding her brain this time. The need to fight back was still there, but it was muted. Her raging beast more purring kitten than roaring predator at the moment.

Nord crawled over her until his chest pressed into her back and his lips caught the lobe of her ear. "Where do you think you're going?" He slid one hand down her spine and then lower until he was palming her center.

Heart racing, aching with need, Lina was forced to admit the truth. "Nowhere."

She shivered as his deep chuckle washed over her. Somewhere in the last handful of seconds, she'd lost sight of her mission. And when two thick fingers slipped inside of her wet folds, she realized she didn't remotely care.

In the end, she'd gotten exactly what she wanted. What did it matter if she was on her knees? So was he.

Lina arched her back and lifted her hips higher. She whimpered as he withdrew his hand and then let out a low groan of complete delight when he replaced his fingers with something far more satisfying.

She quickly realized that she wasn't the only feral creature here. Nord held nothing back as he claimed her, no longer having to fear hurting her. His thrusts were brutal in the best possible way. Every time he bottomed out, he pulled back and then slammed back in. Each slap of his skin against hers perfect punctuation to the cries falling from her lips.

It was rough, fast, and everything she wanted.

"Yes," she groaned as the tip of his cock rolled over the sweet bundle of nerves inside of her.

She knew it wouldn't take much more to send her over the edge. She'd been nearly there ever since he'd clued her in to his intentions back in that alley. So when he moved his hand to dip between her legs and pressed his fingers over her swollen bud, Lina couldn't have stopped the tidal wave of pleasure if she'd wanted to.

Nord's thrusts grew wilder as she rippled around him, her orgasm triggering his. He leaned forward, her name leaving his lips in a low groan a second before he bit down and spilled inside of her. He held her there, his body curled over hers, the sounds of their ragged breathing the only noise in the room. After a couple seconds, he pressed an open-mouthed kiss to the nape of her neck.

"Still angry?" he asked, his smug smile evident in his voice.

"Yes," Lina answered emphatically.

She wasn't, not like before, but that relentless need still had her in its grasp. And there was the matter of winning she needed to see to. One way or the other, she would make him submit. They weren't leaving until he did.

While Nord laughed, Lina slipped out from beneath him and shoved him on his back. Then she stood, removed her stupid leggings, tossing the black fabric onto his face as she straddled him.

"This time, I'm in charge."

His answering smile as he flung her pants across the room contradicted her declaration. He didn't believe she could manage it.

Lina returned his smile with one of her own. One that told him while he might know Lina, he didn't know a thing about her berserker.

But he was about to learn.

It was going to be a long, educational night.
Let the games begin.

Many hours later . . .

ONCE THE BLOODLUST HAD SUBSIDED, NORD HAD TAKEN HER A FINAL TIME. It was everything their frenzied lovemaking hadn't been. Slow. Sweet. Tender. As rough and intense as the first several rounds had been, they'd been no less of a declaration of love.

As they'd lain beside one either, bodies slick with sweat, the day lost once more to the night, Nord had brushed the hair from her face and whispered, "I'd like to show you something if you're up for it."

There was something almost boyish about the request. Curiosity piqued, Lina instantly agreed. "Does it involve putting clothes on?"

He chuckled. "It does. But you can rest here while I get everything set up."

He stood, making a point to tuck a blanket around her before creating a pair of sweatpants to pull on.

Lina propped her hand beneath her head. "It's unfair how good you are at that."

He glanced at her. "You'll have to be more specific. I'm good at everything."

Lina groaned and rolled her eyes. "Using your new magic."

"Ah." He sat back down beside her and ran his hands over her hair, not seeming to be able to resist the urge to touch her. "Well, it's pretty similar to how my Guardian magic worked. Easier in a lot of ways since I don't need to modify something that already exists. I just need to picture what I want, and the magic responds."

"That's fair, I suppose. When do you think I'll get a hold on the berserker stuff?"

Nord shrugged. "Hard to say. I had years of training and still don't always feel like I'm in control. Luckily you have time on your side." He leaned down and brushed a kiss over her lips. "And me."

"True."

He stood once more. "Okay, I'll be right back."

Lina sat up. "Where are you going?"

"I need to grab something. I won't be gone long."

She watched him leave the bedroom they'd found upstairs. Even though it had already been furnished, they'd taken a short break from their sexcapades to spruce up the place. It now resembled Nord's room at the penthouse.

Deciding to use her time to dress, Lina claimed Nord's T-shirt and her leggings.

True to his word, Nord was back within minutes, a familiar dagger in his hand.

"Where'd you find that?" Lina asked.

"Considering how the bastard left it buried in my stomach, it wasn't hard."

Lina searched her memory. "I don't recall it still being stuck in you when you went after him."

"It wasn't. The healing magic must have pushed it out. I saw it lying in the alleyway when we were waiting for the Brotherhood, so I'd pocketed it for us to use later."

"Us?"

Nord's eyes dipped, and he scratched the back of his neck in an uncommonly shy gesture. "I thought, since you're a berserker now, you might want to learn some of the ways of our people." He held out the dagger. "I'd hoped we could start with me teaching you to make your first ring."

Tears pricked at Lina's eyes as her heart filled near to bursting. She hadn't thought she could love him any more than she already did, but there he went, proving her wrong.

"I would love that."

He grinned, looking relieved. "We just need to make ourselves a forge—"

Nord's words stopped short, and Lina felt a momentary burst of panic that was soon eclipsed by molten fury.

Crombie stepped out from the shadows, his beautiful face cold and mocking.

"What are you doing here?" she growled.

"Word on the street is your Director is no longer a threat. According to the terms of our agreement, that means you're mine, sweetheart. And I'm here to collect."

Nord and Lina's adventures continue in Promise of Danger, out now!

GLOSSARY & PRONUNCIATION GUIDE

AUTHOR'S NOTE: After the results of a reader poll revealed a wildly popular preference for glossary and pronunciation guides, I decided I should probably include one! These are the notes I send to my audio narrators. I am no pronunciation expert, as you'll see, so when I go for phonetic spellings, I base it off what makes most sense in my mind (which you should all know by now is a scary, scary place. Ha!) In some case, pronunciation can vary depending on region, and while I generally default to the Old Norse version or the Norwegian versions of words, sometimes a matter of personal preference may sway me to something else. All of this is to say, while I do my research, I am far from an expert and this is all just how I hear things in my head while writing. You may keep or disregard these as you will. 😊

Animagi (plural): Ani (as in animation) Maji (hard J)

Animagus (singular): Ani (as in animation) Mag (as in magazine) Us

Gunnar: Goo (like goose) na (like nah) r (soft, a British v. American r) *Gunnar is a male first name of Nordic origin (Gunnarr in Old Norse).*

The name Gunnar means fighter, soldier, and attacker, but mostly is referred to by the Viking saying which means Brave and Bold warrior (gunnr "war" and arr "warrior").

Häxa: Hex-a (long a at end) *A witch (woman who knows or uses magic) Though it is not used like this in the book, it can also be used in a derogatory way to mean an ugly or unpleasant woman.*

Jarl: Yaa-rl *A Norse or Danish chief.*

Kærasta: Ki (like in Kite) ra (like radish) stuh *Nord uses it as a term of endearment, like sweetheart, though a more direct translation would be girlfriend.*

Knörr: Nor *A large merchant ship used in mediaeval Scandinavia.*

Móðir: [Old Norse] Mow-Dear (o sound slightly extended) *Mother*

Novasgard: Nov (as in nova) – as – guard

Spes meum solatium [Latin] *"Hope is my solace"*

- Spes: (like the first part of special)
- Meum: meh-oom
- Solatium: soh-ley-shee-um

Novasgardians:

- Arrick: Eric
- Björn: Bee - Yorn (like horn)
- Brynhild: Brin-hild (with r slightly rolled)
- Søren: Sore - en
- Strega: Stray - ga

A NOTE FROM MEG

I think it's safe to say that 2020 was a hard year for everyone. And by hard, I mean nearly impossible. I certainly wasn't immune to the *charms* of pandemic life. If anything, spending over a year apart from my family in the States (with no end to the border restrictions in sight) taught me a valuable lesson. It was a study in long-distance relationships, which I thought I had already mastered after the three years my husband and I spent living in different countries. But alas, there was one last lesson for me to learn.

So here's what 2020 taught me: no matter how independent I might **think** I am, I am useless without my people.

If I go too long without interacting with them, it feels like I begin to wither. Everybody suffered in one way or another last year, and when things were at their bleakest for me, and I was on a full-blown retreat into myself, it was the people who randomly checked in that kept me going. Without fail, on my worst days, there was always one person who seemed to message me out of the blue. I cannot tell you how grateful I am for the people in my life who can always seem to "be there" even though they may not be physically present. It's a gift; one I cherish.

Sitting here, reflecting on this book and the journey it was to write, it feels more important than ever to acknowledge the people who played a major role in its evolution. I'm not sure I'd be writing this, or you reading this, if not for them. To be honest, Lina might still be standing outside of Alistair's door, with all of us wondering what happens next. Haha.

Kim L. If ever a book could have an MVP, you've certainly earned the title for this one. Without fail, you've been there, not only cheering me on but inspiring me with your kindness and talent. I don't think you'll ever truly know how much I value our friendship, but I hope to live up to the example you've set for me.

Sarah K. you are such a light. Our chats have been some of my favorite these past months. Thank you for believing in me and these characters that we both love so much. And thank you for being a good hooman. Wade adores his sloth toys.

Traci B. your videos from the farm and all the pictures of baby animals give me life. I'm not sure I can ever express the joy I feel whenever your name pops up in my inbox.

Laura B. & Heather A. It feels like you've been with me since the beginning. That source of constant support and belief means the world to me. My books never feel complete until they get your seal of approval.

Mo & Dom you two are lifesavers. You swooped in and saved the day when it felt like everything was falling apart. Thank you!

Wade you are by far the best thing that came out of a dumpster fire year. I will never get tired of your puppy kisses and snuggle breaks. I wrote a lot of this book with you in my lap or sleeping by my side. I consider you its official mascot.

And last but never least, my Gabe. My #MenByMeg have nothing on you. Thank you for being my #1 fan. The person who makes sure I always have coffee, or water, or food. My first reader. The person I can bounce ideas off, talk through fight scenes with, ask for help coming up with cool insults or names or erm other personal details so that I can keep elevating my worlds. Love is not a strong enough word for what I feel for you, but I guess it will have to do. 🩶

And for anyone else who's read this far, thank you. I do this for you. I write these stories for you (well, me too, but mostly you). I cannot tell you guys how much your messages and emails mean to me. Hearing about your reactions to the twist and turns, and watching you fall in love with the characters that I love too is the most wonderful thing in the entire world.

Until next time, stay safe and happy reading!

XOXO,

♡ Meg Anne

If you enjoyed this book, please consider writing a short review and posting it on Amazon, Bookbub, Goodreads and/or anywhere else you share your love of books. Reviews are very helpful to other readers and are greatly appreciated by authors (especially this one!)

Want to know when I have a new release or get exclusive access to my newest works? Join my mailing list: MegAnneWrites.com/Newsletter

ALSO BY MEG ANNE

ABOUT MEG ANNE

USA Today and international bestselling paranormal and fantasy romance author Meg Anne has always had stories running on a loop in her head. They started off as daydreams about how the evil queen (aka Mom) had her slaving away doing chores, and more recently shifted into creating backgrounds about the people stuck beside her during rush hour. The stories have always been there; they were just waiting for her to tell them.

Like any true SoCal native, Meg enjoys staying inside curled up with a good book and her fur babies . . . or maybe that's just her. You can convince Meg to buy just about anything if it's covered in glitter or rhinestones, or make her laugh by sharing your favorite bad joke. She also accepts bribes in the form of baked goods and Mexican food.

Meg is best known for her leading men #MenbyMeg, her inevitable cliffhangers, and making her readers laugh out loud, all of which started with the bestselling Chosen series.